Call Me Mac
by
Susie Baggaley

Published by
Baggatelle Publishers Ltd
ISBN: 978-0-9932121-9-2

Index

Part One

Port Out

Index

Part One

Port Out

Prologue

I stood at the ship's stern and watched the crescent moon appear like an iridescent sail above the horizon before breaking free of the earth's contour and rising into the heavens.

Alone on the empty deck, I could feel the vibration of huge propeller blades churning the dark waters below my feet as the sixteen-thousand-ton hull of the ss NARKUNDA cruised towards Port Said, carrying me ever eastwards to the far sub-continent of India. The smell of exhaust fumes invaded my senses as my fingers gripped the cold steel of the handrail. I closed my eyes and willed myself back to the beginning.

'Join the Fishing Fleet, dear,' Aunt Karr had said.

So here I was, on this speck of ocean betwixt east and west, having torn up my roots from the ground where I had been born on some fanciful whim that I could change the world. I was having second thoughts, but the die had been cast, and I could do little about it halfway across the Mediterranean Sea. As my spinster Aunt had pointed out on more than one occasion, those who made waves only had two choices, they could either ride the breaking crests or sink below the waterline. I gritted my teeth, crossed my fingers and hoped that I, Elizabeth Stuart-MacKenzie, had the mental and physical capacity to stay afloat!

Chapter One

I was born on a foggy October day in 1902 at Riveldene Vicarage in Berwick-on-Tweed.

Pa was Riveldene's Presbyterian minister, a post he had held for many a year, his Scottish lilt cajoling his congregation every Sunday at St Stephen's Church with its tall spire and lichen-covered headstones. He was well-respected and my hero.

I was an avid reader with a bookcase full of accounts of distant lands, adventurous individuals and derring-do. I cast myself in the image of Florence Nightingale whose courageous life in the Crimea tending to the war-wounded far from home had appealed to my imagination. Years later, when witnessing Britain's brave young soldiers returning crippled or limbless from the Great War, I knew where my destiny lay.

'I am going to be a doctor,' I proudly announced on my fifteenth birthday.

Rational argument from my parents, scepticism from friends and a general "Doubting Thomas" attitude from Pa's parishioners had little effect. I was head-strong and doggedly determined, convinced I could succeed in a predominantly masculine profession and become Riveldene's first female GP, and a very good one at that!

I obtained excellent grades in my matriculation examinations and applied for an undergraduate position to Edinburgh University Medical School. With a name like Stuart-MacKenzie, I believed acceptance would be a foregone conclusion.

The University Governors had other ideas.

'Pa,' I yelled, bursting into his study where he was sitting writing his Sunday sermon, waving my rejection slip like a declaration of war, 'they've rejected my application because I'm a woman!'

My first experience of gender inequality had punched a hole the size of a twelve-bore bullet through my self-esteem, but I refused to be beaten. Plonking my backside on the edge of his desk I insisted Pa write to the University's Medical Director, a fellow graduate of his at university.

'My intervention will have no sway at all, Elizabeth, you do realise that?'

'If you say so, Pa,' I said, placing a blank sheet of writing paper on top of his sermon and refusing to move until I had got my own way.

His letter emphasised the death toll from the Great War which had severely affected the University's intake of male undergraduates and argued that women, who had successfully handled masculine jobs while their men were away fighting, should have the right to prove their worth in peacetime. He respectfully concluded that my application should be re-considered.

What a hero! The Governors agreed and on a blustery, damp October morning in 1920, two days after my eighteenth birthday, I walked through the imposing portals of Scotland's most prestigious medical training establishment and felt my stomach catapult at the thought of what lay ahead.

Life at university was inspiring, and, as the year passed, I proved that I had just as many brain cells as my male counterparts and an even better bedside manner. In an attempt to ignore the fact that I was female, they took to calling me 'Mac', a nickname I rather liked, and I earned their respect for my total dedication to my profession and my growing appreciation for Guinness. I was nineteen, God was in his heaven and all was right in my world.

Then Duncan Fitzpatrick entered my life.

This emerald-eyed, red-haired, veterinary surgeon from County Antrim was doing post-graduate research at Ashworth Laboratories, an adjunct of Edinburgh University's Department of Zoology and had become a regular intruder into our undergraduate social life. He became the principal cause of my sudden inability to concentrate.

I confess, I had no excuse for falling in love with this complex Irishman. I was young and self-assured with a definite superior air around my male associates, which of course was like a red rag to a bull for Duncan Fitzpatrick's ego. He was a flirt with an inexhaustible supply of charisma and charm which left me utterly defenceless. He went on the attack and derived great pleasure in watching me naively succumb to his Irish brogue and Gaelic good looks as he wound me around his little finger for near-on eighteen months.

Warnings of Duncan's self-centred character from those in the know fell on deaf ears. I was far too besotted to believe our relationship wasn't permanent and too pig-headed to heed advice. *Pride before a fall* should have been my maxim.

I was studying a male anatomical drawing by Leonardo de Vinci in the University Library when Duncan breezed in.

'Mac, guess what? I'm off to India on a sabbatical.'

'But what about us?'

'No problem, Sweetheart, you can always follow.'

'But ...' Too late, he was gone, disappearing over the horizon flinging back promises to keep in touch, which, needless to say, he didn't.

Suffering a right upper-cut from a heavy-weight boxing champion would go some way to describing the effect of his departure on me and for months I continued my studies in a state of emotionally charged confusion. Then Aunt Karr, at the behest of my parents, decided to intervene. I was summoned to her rambling Victorian pile in Peebles where she placed a large schooner of Harvey's Bristol Cream sherry in one hand and an enormous slab of her home-made Dundee fruit cake in the other.

'Get some MacKenzie backbone,' she told me.

Karr's formidable command cut to the core. Never one for mincing her words, Pa's big-bosomed, steely-eyed and tight-mouthed sister had been a Professor of Philosophy at the University of St Andrews before she retired to her beloved Peebles and anyone ignoring her advice did so at their peril.

I can't say whether it was the sherry, the Dundee cake or her shot across my aggrieved bow which brought me to my senses, but my backbone straightened as if ironed and my studies became the sole purpose of my existence. With surgical precision I lanced the umbilical cord attaching me to Duncan Fitzpatrick's memory and he was consigned to history, along with my virginity!

I did become Riveldene's junior GP, known for my efficient and caring manner. Thoughts of Duncan surfaced occasionally, usually when called upon to assist the local vet with a pregnant cow or to geld a stallion, but an image of me

castrating him soon put paid to this lapse in self-control and
once bitten, twice shy cemented itself into my psyche.

Life would have happily continued this way had it not been
for a sudden outbreak of smallpox around the Newcastle docks
which was to prove a watershed moment for me and a disaster
for the local population. This virus, spreading through
Northumbria like a plague of locusts, attacked men, women
and children without mercy. There was little I could do in
Riveldene other than isolate those who had become infected,
administer acetaminophen for the fever and impotently watch
as many died in agony or went blind. I immunised thousands
against contagion, pricking the skin's surface with a pronged
lance soaked in a derivative of cowpox, and prayed for the
epidemic to subside.

It took months, however, and the aftermath was shocking.
Housewives struggled without a breadwinner, children found
themselves orphaned, mothers wept as their wee ones went
into the cold earth, and all dear Pa could do was believe in
God's will and reiterate this to anyone who would listen.

The Stuart-MacKenzie family were not immune either. My
youngest sibling never saw her tenth birthday, my brother
became partially sighted, my mother forgot how to smile and,
much to my father's horror, I turned my back on God. To me,
religion was irrelevant, and our Saviour found wanting. What I
needed was knowledge and I knew just where to find it.

Taking leave from my GP practice, I returned to Edinburgh
to begin a post-graduate degree in Virology at Ashworth
Laboratories. Here I avidly read everything I could, burning the
midnight oil searching case studies and medical reports for

anything relating to smallpox. I also learned of Sir Ronald Ross, the 1902 Nobel Prize winner for Physiology, who had discovered the link between mosquitos and the spread of malaria in 1890 at the Calcutta School of Tropical Medicine. Like Florence Nightingale all those years before, Sir Ronald Ross now became my inspiration and, as rain wakes a dormant seed, India and the CSTM germinated in my fertile mind.

I was twenty-seven and, according to Ma, already *on-the-shelf*, so what I needed was a new challenge.

Casting off my Northumbrian shackles, I applied to do research in Calcutta's famous college and convinced myself that, whatever the hurdles, I would have a distinguished career in tropical medicine.

Firstly though, I had to get there and didn't have a clue how to go about it. Fortunately, Aunt Karr did.

'Join the Fishing Fleet, dear.'

'The what?' At eighty-six, Karr appeared to be losing touch with reality.

'The Fishing Fleet, dear. Are you deaf?'

I shrugged, finding it difficult to understand why rolling around the fringes of the Dogger Bank in a gale trawling for haddock in the middle of the night had anything to do with me getting to Calcutta.

She was ahead of me. 'Oh, for goodness sake, Elizabeth, I'm not talking about catching mackerel, I'm referring to the bevy of young lassies who sail to India each year intent on finding husbands amongst the military or ICS.'

Before I could ask what ICS stood for, a cup of Darjeeling tea and an Abernethy biscuit were thrust into my hands and my

Aunt continued her diatribe on the vagaries of life within the British Raj.

Apparently, Britain's favoured colonial outpost had one thorny problem. It had a surfeit of eligible young men and a dearth of suitable young women for them to marry. To right this imbalance, girls with romantic notions of Empire and those hoping to improve their social status boarded Peninsular and Oriental Steamship Company liners bound for a life of marital bliss in the sub-tropics.

Karr appeared to be staring at me from above her half-rimmed spectacles. I didn't like the inference of this look, so I sniffed and finished my biscuit.

'Don't look down your nose, Elizabeth, I'm well aware of your views on matrimony. My point is, you would not be travelling alone but with other young women who, no doubt, will have contacts in Bombay, Delhi and Calcutta.' She allowed her words to hang in the air. 'Take my advice, dear, place an advertisement in The Lady Magazine looking for a travelling companion and you'll be amazed at the response. All you need are one or two of these women to share a cabin and once there, you can cut all ties with the Fishing Fleet, study whatever medical research takes your fancy and administer pills and potions to the great and good of the British Empire.' Her voiced dropped to a murmur. 'You might even find yourself a husband into the bargain.'

I flicked her latter comment away with the tips of my fingers, but her words were still ringing in my ears when I arrived home that night and I made a diary note to buy the latest edition of The Lady Magazine the following day.

Passing the church lych-gate, scanning the classified ads on my way home from the newsagents, I was accosted by Gladys Bottomley, waving the latest edition of the parish magazine above her head.

'Doctor MacKenzie, hold up.'

I paused, wondering if Gladys's piles were playing up again.

'I've just been chattin' with your Ma.' She leant against the dry-stone wall clasping her chest. 'My, the old ticker is tellin' me a tale today. Must be the damp.'

'Deep breaths, Mrs Bottomley, deep breaths.'

'Aye, Doctor. Deep breaths it is. OK, now, what ya need ta know is me cousin, Elsie, she be married to a Sanitary Inspector and they lives in Calcutta . . .'

I nearly dropped the magazine in surprise.

'. . . nice bloke, named Arthur,' she continued between breaths, 'Arthur Thornton. They met when 'e was back 'ome on furlough in '21. The point is, Doctor, Elsie and Arthur would be raight chuffed to have ya stay, and they be knowing an awful lot o'people out there.' She thrust a piece of paper in my hand. 'Drop 'em a line.'

I was staring at an address on the other side of the world, unable to believe my luck. A Sanitary Inspector's introduction into Raj society didn't inspire me with confidence but beggars could not be choosers, so I thanked Gladys profusely and penned a letter to the Thorntons, posting it with my advertisement for a travelling companion within the hour.

My fingernails were chewed down to the quick as I paced the Vicarage waiting for some response. The first came from a Miss Frances Trotter who was booked on the ss Narkunda bound for Bombay in October and travelling alone. The second was from Elsie and Arthur Thornton welcoming me with open arms and the third, which was handed to me by our postman some days later, his index finger pointing directly at the embossed envelope as he doffed his cap, was from the Calcutta School of Tropical Medicine.

I ripped open the envelope and unfolded the letter.

Dear Dr Stuart-Mackenzie,

Your application request addressed to the Director of Physiology at CSTM has been passed to me to respond. I have read with interest your professional medical qualifications from Edinburgh University and your work in General Practice in the North-West of England before studying virology at Ashworth Laboratories.

Your desire to carry out PhD research into the virology and immunology of tropical diseases is commendable and we feel confident we could offer you such a position should you decide to relocate to Calcutta later this year.

I must stress, however, the final decision rests with the Board of Governors who will wish to meet you, in person, before making a final decision. We therefore recommend that you also secure paid employment as a medical practitioner in order to supplement your income during your stay in India.

Please let us know if you wish to proceed and your estimated date of arrival in Calcutta. When attending the interview please have all original medical certificates available for examination..

Yours sincerely,

R B Chakramachari M.D.M.Sc.Immunology

Russet leaves lay like confetti along the railway track as I boarded a London bound sleeper-train months later. My cabin trunk was stowed in a rear carriage, my leather medical bag and overnight case balanced in the overhead netting and my parents, siblings and Aunt Karr gathered on the station platform like abandoned souls.

I leant out of the carriage window waving my wet hankie in the breeze and felt the train judder as the wheels began to turn. The last I saw of my family, their arms aloft as they reacted to the station-master's shrill whistle, was their outline shrouded, fog-like, in a cloud of sooty steam, slowly merging with the grey limestone buildings until they disappeared completely.

I was on my own at the start of my Indian adventure with no idea how it would end . . .

Sudden squeaking of metal on metal interrupted my musings, bringing me sharply back to the stern deck of the ss Narkunda. The sound, like a door hinge needing lubrication, grated on my nerves and I turned to see one of the ship's lascars shuffling along the port gunwhale, metal bucket in hand, his white turban, soiled dhoti and bare feet in stark contrast to the flat cap, ragged breeches and wooden clogs worn in my homeland. The comparison was a sharp reality check and that hollow space below my ribs grew ever larger.

I had crossed numerous latitudes and longitudes since leaving Tilbury Docks and what had seemed like a cracking idea in Edinburgh was now taking on viruses all of its own. Would I be accepted at the Calcutta School of Tropical Medicine? Did Arthur and Elsie Thornton assume I was one of the Fishing Fleet and were now planning to marry me off to some chinless wonder in the Sanitary Department? If things went awry, what would I do to remain solvent? Fear rippled along my vertebrae and I shuddered in the sub-tropical air. Far from being in control of my own destiny I now felt like a piece of driftwood floating on the current, to be beached on some distant shore.

'You're being ridiculous, Mac,' I said out loud. 'Where's your Scottish backbone?' I coughed, hoping the lascar didn't speak English and raised my eyes to the moon. The notion that Pa would see this same moon from his study window within a few hours went some way to relaxing my tense stomach muscles and, like a Highland clansman taking courage from a dram of whisky, I stiffened my resolve by repeating my own personal mantra.

'I am Doctor Elizabeth Stuart-MacKenzie making passage to India to advance the cause of medical science.'

As I made my way back along the empty deck in the dark, I added an after-thought. 'What I am not, Aunt Karr, is a member of the Fishing Fleet, so Arthur and Elsie Thornton will find themselves barking up the wrong tree if they think otherwise.'

I pulled open the deck door and stepped inside. My second-class cabin berth was waiting and tomorrow . . . no, I corrected . . . today, was my twenty-eighth birthday. To celebrate I planned to go shopping in Port Said to buy some tropical clothing and a Topi. Suitably clad, I aimed to join the ship's shore party and, like Gertrude Bell, Mesopotamia's Queen of the Desert, go ride a camel. Well, that was the plan anyway.

Chapter Two

I woke with the sun streaming through the cabin porthole and the sound of Ruby Tavener cleaning her teeth in the ceramic washbasin attached to the aft cabin bulkhead. I buried my head in my pillow trying to keep both annoyances at bay.

'Morning. Mac. Sorry, did I wake you?'

I mumbled some inanity, assuming she was referring to the previous night and remembered that her bed had been empty when I had returned from the deck.

'You'll never believe what I learned last night.'

Oh, yes I would, I thought. Miss Ruby Tavener, five-feet-eight-inches in her stocking feet with an hour-glass figure and blonde, bobbed and fashionably crimped hair, had been a *tableau vivant* at the Windmill Theatre in Soho. Her appearance on the ss Narkunda was the result of a difference of opinion with the Windmill management over her fraternising with a customer and she was now proving to be a real hit with the officers and male passengers aboard ship. With her deep lilac eyes, rosebud lips, body-clinging silk evening dresses in every pastel hue imaginable and an inexhaustible supply of vaudeville songs which she sang in a mezzo-soprano voice accompanied by Major Stokes on the pianoforte in the second-class lounge after dinner, she was the talk of the cruise. The prim ladies of the English Shires didn't seem to know quite what to do with this apparition from the West End. As for yours truly, who had lived a very sheltered life in the Borders, Ruby Tavener was a complete revelation and someone who could shock me with every sentence. She was now in full flood.

'. . . the ship's Purser comes from Streatham, just around the corner from my sister, Joan,' she spluttered with a mouth full of foam. 'What's more, his Mum goes to the same knitting circle as my Aunt Annie.'

I heard her gurgle and spit then pull the monogrammed hand-towel off the bulkhead rail. I was trying to imagine what her Aunt Annie looked like when I felt my bed-springs sag as Ruby pushed my legs aside and sat on the end of the mattress. I opened one eye and studied my roommate. Ruby could alter her accent, her demeanour and her history to suit whoever she happened to be alongside. I had never witnessed anyone who could lie with such impunity and get away with it. Take the first-class passengers for instance. They were under the illusion that she was a young widow who had lost her husband at Passchendaele and had become a model for Dior in Paris after having been discovered at the Folies Bergère by a Madame Du Lac, whoever she was. Major Stokes of the tinkling ivories meanwhile, was convinced he had seen her starring in the leading role at Drury Lane in *Show Boat* and that she was on her way to Delhi to entertain the guests of Lord Irwin, the current Viceroy of India, and his wife at their annual winter charity ball. I, on the other hand, seemed to be the only one who knew she had worked for Mrs Laura Henderson at the infamous Windmill Theatre and, I had to admit, even that was not necessarily the full truth. I pulled the curtain across our porthole to block out the sunlight.

'You should have requested a cabin on the port side, Mac.'

My lack of response must have indicated that I hadn't got a clue what she was talking about.

'You know. Port out, Starboard home?'

I shook my head.

'Oh, Mac, you're impossible. That's what POSH stands for. Port Out, Starboard Home, which is what any sensible traveller does when reserving a cabin going East. That way they always stay in the shade.'

'Really?' I gave up trying to get back to sleep.

'Really.' She stretched across my bed and pulled the curtain open, the sudden glare piercing my eyeballs. My hands shot to my face. 'I'll have a word with Stanley, our friendly Purser, and see what he can do. Now, Mac, what have you got planned for your birthday?'

I came upright like a male patient about to be given an enema, my pillow falling at her feet. 'How do you know about that?' I desperately tracked back through our conversations since meeting in Tilbury Docks ten days earlier, but I couldn't recall ever mentioning my birthday.

Ruby puckered her lips in that coy way of hers and tapped her nose. 'Now, now, Doctor, no need to have apoplexy.'

A striking image of the Purser sprang to mind. I recalled filling out my passenger details and handing over my passport to him before we left. 'Stanley?'

'I won't tell if you don't.'

Trusting Ruby as far as the cabin door was a stretch and the last thing I needed was to become the ship's mascot for the day. We had already had numerous birthday and anniversary celebrations aboard ship with all the associated drum rolls, candle fizzing cakes and first dances with appropriate partner, or, indeed, the Captain, and I wanted none of it.

'Ruby, listen to me,' I said, my finger pressing against her sternum. 'Unlike you, I resemble a hot flush with a stutter if I'm placed in the spotlight and no amount of deep breathing is going to stop me from making a complete and utter fool of myself. So . . .' At this juncture, my lungs demanded air and I gasped audible, '. . . please keep this strictly to yourself and let me get on with my day, my way.' I lay back down and wiggled my toes.

'Doing what, exactly?'

'I intend to visit Simon Arzt Departmental Store once we dock in Port Said and treat myself to some tropical attire, a pith-helmet and a fly-swat.' Even to my ears that sounded a bit lame.

Ruby, meantime, resembled a child learning that Santa Claus didn't exist.

'But . . .'

'No buts, Ruby. If you don't want me to tell Lady Cottesmore that your father was a gambler and your mother died of cirrhosis of the liver, I suggest you keep the information of my birthday to yourself.'

She pouted. 'Oh, alright, if I must, but you're a real wet blanket when it comes to enjoying life.' She stood and let her cream satin nightdress slip to the cabin floor exposing a full-frontal view of her sculptured bare flesh just as a shadow past by our porthole. I leapt up and blocked the glass with my brushed-cotton clad shoulders.

Ruby hadn't even noticed. 'I bet your idea of a good time is staring into the backside of some sixty-five-year-old biddy with haemorrhoids,' she announced, pulling her cabin trunk out from under her berth.

Ruby certainly had a graphic way with words. 'If you must know,' I said, feeling pompous, 'I'm going to treat myself to lunch at the Casino Palace Hotel.'

Ruby viewed me from under her left armpit. 'Mac, why are you leaning against the porthole?'

I shrugged and sank back onto the mattress.

'Will you be starting the day with breakfast?' She was now imitating a dog digging for a bone.

'Oh, gosh,' I gasped, looking around for my watch. 'What time is it?'

Her arm appeared in front of my eyes a gold Cartier watch strapped to her wrist. I was impressed. It was seven-thirty and breakfast started at eight. 'Nice watch.'

'Yes, compliments of some Sheik who fancied his chances,' she replied, dragging a white pleated skirt from the mess that was her trunk. 'Do you want me to order you something?'

'Would you?' I swivelled onto the edge of my berth and slipped my toes into my pumps as Ruby's head appeared through her aertex sleeveless top. 'Some porridge with honey, please.'

She turned, pushing her blond locks under a thick, towelling headband which completed her Wimbledon ensemble. 'Right, I'll be on my way then. See you in the dining saloon.'

'RUBY.' She paused at the cabin door. 'Not a word. OK?' Her twisted smile didn't encourage confidence, then she was gone, off to breakfast before meeting her tennis doubles partner; some tea-planter from Assam on his way back to India after a spell of R&R in Scotland.

The cabin seemed very drab in her absence. I stood in front of the bulkhead mirror brushing my auburn, shoulder-length hair trying to bring some order to the mass of unruly curls and examined my reflection. Unlike Ruby, I lacked height; I was only five-feet-four inches in my stocking feet, I didn't have her silver-screen glamour or social aplomb and could only hope that my sharp intelligence, high ambition and dogged determination would make up for this shortfall. I wasn't optimistic.

I gave up on my hair and began to dress, then folded my creased nightie and placed it under my pillow. Ruby's satin equivalent lay like a puddle of liquid gold where she had dropped it earlier. I picked it up and without thinking held the thin straps against my shoulders, turning to check the effect in the mirror. The gossamer-thin material felt decadent against my skin and I thought it looked rather risqué on the frame of a country doctor from Northumbria. Still, I argued, it was my birthday and the purchase of one silk shift in Port Said would certainly go some way to balancing the practicalities of a ladies Topi and a bone-handled fly-swat.

'You're being ridiculous, Mac,' I announced and quickly folded the nightdress and placed it under Ruby's pillow out of view. My roommate was having a worrying influence on me and I wasn't sure how I felt about it. We were so diametrically opposite we could have been from different planets, but I had to admit, it was refreshing sharing a cabin with a woman who thought men were only useful in bed and for financing her very expensive lifestyle. Ruby, on the other hand, thought that my staid, Victorian values were old-fashioned and irrelevant in the modern world of the nineteen-twenties and said so, ad nauseam. Perhaps her influence on me was not that bad after all, I concluded. Her life in the hotspots of Soho had opened my eyes to a parallel universe and if I planned to expand my own horizons, then this was no bad thing.

I tried again untangling my hair as I looked out through the porthole at the cobalt-blue sea beyond and recalled the first time I had seen Ruby Tavener. It had been at Tilbury Docks ten days earlier. I smiled at the memory . . .

Having arrived in London, I had spent several days living in a Catholic Convent in Lambeth, staying with a distant relative of Ma's. Sister Edith had been very kind, my convent cell dry and, although the food was sparse, at least it was wholesome and edible. I used the time to gather some last-minute purchases from the Army & Navy store in Victoria Street. I spent a happy hour browsing through Foyle's bookshop on Charing Cross Road where I found a copy of Sir Ronald Ross's book on the spread of malaria. The British Library had extensive information and advice on life in Colonial India, which took me back to Foyle's book shop to buy copies of Rudyard Kipling's *Plain Tales from the Hills* and *Under the Deodars*.

When my departure day finally dawned, I climbed onto the 11.15 Fenchurch Street train en-route to Tilbury Docks and my berth on the ss Narkunda. This was it. I was on my way, if only my bowels would stop diverting me into the nearest ladies lavatory.

My cabin trunk with its P&O baggage labels was loaded
into the luggage trailer with any number of others and I took
my place alongside a large-bosomed female with signs of onset
emphysema, and opposite an emaciated missionary with acne.

Tilbury was a hive of activity as I stepped from the train,
feeling as anxious as an eighteenth-century midshipman about
to join his first ship. I was lost in a sea of humanity with no
clue as to what to do next. Some chap called for passengers on
the ss Narkunda and I followed his index finger as he pointed
to a large shed to my left with a faded 'Departure Hall' sign
nailed above the door. With other flustered new arrivals, I
entered this building with grimy, glass windows all down the
seaward side and voices echoing around the rafters of the
corrugated-iron roof. I could just make out a floating landing
stage beyond the shed and the imposing dark hull of a
passenger liner. Looking across to the other side I saw a
bearded, uniformed officer beckoning to me. I pushed through
the throng and came up against his wooden lectern, sweat
trickling down my neck.

'Good Mornin', Miss. Ya passport and ticket if ya please.'
His cockney drawl was delightful but indecipherable to my
northern ears and I remained inert. A grumpy baboon would
have described his expression as he repeated 'Passport . . . and .
. . ticket . . . please,' placing emphasis on each syllable. I
fumbled around in my bag for both then placed them on the
lectern and was about to ask if a Miss Trotter had arrived when
I was roughly elbowed out of the way by a young woman
wrapped in fox fur.

'My man, kindly deal with me first,' she demanded, pulling a passport and ticket out of her handbag.

The officer hesitated then abandoned me for this chit of a girl with delusions of grandeur. I was hot, nervous, frustrated and severely put out by this toffy-nosed debutante with no manners. Jabbing the officer on his arm with my index finger, I rammed my documents into his outstretched hand.

'Excuse me!' pronounced Miss High-and-Mighty, peering at my second-class ticket with disdain. 'I happen to be a First-Class passenger and therefore have priority.'

'I don't think so, dear.' The voice came from behind me.

I turned to find a tall, slim female towering over the scene, clad from head to toe in camel suede, her gloved hand pressing firmly into my opponent's fox fur and eyeing the Purser through a panel of cream netting.

'This passenger requires your attention.' She nodded at me. 'Now, Purser, kindly deal with Miss . . .?'

'MacKenzie,' I announced, still smarting from the intrusion. 'Doctor Stuart-MacKenzie.'

Her pencilled eyebrows widened. 'Right.'

The officer ran his finger down the passenger list as Miss First-Class wriggled like a sprat on a line.

'Cabin Twenty, Miss. . . er. . . Doctor MacKenzie.' He scribbled something on a notepad, ripped the page off with a flourish and beckoned a bellboy over from the rear wall.

'Folla' this lad, Doctor. 'E'll show ya to ya cabin.'

The one-sided conversation behind me continued unabated as I muttered my thanks.

'In the real world, dear, people learn to know their place and as you seem to be incapable of reading joined-up writing, allow me to assist you. Your First-Class reception desk is over there.' She pointed to another lectern to my left. 'Now, don't stand there looking vacant. Shift yourself.'

I retrieved my documents, nodded my gratitude to the woman for her intervention and rushed out of the departure shed, trying vainly to stay on the heels of the youngster whose wine-red pill-box hat dodged between passengers, cabin trunks and matelots as he made headway down the floating platform.

I was still chuckling to myself at the seriously insulting put-down of Miss High-and-Mighty when I was ushered into Cabin 20, followed shortly by my cabin trunk.

Expecting to share it with Miss Frances Trotter, a schoolteacher from Peckham who was to take up a post as headmistress at some girls' school in Poona, I was somewhat taken aback when my steward knocked, opened the door and allowed the camel-suede clad female from the departure shed to enter. I was on my knees in the process of removing my toiletries from my trunk at the time.

'You're not Miss Trotter,' I exclaimed open-mouthed.

'Well spotted.'

I stood, washbag in hand, the blood vessels of my face and neck dilating. I felt a complete idiot. 'Sorry, what I meant to say is, you seem to have the wrong cabin. I'm to share this one with a Miss Frances Trotter.' I peered around her at the steward, frowning.

'Not anymore, you're not. Miss Trotter is being re-berthed in cabin twenty-nine.' She held out her gloved hand.

I shook it. 'I don't understand.'

She pushed the gauze veil up over the rim of her hat and began to remove her gloves. 'Let's just say the Purser agreed to make some changes.' She pointed to my medical bag. 'There's nothing like sharing a cabin with your own private physician, now is there?'

'Actually, I'm a GP not a physician,' I corrected, placing my medical bag on the bulkhead shelf.

'Same thing in my book, Doctor MacKenzie.'

'Stuart-MacKenzie,' I said, turning and closing my cabin trunk lid.

'Sorry?' She was now testing the bed springs with her hands.

'Doctor Stuart-MacKenzie,' I repeated. 'Elizabeth Stuart-MacKenzie, but most colleagues called me Mac for short.' My trunk disappeared under the bed with the help of my left foot.

'Very well, Mac.' She removed her ankle-length coat and hung it on a hook behind the door. 'You can call me Ruby.'

'Nice to meet you, Ruby. Do you have a surname?' The muscles in my cheeks seem to have a mind of their own as I imagined her gripping the purser by his necktie and threatening all manner of consequences if she didn't get her own way.

'Tavener,' she said, 'and no, my father doesn't run a public-house. Now, which bed do you want?'

I pointed to the one below the porthole and my facial muscles finally won out as I burst out laughing. 'Did Miss Trotter have anything to say on the subject?'

'Hardly. She wasn't there.' Ruby winked and kicked off her shoes. 'First come, first served, that's my motto in life. Just keep a low-profile for the next couple of days, Mac, and you'll be fine.'

'Great,' I said, wiping a tear from my left eye. 'I've only been on this ship fifteen minutes and already have two enemies.'

'You should be so lucky. Mine would fill Trafalgar Square.'

That evening, over tomato soup, pork medallions in cream and a fresh fruit salad we discussed our diverse histories. Ruby's life in decadent London was a revelation to me, each reminiscence more colourful than the last until I couldn't tell truth from fiction. She was also the main topic of conversation amongst the ladies of the Fishing Fleet, whose salacious gossiping kept them occupied for hours.

'Crikey,' I exclaimed, looking at my watch and made a dash for the dining-room, convinced I had now missed breakfast. Ruby was leaving, racket in hand, with one of her tennis partners, as I reached the door.

'Oh, there you are, Mac. I don't think you have been introduced to Maurice.'

'Morning, Doctor. Miss Tavener has told me all about you. Maurice Blackthorn's the name, a fellow Scot.' He clasped my hand undressing me with his eyes. I pulled my hand away, his rough skin sandpapering my palm, instantly disliking this Glaswegian with chipped fingernails and stocky features.

'Your porridge is on the steamer keeping warm and Stanley wants to know if you're going on the Cairo and Pyramid tour?' Ruby announced, changing the subject.

'OK, I'll see him after breakfast. Are you going?'

'Wouldn't miss it for the world,' she shouted over her shoulder, 'so I'll be coming with you to Simon Arzt to buy a pith helmet.'

Oh great, I thought, lifting the P&O monogrammed breakfast bowl off the steamer and heading for my usual dining chair. A shopping spree with Ruby in charge was not quite what I had in mind on my birthday. I was halfway through my luke-warm porridge trying to think of a suitable excuse when a shadow fell across the tablecloth.

'Doctor Stuart-MacKenzie . . .'

I looked up to find Frances Trotter standing across from me, unease evident in her taut shoulders. She couldn't have been more than thirty, but her serious, scholarly countenance added years to her features, reminding me of Pa's organist at St Stephens Church who shunned any tune that didn't have a religious provenance. The high-necked cotton blouse and calf-length twill skirt masked what I imagined to be a slim, finely boned frame. Her chestnut-coloured hair, pinned back in a bun at the nape of her neck and half-rimmed gold spectacles hanging at her chest from a beaded chain proclaimed her profession.

Tilting her head to one side, her dark brown eyes indicating the chair opposite, she stoically waited. I nodded and she sat, her long, smooth fingers clasped in her lap.

'Good Morning, Miss Trotter, I trust you are well?' I wasn't sure if she had ever forgiven me for her change in sleeping arrangements and concentrated on my breakfast.

'Yes . . . well yes, I'm fine, but you see . . . it's Lady Wetherington.'

She was referring to the other occupant in cabin 29, a rather rotund lady of middle age who was returning to Bombay to rejoin her husband after spending the summer with her twin sons in Hertfordshire where they boarded at Haileybury school. I waited while Miss Trotter twisted the edge of her Belgian lace handkerchief.

'It's a little delicate, you see.'

I lowered my spoon, dabbed my lips with my napkin and abandoned my porridge, suggesting a stroll on deck. Whatever was wrong in cabin twenty-nine, Miss Trotter obviously needed time to overcome her embarrassment.

The starboard boat deck was littered with steamer chairs, some empty, some occupied, as passengers enjoyed the warmth of the morning's rays whilst sipping coffee or beef tea, reading or simply enjoying the sea breeze. As we walked towards the bow, I peered into the distance in the hope of seeing Egypt outlined on the horizon, but the African continent was being illusive in the heat haze. We paused, turned and made our way back aft, my impatience getting the better of me.

'You said the matter was delicate, Miss Trotter.'

'Indeed, indeed.' Her bottom lip was trapped between her teeth.

'Can I assume it's a medical delicacy?'

'Indeed.'

It occurred to me that Miss Trotter had a very limited vocabulary for a schoolteacher. I nodded to Major Stokes overflowing his steamer chair, smoking a cheroot as we passed by.

Miss Trotter lowered her voice. 'Lady Wetherington . . . Sybil, asked me to approach you as she is not of a mind to discuss her affliction with the ship's surgeon.'

'Ah, I see.' Now we were getting to the hub of the problem. 'A touch of diarrhoea, perhaps?' Poona's future headmistress appeared to be suffering from mild asphyxia. 'Would you like me to visit Lady Wetherington to see what I can do to help?'

'Oh, yes please, Doctor MacKenzie.' Colour instantly returned to her complexion. 'Sybil believes she has eaten something not quite digestible, you see.'

'Indeed,' I replied, clapping my lips together so as not to offend. 'I'll get my medical bag.'

'And, Doctor . . .' Miss Trotter clung to the aft rail breathing in the morning air as if she were about to hyper-ventilate. I paused by the deck door.

'You may find the cabin a little . . .' She rubbed her index finger under her wrinkled nose. 'A little . . .'

'Fetid?' I offered.

'Indeed.'

My sense of smell picked out cabin 29 yards ahead of the cabin door. Lady Wetherington lay on her cot, a metal pail at her side and the most noxious fumes coming from her person.

'Now, Lady Wetherington, the first thing you need is some fresh air.' I threw open the porthole hatch and then called down the corridor for the steward. 'How long has this been going on?'

'Since yesterday evening. Oooh!' Her head disappeared into the bucket as the steward knocked on the door.

'I need a mop, a bucket of sea water, some fresh towels and a jug of boiled water please.'

'Yes, Memsahib. Right away, Memsahib.' He backed away from the door, pinching the end of his nose as I returned to my patient and checked her pulse. It was racing. 'Have you passed any urine recently?'

Her affliction was making speech difficult but an echoed 'No,' was audible from inside the pail followed by another bout of severe retching and a strangulated explosion from her nether regions. 'Lady Wetherington, do you suffer from dysentery?'

Her head shook and she lay back with bile yellowing her lips.

'Well that's good, anyway. I'm going to take your temperature, clean you up and arrange for Miss Trotter to be moved to another berth until you are fit and well.' Sybil stared at me from sunken eyes, her breath coming in short gasps. She grabbed my arm and shook it in agreement.

For the next hour I acted as nursemaid until she was clean, rested and sipping small cups of cool, boiled water and nibbling dry toast. The cabin air still had the aroma of the sick room but as there was little left in Sybil's gut, I concluded that the sea breeze would combat any further bodily smells and left my patient to rest.

When I finally came out on deck, Port Said was hovering in the distance and I realised that I hadn't yet spoken to the Purser about the shore trip to Cairo.

'First things, first, Mac,' I chided, descending the stairs to the lower deck. Sybil's affliction had to be reported to the ship's surgeon as it needed to be written into his daily log and now that the patient was more presentable, I felt that he was best placed to take control. I knocked on the surgery door and waited. Dr Wallace's broad smile met me as I crossed his threshold.

'Mac, what a pleasant surprise. Now, what brings you to my door?'

'Lady Wetherington, Tom. Second-class, cabin 29. A sad case of food poisoning . . .'

Dr Wallace and I had been on first-name terms since leaving the Bay of Biscay and he had become a firm friend and a fount of knowledge on tropical diseases due to his long experience tending to the infirm passengers and crew of the P&O fleet.

Our paths had crossed in a gale off Ushant when I was co-opted into service tending to numerous passengers suffering seasickness. My strong stomach had ridden the storm intact, which was just as well because Dr Wallace and his assistant were sinking under the rising tide of *Mal de Mer* from the ss Narkunda rolling like a drunken sailor towards Finisterre. Meanwhile, Ruby, convinced that she was going to die clung to my side like a limpet. No amount of reassurance could counter the fear in her eyes as fifteen-foot waves battered our starboard hull and everything not lashed down shot across the cabin. The ship didn't stop listing to port or starboard until well past the Spanish Rias by which time Ruby's glamourous looks had taken on a rather Medusa-like quality.

I dropped into a chair by Tom's desk and continued my report. '. . . Lady Wetherington is now resting, propped up below the open porthole and sipping boiled water to avoid further dehydration. Her pulse is stable, her temperature only a little above normal and the Purser is arranging for Miss Trotter to take my berth while I'm away in Cairo.'

Tom began to scribble notes in his log. 'When did all this start?'

'Last night. After dinner, I think.' I tried to recall what had been on the menu. 'It could have been the egg mayonnaise sandwiches earlier. Have any other passengers reported in sick?'

'No, but I must get to the bottom of it or we could have the whole of second-class horizontal.' He put down his pen, removed his spectacles and rubbed his eye sockets with his fingers. He was quite attractive in a country gentleman sort of way, his smart uniform giving him an air of authority and respect. 'We'll probably find that the bar staff have used contaminated water to make ice, Mac. Leave it with me. I'll check with the head-waiter and pop along to cabin 29 within the hour.'

'Tom?'

'Umm?' He was back scribbling.

'What precautions should I take when eating ashore?'

His hand paused above his log. 'Dowse everything you eat with fresh lime or lemon juice.'

'Really?'

'Really. The acidity will help kill off any nasty bacteria.'

With that I made my farewells and returned to my cabin via the Purser's office, looking forward to being on terra-firma for the first time in days.

Chapter Three

Sweat was trickling down my spine as Ruby and I entered Simon Arzt Departmental Store on the Quai de Palestine in Port Said and I stared with wonder at the glass ceiling which allowed natural light into the atrium. The store's imposing fretted façade, some forty yards in length, had dominated the waterfront and Ruby reliably informed me as we headed across the ground floor that within the establishment one could find a post office, hairdressers, photo studio, pharmacy, florist and tearoom.

The latter sounded good to me as my roommate paused by a male member of staff clad in a white suit and red fez who bowed his head in deference to us, acknowledged her enquiry and pointed to the rear stairs.

'The pith-helmets are in Ladies Accessories,' Ruby announced as we ascended the carpeted staircase. 'Not sure about the fly-swat but no doubt the shop assistant will know.'

I kept thinking of that champagne-silk chemise I longed to buy but recoiled from searching for such a feminine garment when the only assistants I could see were male.

The plethora of white suits and red fezs made it easy to spot the store's employees amongst the throng of shoppers and Ruby soon had one such assistant producing an array of Topis on the glass counter of Ladies Accessories for us to try on. They were much lighter than I had imagined, clad in either khaki gabardine with leather chin straps or white cotton with webbed straps. Taking advice from our Egyptian sales assistant, who assured us that the cheaper white cotton versions were frowned upon by the British Raj, we agreed to purchase the gabardine version.

Ruby looked rather fetching in hers, but then, I thought, she would look fetching in a shroud. I, on the other hand, resembled a Yorkshire miner lacking a forehead and said so, loudly, sulking at my lack of height, glamour or sex appeal. My cabin companion assured me that I was talking nonsense and dragged me to the top floor in search of Men's Accessories. Here we found, guns, knives, ammunition, military furniture, tents and fly-swats. I was rather taken by the stuffed head of a rhinoceros mounted on ebony, its beady eyes glaring at me from the department's far wall.

'Do you do taxidermy as well here at Simon Arzt?' I enquired. Ruby was busy trying her hand at swatting anything that moved.

'Of course, Memsahib. Simon Arzt prides itself on catering to all our customers' needs.' The man was so smarmy he could have been made of molasses.

'Must be an off-shoot of Harrods,' commented Ruby, flicking a dead fly off the counter with her finger and thumb. 'I'll take this one.' She held up a fly-swat with a brown leather-bound handle. 'If you're not intent on buying that stuffed animal head, Mac, perhaps you could choose one of these and we could go and get some tea.'

My eyes kept veering towards the bolts of gloriously coloured silks stacked on the shelves across from the tearoom as we sat, enjoying a pot of Darjeeling tea and a cake-stand full of miniature pastries. It all reminded me of Aunt Karr's drawing room, and I wondered how she would react if she knew my Fishing Fleet companion was an ex-Windmill Girl.

'Badly,' I muttered through layers of honeyed pastry.

'What?'

'Nothing.'

'Mac, why do your eyes keep wandering over to Haberdashery? Have you spotted the man of your dreams wearing a fez?'

I sighed, sat back and raised my chin. 'I'd like to replace my brushed-cotton nightie with something a wee bit more light-weight, as a birthday treat.'

Ruby peered at me from under her long dark eyelashes. 'Good Lord, Mac, why didn't you say so before. It's high time you came out of your strait-laced shell and I'm just the person to help you. Come with me.'

Before I could say 'haute couture', she had me draped in silks, satins, muslins and French lace until my head spun. An hour later we returned to the ss Narkunda trailing a Simon Arzt shop-assistant hidden behind a stack of boxes with only the top of his fez visible.

I flopped onto my bed exhausted, convinced that I had emptied the departmental store of all its ladies-wear and was now bankrupt. Some sensible grounding was called for, so I went to check on Lady Wetherington, leaving Ruby fly-swatting the bulkhead mirror.

Sybil lay as I had left her, but she had more colour in her cheeks and had progressed from dry toast to half a banana.

'Has Doctor Wallace been to see you, Lady Wetherington?'

'Yes, dear. Such a charming man. He has given me something to calm my stomach and I'm to stay put for the next twenty-four hours.'

Probably ginger, I thought, and checked her pulse. 'Good, at least your heart-rate is better. Miss Trotter will be using my cabin for the next few days, so you won't be disturbed, and I know you are in very capable hands with Tom . . . Doctor Wallace.'

'Thank you, dear. I shall write to my husband from Port Said telling him what an asset you are to us all. I'm sure he'll expound your virtues to Bombay's society at large and you will be quite the celebrity by the time we dock.'

I wondered if Lord Wetherington had any influence with the men in grey suits at the Calcutta School of Tropical Medicine as I made my way aft but concluded that treating a bout of food poisoning was hardly on a scale with Yellow Fever. Back in cabin number 20 Ruby was busily packing.

'Why d'you think Lady Wetherington is travelling in second-class?' I asked as I entered.

'Probably fallen on hard times. The war effort and all that. It can't be cheap educating two sons boarding at a private school,' she stated, closing her portmanteau with difficulty. 'You'd better get a move on, Mac. Thomas Cook are due to collect us in thirty minutes.'

I recalled noticing their office next to Simon Arzt's Store, their windows full of posters advertising exotic destinations from Luxor to Alexandria. 'Right, help me stow these boxes under my bed and I'll pack for Cairo. I'll meet you on deck. Can you tell Stanley that I might be a tad delayed?' I suspected our Purser would not be amused at this fact being a stickler for timekeeping.

As it happened it didn't matter anyway. I was still deciding whether to include my medical kit in my luggage when there was a knock on the door. 'It's open,' I called, rifling through the bag's contents. When I looked up, Tom was hovering by the wash-hand basin.

'Mac,' he rubbed his chin. 'I'm afraid I need your help.'

I sat on the edge of the bed, sensing that Cairo was fading into A Thousand and One Nights and waited for Tom to explain his dilemma, which he did in great detail.

'Princess Dashwanabai of Jhalanpur, one of our First-Class passengers, is ill. I suspect, like Lady Wetherington, Her Highness is suffering from food poisoning but being a Hindu and in purdah, she cannot be treated by a male doctor. I know it's a lot to ask, Mac, and you have no reason to feel under any obligation as a passenger yourself, but I would be so grateful if you could examine her for me.'

'I assume there is no other choice, Tom?'

'I'm afraid not. The family physician is on his way to Cairo with her husband and, anyway, he's male. Under the circumstances, all I can do is appeal to your sense of professional duty and ask you to take my place.'

I returned my stethoscope to my medical bag and nodded. 'Give me five minutes to unpack, Tom, and I'll come to the surgery for a briefing. Should I cover my legs?'

'It might be advisable.' His brushed both his hands through his hair. 'I won't forget this, Mac. Let's hope it's all a storm in a tea-cup.'

The entrance to the Jhalanpur's first-class suite of rooms was opened by a chaprassi in full Hindu dress, his red and gold cummerbund and pagari headgear pleated with military precision, his Jhalanpur badge of office as the royal family's chief steward prominently sited at his chest. He bowed, palms together.

'Namaskaram Sahib. Namaskaram Memsahib.'

'Namaste,' replied Tom and eased me into the Persian carpeted sanctum.

I could feel my knees shaking as the chaprassi moved to an inner door and knocked. Another imposing male member of the household appeared, greeted me as before, took my bag and welcomed me in perfectly accented English.

'Doctor Stuart-MacKenzie?' I nodded. 'Allow me to introduce myself. I am Prince Kapoor Dhawan, the Princess's uncle. We are blessed with your presence. Please, follow me to the zenana.'

Tom watched as I was led from the room and along a plush carpeted corridor not knowing what to expect. The Prince opened a door, my view into the interior blocked by a heavy toile screen and having moved around it, I found myself in the Jhalanpur zenana and a world unchanged in centuries.

Five Hindu women swathed in magnificent gold or silver threaded saris, their jet-black hair hidden below the folds, sat on tasselled silk cushions scattered across the carpeted floor, their eyes lowered, voices silent, gold rings attached to their noses and ear lobes, and intricately patterned jewellery on their fingers and toes. It looked like a scene from Scheherazade and I had to pinch myself to check I wasn't dreaming.

'This way,' whispered the uncle moving across to an adjoining door.

I followed, entering the room beyond where a four-poster bed was swathed in yards of white gauze, the occupant within almost hidden from view. I turned. 'That will be all for the moment. Thank you, Your Highness.'

The uncle bowed and retreated leaving me alone with the first princess I had ever met. For a moment, the difference in our social status overwhelmed me and I steadied myself against the bedpost, my breathing coming in shallow gasps, then I saw her body writhe in pain within the muslin screening and the medic in me took over.

'Your Highness, I will need your co-operation.'

She whimpered, her hand grabbing the soft muslin searching for my touch. I lifted the pleated screen away and took her hand in mine. It was so delicate, so soft, the veins so pronounced. I couldn't see it well, but I could feel the contours like a blind person reading braille. 'I will need some light,' I said and opened the heavy brocade drapes covering the porthole.

The Princess was lying on her side, her legs curled up against her abdomen, her chin deep in her chest, eyes closed in pain. I peeled her fingers from my flesh and asked if she understood me. A voice from the doorway answered for her.

'No, Doctor Memsahib, the Princess, she only speak Hindi. I say to her what you say.'

The voice belonged to one of the more elderly ladies from the main saloon. 'Right. Please come and stand here.' I pointed to the opposite side of the bed, 'and tell her I need to examine her below the waist.' I brushed my hand from my belly button to my thighs. The woman nodded and leant closer to my patient.

I moved to the washbasin, turned on the gold taps and scrubbed my hands until they were raw, drying them naturally in the clammy air before removing my Pinard Horn from my bag. Tom had been under the impression that my patient was suffering from some intestinal problem, but a sixth sense brought me to a different conclusion.

'Is Princess Darshwanabai with child?' I asked.

The silence was deafening. 'It is possible, Doctor Memsahib.'

'How long?'

The question was repeated in Hindi and the Princess mumbled something unintelligible. 'She does not know, but perhaps four cycles.'

I figured that would put her around sixteen weeks. If I was facing a potential miscarriage, then I had to reverse it and save the child. I had the experience, but didn't know if I had the facilities? The mother should have been in the local hospital or at least the ship's medical bay, but I assumed the reason she remained in her suite was due to Hindu culture and religion which forbade her being helped by any male outside her family circle. Whether I liked it or not, I was her only hope of saving the baby or, if she haemorrhaged, saving her life, and that was far from certain. I rubbed my arm against my damp forehead, gently rolled her onto her back, lowered her knees and picked up the horn.

'Try to relax,' I said and placed the cup to her abdomen.

My acute hearing concentrated on sounds coming from the instrument, all ambient noise from the ceiling fans blocked by my brain. It was not a simple task. Intestinal gurgles, the mother's pulse, the valves of the blood vessels opening and closing were like white noise masking the baby's own life-beat. I moved the cup several times, stood to stretch my spine then bent again to make sense of the body's concerto. Suddenly, I heard it. The baby was alive, its heart-beat faint at over 160 beats a minute. I moved to the chest, the mother's heart-beat erratic and powerful. The foetus was in its infancy, it was under stress and about to abort.

I spread Princess Darshwanabai's legs and saw spots of blood and mucus dripping onto the sheet beneath. I carefully examined the area and smelt the discharge. It was fresh. My muscles relaxed. I had seen this often in the back streets of Berwick and knew that it didn't necessarily mean that the Princess was losing her child. However, I had to move quickly if I were to keep the foetus in the womb.

The Princess's stomach muscles went into spasm with another wave of pain and my stained hands immediately moved to her stomach and began gently massaging the abdominal area to increase blood circulation to the uterus, speaking slowly as I worked.

'We need Chamomile tea to relax the muscles and ease the pain.' Instructions were quietly passed back to the servants.

'Has the Princess drunk any caffeine in the last twenty-four hours?'

'Yes, Doctor Memsahib.'

'What about spiced foods?' There was no response. 'Curry or chillies?'

'Curry. We eat much.'

I continued gently kneading the area above the womb, the warmth from my hands adding to that created by the light friction of the massage, racking my brain for relevant natural therapies which would help. I thought back to my studies on herbal remedies in Edinburgh Medical School. Black Haw or Maca. That was it. Herbs which helped balance the mother's hormone levels, but were they available in Port Said? Maybe, if there was a Chinese herbalist in the Souk? I checked the baby's heartbeat. So far, so good. The Princess's kohl-blacked eyes scanned my face, trying to delve deeply into my soul. I smiled, nodded and went back to my work, determined to succeed, but knowing that without constant bedrest, a blanket curb on all spices and caffeine and daily abdominal massages, my efforts could well be in vain.

I checked my patient's pulse; it was in rhythm. The baby's heartbeat was also steady. 'I need hot water, clean towels, and fresh bed linen. Where is the Chamomile tea?'

'Here, Doctor Memsahib,' said a voice to my left.

'Please help the Princess to drink a little.' I held her gaze with mine. 'It will help you relax.' A loving arm went around her delicate neck and a small beaded ceramic cup touched her lips. The Princess didn't need to speak, her eyes said it all. The baby's future rested in my hands and she would do whatever was necessary to help me succeed.

When I was satisfied the emergency was averted, I stood back and took stock. 'I am confident that the baby will live,

Your Highness, but now it is up to you.' I waited for the message to be understood. 'From today, you must do exactly what I say.' She nodded, a weak smile creasing her lips and sipped more tea. 'I will come each day to check on the baby and give you a massage. Your woman must also learn to do this. You are to stay in bed and only eat and drink the things I recommend.' I covered her nakedness with her silk wrap. 'Now I will wash you and change your linen. Please turn onto your side.' I bent her legs into a foetal position and dipped the edge of a towel into the warm scented water.

Minutes ticked by as I worked until she was clean, well-padded between the legs and in new attire. Her eyelids were beginning to droop. Squeezing her hand, I assured her that all would be well but that she must not stress herself or the baby, then lowered the folds of muslin back into place. As she drifted into a fitful sleep, I lifted my medical bag from the floor, backed out of the bedchamber and tried to ignore the mother-of-all headaches now stabbing at my eye-sockets.

The uncle was waiting for me, his features taut, his mouth a thin white line amongst grey facial hair.

'The baby is saved, Your Excellency, but your niece needs total bedrest for the duration of this voyage and a special diet. I will check on her daily until Bombay. Thereafter, you must ensure she does not get stressed and where possible, continue her massages and diet.'

'*Bahut dhanyavaad*, Doctor MacKenzie. We are forever in your debt. Is there anything more we can do today?'

I rubbed the bridge of my nose. 'Well, there is one thing. Do you know of a Chinese herbalist here in Port Said?'

'No. Why?'

'There are certain natural remedies which will help balance your niece's hormone levels if only I could find them.'

'Doctor, if these herbs are not in Port Said I will send to Cairo for them. The Maharaja of Jhalanpur's grandson must live to continue the bloodline.'

I massaged my temples. Right now, the Maharaja's bloodline was not my priority, my headache was. 'Black Haw, from the Americas or Maca root from Peru.'

'Anything else?' I shook my head. A bad move.

'Then, if you'll excuse me, I will begin the search immediately.'

He bowed low, his palms locked together in prayer, his thumbs touching his forehead then opened the door to the corridor and followed me out.

I returned to Tom's office and sat, still massaging my temples. Tom handed me a cup of Earl Grey tea and two aspirins.

'You look shattered, Mac. What do you think the baby's chances are of going the full term?'

'Hard to say, Tom. Most of the women I've treated before have been tough, Anglo-Saxon stock from northern climes, not delicate flowers from the sheltered world of a Rajputan palace. The Princess is young, so that should help, but all these spicy foods and caffeine drinks in the tropics create heat in the womb and that's not good for the foetus.'

'Then we must make sure her uncle understands why you are concerned. He is an intelligent man and no-one in his household would dare to go against his wishes.'

'Where's her husband?' I swallowed the aspirin.

'In Cairo. He left this morning.'

'Why didn't he return to the ship once his wife became ill?' I was becoming tetchy. 'Doesn't he care about his bloodline?'

'Mac, Prince Vijay Kumar Singh II lives in a very different world to yours. The future Maharaja of Jhalanpur would never interfere in matters of the zenana. Child mortality is very common in India, that's why these Princes take so many wives. It's one way of ensuring that there is a male successor.'

I stopped dead, my mug half-way to my mouth. 'Were all those women in the zenana his wives then?'

'Probably . . . not necessarily . . . I couldn't say, Mac, I didn't see them, but Hindu families tend to be large so they could have been sisters, aunts or cousins. How many were there?'

I swallowed feeling the hot liquid warming my oesophagus. 'Oh, about six, I think, plus their servants. They seemed to be a range of ages, but I didn't see any children.'

'Then they are probably family. Vijay is still in his twenties, so I doubt he has more than one or two wives right now.'

'Male chauvinist,' I muttered into my mug and received one of those looks my father used to give me when I took the Lord's name in vain.

Chapter Four

Climbing the steps to the boat-deck I mulled over my day so far and concluded that my twenty-eighth birthday was turning into a non-event. Suddenly the ship juddered into life and I grabbed the rail for support as Port Said's waterfront buildings appeared to be moving slowly backwards. By the time I reached the promenade-deck to get a better view the ss Narkunda was already turning into the Suez Canal, the glow of the setting sun painting the Quai de Palestine a soft burnt-orange against the lighter desert sand.

Major Stokes was standing amidships leaning against the rail, the smoke from his cheroot spiralling aft in the light breeze, his waistcoat flapping freely. He saw me and beckoned me over.

'Now then, lass, this 'ere's nowt like the River Tweed, raight enough.' He pointed at the bumboats along the canal's shoreline and the dhows ploughing their trade in the late afternoon light, all keeping well into the side to avoid collision from our ship's wake as we snaked by.

'Should I know him?' I asked, pointing to a bronze statue atop a tall column, somewhat Nelson like, supported at its base by a roped concrete plinth, as the ss Narkunda moved ahead.

'Reckon not, lass. That'll be Ferdinand de Lesseps in all 'is glory.'

I watched the rigid figure glide past, his right arm pointing into the cut and his left holding a roll of parchment. 'I must say he looks very pompous.'

The Major's jocular snort attracted the attention of the lascars polishing the brass fittings on the deck below. 'Happen I would too, Doctor, if I'd dun summat Napoleon and 'is engineers managed to bungle.'

'Napoleon? Whatever did he bungle?'

'Apart from t'Battle o' Waterloo?'

I smiled as he scratched behind his ear.

'Aye, well, I 'ave it on good authority that Boney tried to build a canal 'ere fifty years afore de Lesseps. 'E wanted to get one over us English, ya see. Happens his army engineers blethered on about sea-level at one end bein' much higher than at t' other. Said it couldn't be done. Typical Frogs. Wouldn't know their ars . . . Sorry Doctor Mac, didn't mean to offend.'

'No offence taken, Major. So, what changed?'

'Well for starters, de Lesseps was an architect.' He winked at me sideways. 'It does help, you know, and Said Pasha, Egypt's Viceroy at t' time, was a very close friend.' He tapped the side of his nose. 'The rest, as the says, is history.'

'It's not very wide though, is it?' I tried to imagine a ship coming the other way and failed.

'That'll be why we take on a Suez Canal Pilot and transit in convoy. He'll be responsible for t'ship's progress through the Canal until we reach t' Red Sea.'

'How long is it?' I watched as a bullock pulled a wooden cart along the dusty road running parallel, the driver sitting cross-legged on a raised plank, his body swathed in a grubby dhoti and turban.

'About one-hundred-and-twenty nautical miles.'

'And what does our Captain do while this is all going on?'

'Sits back wi' his feet up watching t'world go by, I imagine.'

'Crikey. And if the Pilot runs the ship aground while he's not watching?'

The Major blew smoke rings into the air. 'Happen our Captain wouldna be best pleased. Come to think on it, nor would any other Commander waitin' to transit t'canal. That'd cause an international incident, and no mistake.'

'Dear me.' I crossed my fingers. The last thing I needed was to be stuck halfway up the Suez Canal on my birthday with an international incident raging around my ears.

I was about to mention that fact when a train, whistle blowing, passed along the railway track beside the bullock cart, heading away from Port Said, clouds of black smoke and steam billowing out behind. I followed its progress towards the horizon, a welcome distraction from an otherwise undulating, desert landscape which stretched for miles in all directions.

The Major and I stood in companionable silence, my eyes transfixed on a line of camels plodding across the sandy waste in the distance until the monotony of the never-ending sand-dunes made me feel drowsy. My headache was affecting my vision so I went below, hoping a warm bath would work where Tom's aspirin had failed. My cabin-steward went to organise things while I flopped onto my bed, closed my eyes and drifted into a disturbed slumber. I came to at the sound of someone walking into the cabin.

'Oh, Doctor MacKenzie, I'm so sorry. I thought you were in Cairo.'

'I should be,' I replied, shaking sleep from my heavy eyelids. 'Something came up.'

Miss Trotter hesitated at the door, hovering between staying or leaving.

'It's alright, you can have Miss Tavener's berth, she's definitely in Cairo.'

'Well, if you're sure?'

'Perfectly sure.' I eased myself off the bed, black dots forming before my eyes. 'I'm off for a bath before dinner. Do make yourself comfortable.' I grabbed my towel, dressing gown and bag and was about to depart when curiosity made me pause. 'How's Lady Wetherington?'

'Less explosive, thank you.'

'Oh, good. See you later then.' With that I was out into the corridor and on my way to the bathroom cubicle where Salvador D'Souza, my Goan steward, was busily filling a tub with hot seawater. He moved aside as I approached.

'Bath ready, Memsahib. Good washing.'

'Abrigada, Salvador. Abrigada.'

'Memsahib.' He handed me some special soap which lathered well in saltwater, placed a large wooden container of fresh water on a tray straddling the tub and departed.

The warmth of the seawater was like liquid velvet on my skin when I stepped in and sank below the waterline. As it lapped against my breasts I lay back and rested my aching head on a folded fluffy towel and closed my eyes. Ruby was now in Cairo and I wondered how she was getting on. I envied her one-night stay at the Shepheard's Hotel, well known as 'the' hotel in Egypt's capital according to Thomas Cook's literature. With its wall-to-wall luxury and her own en-suite bathroom, it was a far cry from my floating bathtub and sharing our cabin with the rather prim Miss Trotter. The heat of the cubicle was making me drowsy, so I let my eyelids drop and returned to my dream of earlier.

I had been alone in the sun-drenched desert walking aimlessly around, apparently lost. Suddenly Dr Wallace had appeared on the horizon, riding towards me across the sand dunes on a camel, his white suit and red fez conspicuous against the shifting sands, a stethoscope around his neck and a leather-bound fly-swat in his right hand. His progress was being hampered by constantly rising sand-dunes, holding him back like waves on a turbulent sea. In frustration, he dismounted and strode across the dunes, fly-swat aloft and, once close, pulled me into his arms. I never discovered what happened next as dear Miss Trotter had disturbed my nap.

I chuckled, and drowned my shoulders and head in the bath, my wet locks swimming around my face like a trawler net. Why on earth my subconscious mind had cast Tom Wallace as a Valentino matinee idol I had no clue. I've obviously had too much sun, I thought as I surfaced, finding the whole idea nonsensical. With his shy demeanour, intellectual features and impeccable English manners, our ship's surgeon was hardly the type to go rushing off into the Sahara Desert. On the contrary, if asked, Aunt Karr would have described him as solid, dependable and from good English stock. The sort who would make excellent husband material.

The adjacent cubicle door slammed shut bringing me out of my reverie and I continued with my ablutions. However, the notion was still rotating around my head when I arrived back at my cabin and found Salvador holding a bottle of Veuve Cliquot champagne in an ice bucket in one hand as he knocked on number 20's door.

'Where's that come from, Salvador?' I asked, pushing the door open and walking in ahead of him. Unless Miss Trotter had a secret lover in first-class, which I very much doubted, and with Ruby ashore, the champagne had to be for me. I was intrigued.

'Memsahib, the doctor, he ask me to bring.' With a flourish he produced a small white envelope from up his sleeve, bowed and withdrew leaving Miss Trotter sitting on Ruby's bed, open-mouthed, her hair loose and cascading across her shoulders in waves. I shrugged, ripped the envelope open and read the contents.

Dear Mac,

With sincere thanks for stepping into the breach today. I'm hoping you'll agree to share this with a certain fellow-medic on the promenade-deck before dinner.

ps: Happy Birthday!

Tom

Well, well, well, I thought and stuck my head out into the corridor. Perhaps our Dr Wallace wasn't so reserved after all.

'SALVADOR?'

'Yes, Memsahib?'

'Please keep this chilled and put it on a table at the rear of the promenade deck in my name.' I handed over the ice bucket.

'How many glasses, Memsahib?'

'Two, Salvador. Just two.'

My cabin was like a scene from a girl's school changing room as I rummaged through my cabin-trunk casting dresses aside.

Miss Trotter, leaning against the bulkhead with her knees against her chin, gave her views on which was most appropriate for a birthday celebration. It was Friday night and there would be a dance after dinner, the officers all in tropical white mess-kit and the ladies showing off their finery. I may not have been part of the Fishing Fleet, but I certainly wasn't going to be found wanting.

'How about this one, Miss Trotter?' I turned holding up a long-sleeved, navy velvet evening dress.'

'Too dark,' came the reply, 'and do call me Frances.'

'Oh . . .yes . . .certainly. Well, how about this one then, Frances?'

'Haven't you got anything a little more . . .' she rotated her hands in front of her shoulders, her nose wrinkled.

'Stylish.'

'Indeed.'

I dropped my MacKenzie tartan ball-gown on the growing pile and sighed. 'I'm afraid a working doctor from Berwick-on-Tweed isn't often called upon to emulate the height of fashion.'

'No, quite. But what about Miss Tavener?'

'RUBY! Goodness, she wouldn't be seen dead in anything but the height of fashion,' I announced, then realised what she was implying. 'I couldn't, Frances. I wouldn't dream of borrowing anything of Ruby's.' I thought back to the evenings she had breezed out of the cabin clad in a variety of long, sequinned and flowing haute couture. 'Anyway, she's twice my height.'

'But surely she wouldn't mind you borrowing some of her accessories to add . . .' her hands were rotating again.

'Chic?'

'Exactly, and you did mention that she was always trying to bring you out of your shell.'

'Strait-laced shell,' I corrected and we both giggled. I was beginning to enjoy Frances's company.

We returned to my cabin-trunk. 'What about something more off the shoulder?' she suggested.

'Good Lord, I don't have anything like . . .' I hesitated, my eyes travelling to the floor below my bed. 'Well, that's not strictly true. I did purchase one silk dress in Simon Arzt Departmental Store today.' I recalled Ruby peeling it off the mannequin in Ladies Clothing, holding it against my chest and instructing the shop assistant to wrap it. I shook my head. 'But that's no good. It needs shortening.' I pulled the boxes out of storage and seconds later I was holding up an emerald green strappy number with draping panels cut on the cross.

'Oh, that's perfect,' enthused Frances, gently touching the hem. 'Did you happen to buy any matching thread?'

'Yes, I did. Why?'

'Because, Doctor MacKenzie, as well as being a highly-respected and rather prim schoolteacher, you are also in the company of a qualified seamstress who adores haute couture.'

I looked at her in a new light.

'Now, put that gorgeous gown on and stand on the bed while I pin the hem, then, while you're drying your hair and putting on your make-up, I'll get cracking with a needle and thread.'

My dressing gown instantly slid to the floor. 'Frances, you're a star, and do please call me Mac.'

'Certainly, Mac. Now, up you go.'

My personal seamstress was true to her word. An hour later, I floated out of cabin 20 looking like a model from Chanel, one of Ruby's cream feather boas slung casually over my shoulders, a cream sequinned clutch-bag in my hand and my hair piled high on my head with an ivory and diamante clasp. Riveldene's ugly duckling was now swanning up the companionway steps in emerald-satined heels and gliding out onto the promenade deck wreathed in smiles.

Tom Wallace did a double take. 'Good God, Mac, is that you?'

'I hope so, Doctor,' I did a quick twirl, 'it's not every day a girl celebrates her twenty-eighth birthday, and with a bottle of Veuve Cliquot to boot.'

'Indeed.'

'You sound like Frances Trotter,' I said, accepting a chilled crystal flute bubbling with champagne, and feeling mischievously sexy.

'Happy Birthday, Doctor Stuart-MacKenzie.' Tom's glass chimed with mine. 'And may I say you look stunning.' He turned puce and coughed. 'For a GP.'

Charmingly shy, I thought and imagined our ship's surgeon in the shower. 'You also scrub-up well in your tropical whites, Doctor . . . for a ship's surgeon.' The cold bubbles fizzed on my tongue like sherbet as I walked towards the stern-rail to look out beyond our wake. 'Tom?'

'Umm?' I felt his arm brush my elbow.

'Who told you it was my birthday?'

A coughing fit overtook him. 'Er . . . I . . . er . . . I happened to see the passenger manifest.'

'Oh, really.' I was now thumping his upper spine to help clear his bronchial tubes. 'Would that have been with Stanley then, in the Purser's office?'

Chapter Five

W e were sitting at a table high up on the hurricane deck forward of the ship's three black funnels with only the star-studded sky above our heads. The lights of other ships in our convoy were easily visible ahead, our conga-line progressing at a snail's pace towards the Red Sea. I placed my dessert spoon on my plate and picked up my crystal wine glass. 'Tom, this has to be the best birthday dinner I've ever had. How did you manage it?'

'Let's just say the head-waiter owed me a favour following his disastrous sojourn into a house of ill-repute in Marseille. Coffee?' He raised his index finger and our Goan waiter, emerging from the shadows, took the order and left. 'I'm afraid I'm kept rather busy tending the crews' nefarious ailments following their visits to some of the more notorious fleshpots in port,' continued Tom. 'Not a job you would relish, Mac.'

'Oh, I don't know. The young farmworkers around Riveldene were not immune to the brothels of Berwick or Newcastle Docks and I'm not sure what was worse for them, the itching around their genitals or having to expose themselves to a woman. As a consequence, I've dealt with my fair share of sexually transmitted diseases in my time.'

'And you'll get a lot more once you arrive in India. The tropical heat tends to make our matelots and squaddies very frisky, not to mention the younger members of the Indian Civil Service.'

'But surely the idea is to marry them all off to girls like these onboard in the Fishing Fleet?'

'Sadly, not until they're thirty. Meantime they're sent to outstations on active military duty or buried in paperwork within the ICS in the hope of taking their minds off the opposite sex. It doesn't work, of course. Boys will be boys.'

'Seems to me bromide might be the better solution.'

'I'm afraid the Government has taken a dim view of bromide. Whilst it depresses sexual desire it also makes our squaddies less aware and less able to react in an attack. The army does have a supply of condoms, of course, but after a few beers the lads forget to use them.'

'Then I'd better keep a large stock of Salvarsan powder handy.' Not the most romantic conversation over dinner, I thought and decided to change the subject. 'That reminds me, Tom. Short of carrying an interpreter around in my medical bag I really need to speak Hindi. My experience today with the Princess made that clear. Is it difficult to learn?'

Tom placed his linen napkin down and sat back, stretching his long legs under the table. 'Well, I don't speak it fluently, you understand, but as to being difficult to learn, that depends who's teaching you.'

'Who taught you?'

'An ADC to the District Commissioner of Bombay during one of my early cruises.'

'Would you teach me . . . I mean, start me off during the rest of our cruise?'

Tom leant on his elbow, his right fingers under his nose and looked deep into my eyes. 'What's it worth?'

My stomach muscles did a somersault. 'I promise not to tell Prince Vijay Kumar Singh II that you fancy his wife.'

He shot up as if electrocuted. 'Good God, Mac, I'd be beheaded before I could say Jhalanpur. That's a bit harsh isn't it, particularly when I've never even clapped eyes on the woman?'

'Girl?' I replied and waited for my coffee to be poured. 'Well, it'll be your word against mine, Doctor Wallace.'

'And you drive a very hard bargain, Doctor MacKenzie.'

'So, are you going to start teaching me Hindi or will you be going to meet your maker at sunrise tomorrow?'

'Only if you'll agree to have the last dance with me tonight. I might as well die happy.'

My stomach muscles were now doing the Highland Fling as the strains of the Blue Danube rose from far below. Must be the claret, I decided, uncharacteristically impulsive as I rose and positioned myself in the centre of the empty deck. 'We could practise here, if you like, away from prying eyes.'

'Are you propositioning me, Elizabeth Stuart-Mackenzie?'

'Perish the thought, Doctor Wallace.' He was on his feet and striding towards me with purpose. 'I wouldn't want to show you up during the Moonlight Saunter, later,' I said. 'Not good for your reputation amongst the crew.'

His arm was around my waist, his buckskin shoes toe-to-toe with my satined heels and we waltzed around the teak-planking like Astaire and Rodgers, my panelled emerald dress fanning out behind. I didn't even know I could dance. As the last notes faded Tom raised my chin with his forefinger and brushed his lips across mine, his well-manicured whiskers tickling my chin. Pity Frances Trotter is sharing my cabin tonight, I thought, as I peeled myself off Tom's chest, lifted

Ruby's cream boa from the chair and headed for the promenade-deck trying to imitate a Northumbrian version of Clara Bow.

By the time the last dance had run its course, my feet ached, my head spun and I hadn't a care in the world. Tom saw me to my cabin, kissed me gently once more then, being the perfect English gentleman, walked away.

I leant against the door trying to decide if I was impressed with his self-control or annoyed by his typically English reserve. Through a haze of alcohol fumes, I was having difficulty deciding so gave up and quietly crept inside. To my surprise, Frances was not there. I tapped her bed to make sure but only the mattress responded. I swore, dragged the ivory clasp from my hair, stripped down to my undies and flopped onto my berth, banging my clenched fist against the cabin bulkhead in disgust. This fit of pique couldn't have lasted long because I was back dreaming of the Sahara Desert and Tom on his camel seconds later.

By morning, my impulsive, immoral self had mutated into a heavily hung-over, level-headed, sober and highly embarrassed Riveldene GP. Frances was still missing, and I concluded that she had probably succeeded where I had failed. Perhaps schoolteachers are more appealing to the opposite sex than female doctors, I mused, wishing my MacKenzie genes had contained more man appeal. I dressed and headed for breakfast, determined to get on with my day. Turning the corner, I bumped into Frances coming the other way looking rather dishevelled.

'Good birthday? Mac,' she asked innocently as we passed.

'Excellent, Frances, and your evening?'

'Oh, wonderful. I spent it keeping Lady Wetherington and her friends company playing bridge,' she cringed.

Sackcloth and ashes would not have been out of place on my side of the corridor. 'But where did you sleep?'

'On deck. It's so hot in these cabins. Even with the ventilation scuttles the ship's not going fast enough to create a breeze. I'll be glad when we reach the Red Sea.'

Realising that Frances would have been horrified at my poor opinion of her morals, I muttered something about porridge and made a quick exit.

I spent a pleasant half-hour breakfasting with a Lieutenant Moffatt from the Calcutta Light Horse who was returning to India with his new wife after two month's paid leave in England. He was a mine of useful information about the city, the hierarchy and the fashionable clubs to frequent, and I was still mulling over my possible membership of the Calcutta Club when I made my way to First Class, the Jhalanpur suite and my pregnant Princess.

She was sitting up in bed when I entered, one of her female relatives combing her hair, the other massaging her feet. 'How is my patient this morning?'

'The Princess, she feel much better,' said her elder relative. 'No curry, no caffeine, like you say.'

'Excellent.' I pulled my Pinard Horn from my medical bag and eased the staff to one side. 'Please.' I pointed to her attire. The Princess obliged and lay back. I beamed with pleasure at the sound of the little heartbeat.

'Our baby is feeling better too,' I announced, and the room erupted with Hindustani praise. Well, at least I think that's what it was, which brought Tom to mind and our verbal sparring over dinner about learning the language. My cheeks burned at the memory, so I dropped the horn on the bed and began the abdominal massage, keeping my eyes down and paying attention to the matter in hand. The aunt was watching with intense interest, so I called her over, placed her fingers under mine and felt her arm-muscles relax as she began to learn the technique. 'The idea is to bring more blood into the veins around the uterus,' I said. She appeared confused. 'The baby's sack?' Our hands rotated around the Princess's belly.

'Utriss?'

'U.T.E.R.U.S,' I repeated. She licked her lips and tried again.

'Utiras.'

'Yes, that's right. Uterus.'

'Garbhāśaya,' she announced and waited. My patient nodded, pointing to my fingers.

'Gar. . .bhā. . .śaya,' she repeated slowly.

I rolled the word around my tongue, her nose wrinkled, and I tried again. After the fourth attempt my instructor nodded, the Princess giggled, and I realised that I had just learnt my first Hindi word. How often I would use this in my daily life was debatable but at least it was a start.

The Hindu lascars, practising their fire-drill on deck gave me some very strange looks as I walked by repeating the word rather loudly so as not to forget it. 'Garbhāśaya, Garbhāśaya, Garbhāśaya.'

By the time I arrived at Tom's surgery I was word perfect and keen to learn more, but he was occupied with his morning clinic, so I spent an hour catching up on family letters in the second-class writing room before checking on Lady Wetherington. Ruby would be back after lunch so Frances would need to return to her own berth, assuming this was feasible.

Lady Wetherington appeared much better and asked me to assist her onto the deck to take some air. We made slow progress and I was just settling her into a steamer-chair with a book and blanket when my ears picked up the strains of bagpipes.

'Did you hear that?' I asked.

Lady Wetherington cocked her head. 'Hear what, dear?'

'Either I'm going crazy, Lady Wetherington, or someone around here is playing the bagpipes.'

'Oh, that'll be Sergeant Major Wilson from the Bombay Lancers. He always pipes the ship into port this side of Suez. Seems to think it's what Lord Irwin would expect.'

I strolled towards the bow and found the piper standing on a cargo hatch in full ceremonial dress uniform playing *Ye Banks and Braes O'Bonnie Doon* as the ss Narkunda made her way towards the town of Suez and her berth in Port Tewfik. The pipes had an instant effect on me. My eyes misted, the hair on the back of my neck stood on end and I was transported back to the Highlands of my childhood, running through a carpet of purple heather as the northerly wind tangled my hair. In the midday heat of the desert I suddenly felt as homesick as a British squaddie in France writing to his girl back home.

'Akkareyiddalli duHKavunTu,'

Two masculine hands rested lightly on my shoulders; familiar hands, strong, well-manicured and devoid of callouses. I leant back against a familiar chest and let tears form rivulets down my cheeks.

'What does it mean?'

'Where there's love, there's grief. An old Kannada proverb.' We stood in silence listening to the refrain. 'I suggest we stretch our legs ashore once we're docked. Blow the cobwebs away, Mac.'

'Lovely,' I whispered, unsure if I was referring to the stroll, the proverb or the piped music. I blinked and focused on the waterfront, a panorama straight out of the Industrial Revolution. Heavy machinery lifted cargo from freighter holds, black smoke discoloured the haze, a bird's nest of metal pipes snaked around gantries, and factory buildings towered above swarms of Egyptian workers bent double carrying heavy loads back and forth. Sergeant Major Wilson held the final note until it drifted out to sea, then saluted, turned on a sixpence and marched away, his kilt swinging from side to side.

'I'll go and change,' I said, still enjoying the feel of Tom's ribcage against my spine. 'Will I need gumboots to get across that lot?' I nodded to the mayhem in the commercial dock.

'No, Mac. We berth at the passenger dock, over there.' He pointed to my left as a concrete mole grew in grandeur beyond our starboard bow.

'Not quite Glencoe, is it?' My head was still in the Highlands.

'No. Suez is like nothing else on earth. A ramshackle crossroads between east and west. A cornucopia of different languages, religions, transportation and trade. Once seen, Mac, never forgotten.' He lowered his hands and eased me to his side.

'Will we be here long?'

'Just enough time to pick up the shore-party after their trip to the Pyramids, take on supplies and pay our dues. With luck, and Allah, we'll be on our way to Aden before the moon rises.'

'My father once said that there were no ten commandments east of the Suez. Was he right?' I caught the aroma of spices, sewage and sweat on the air.

'Yes and no. Christianity still thrives amongst the Musselmen, Hindus, Sikhs and Jews of this region but Christian values don't hold much sway around these parts.'

'Then I'd better keep my feminist opinions to myself and walk two steps behind you.' I winked and tapped my watch. 'I'll meet you at the gangway in half-an-hour.' He nodded as I followed a group of young children with their ayah back amidships.

Chapter Six

We were coming back aboard a couple of hours later when the Second Officer leant over the upper-deck rail and called out.

'Doctor Wallace, you're needed in surgery. Three teeth broken.'

'Right,' called out Tom, squeezed my arm and took the gangway two steps at a time.

I shielded my eyes from the sun and caught the Second Officer's attention, raising both my hands, palms up.

'Cricket, Doctor MacKenzie.' He rammed two fingers into his front teeth. 'Ball hit Reverend Pillsbury here instead of his bat.'

I rubbed my own teeth and entered the ship. That's got to be painful I thought, as I made my way to my cabin, intent on donning a swimsuit and going for a dip in the second-class pool.

It was a furnace below decks, the humidity drawing sweat through my pores like a perforated bladder under pressure. I entered the cabin, decided I had got the wrong one, went out, checked the cabin number and entered again. The place was empty. 'Where's my gear?' I asked the bulkhead and got no response. I checked under my bed to find an empty floor. To add to my confusion, all the linen was freshly laundered, and the porthole curtains drawn.

Stanley sat behind his desk, his expression that of a supercilious Staff-Sergeant as I stood, hands on hips, gearing up for a fight.

'Purser, my clothes have disappeared.'

'Correct,' stated Stanley, and relaxed back into his swivel chair.

'And?'

He drummed his fingers on the desktop. 'Doctor Stuart-MacKenzie, did ya, or did ya not request a cabin on the port side once we docked 'ere in Suez?'

'I . . . No . . . well, yes. . . sort of.' I shut up, Ruby's comments in Port Said replaying in my head.

'Well then.' He stretched over to a large cloth-eared ledger that I had last seen in the departure shed in Tilbury, flicked through a few pages and stabbed the second column on the left, headed 'CABINS'. 'You'll find your belongin's in Cabin 8. I told the steward to shift it all while you was promenading ashore with Doctor Wallace.'

Bush telegraph had nothing on the ss Narkunda, I thought, as I peered at the up-side-down writing. 'So, who used it until today?'

'Professor Snape, the archaeologist, and 'is gofer. They disembarked 'ere to go diggin' up ancient bodies in the Valley of the Kings.'

'Fascinating.' After two weeks of Stanley's cockney drawl I had become familiar with the dialect and had less difficulty in understanding him. As for Professor Snape, I didn't think I'd had the pleasure of meeting this eminent gentleman during our cruise but did recall seeing an elderly, whiskered man, clad from head to toe in khaki sitting in the reading room examining a book of hieroglyphic text. 'Perhaps you'd let Rub . . . I mean Miss Tavener . . . know we've moved when she arrives from Cairo.'

'Will do, Doctor. Meantime, you might want to check out this package from Ismailia. Came aboard earlier.' He handed over a small rectangular box covered in brown paper; my name clearly written on top. I was intrigued and went in search of cabin 8, my belongings and our new steward. To my surprise, Salvador appeared in the corridor.

'This way, Memsahib.'

'Are you moving too, Salvador?'

He bowed. 'Your wish is my command, Memsahib.'

'Wonderful, then how about a jug of fresh lemonade?'

While Salvador went in search of some cool refreshment, I sat under the open porthole hatch and untied the parcel, removing a lacquered wooden box with an ornate metal clasp which, when opened, exposed a mound of ground Black Haw bark surrounded by platted reeds.

'Yes!' I shouted, causing Salvador to jump with fright and the jug of fresh lemonade to rock alarmingly as he placed it on the rattan table. I nodded my thanks as my fingers rubbed the soft brown powder between my fingertips. This should be sufficient to get Princess Darshwanabai to Bombay, I decided, and sipped the chilled drink, mulling over methods of infusion and correct dosages.

Ruby breezed in as I was closing the box lid, the scent of her frangipani perfume pervading the room. She dropped a mountain of ribboned packages on her bed and gave me a theatrical peck on both cheeks. 'Mac, you've just missed out on seeing the most exotic sights of Egypt, and all for some professional call of duty.'

'I can well imagine,' I said, not wishing to elaborate.

Clothes, shoes and toiletries began to cover every available space as I retreated ever further into the corner and watched Ruby polish off my lemonade between bursts of unpacking.

'What was the problem?' She had the effrontery to hand me her empty tumbler.

'My lips are sealed, Ruby.' Her eyebrows touched her hairline as I placed the glass on the shelf by my bed. 'Let's just say, all's well that ends well and leave it at that. OK?'

'OK, but I know all about your tryst under the stars with the ship's surgeon on the hurricane deck last night, so don't look so secretive. Here,' she threw a parcel at me. 'This one's for you,' and went back to her unpacking.

I fielded the item in mid-air and felt its weight. 'Ruby, I really didn't . . .'

'Yes, you did. You've just missed the best two days of this cruise and on your birthday as well.'

'But . . .'

'No buts, just open it.'

A large faceted glass-bottle rested in the palm of my hand, the pale lemon liquid permeating my senses with a delicate aroma of jasmine and citrus. 'Ruby, this is far too extravagant. It must have cost a fortune.'

My roommate's face glowed. 'I was tasked to buy you something very special by a certain gentleman so there's no need to thank me.'

My eyes were locked on the bottle. Surely, I thought, Tom hadn't arranged this before Ruby left, there hadn't been time. I was speechless.

'This one is from me.'

Ruby handed over a small cream paper-bag with black edging and black silk handles. I parted the black tissue paper within and exposed a rose-coloured silk and lace chemise. It was exquisite.

'Ruby.' I dropped onto the end of my bed and held the garment up to the light. 'This is beautiful.'

'And just what you failed to buy in Port Said.'

'But who bought the perfume?' I asked, folding the chemise carefully back into its bag.

'All in good time, Mac. Now, how about a swim then you can fill me in on dancing the night away in something long green and flowing as the ss Narkunda drifted through Suez.'

I placed my gifts on the bed and dragged my trunk from underneath. 'How did you hear about that.'

'Mac,' said Ruby, pulling her swimsuit out of her portmanteau, 'the world and his mother knows about it. Now hurry up, I've been dreaming about this swim since leaving Shepheard's Hotel.'

I was reclining on a steamer chair at the bow dripping seawater onto the teak deck and enjoying the sun's rays tanning my skin when it suddenly disappeared and I was left in shadow. I looked up from reading Rudyard Kipling's Plain Tales from the Hills to find a casually dressed Indian standing at the foot of my chair blocking the rays. His white shorts, pale blue polo shirt and cream canvass loafers oozed quality, his thick, ebony-coloured hair falling casually across one eyebrow, his sunglasses reflecting my semi-naked frame. I looked across to Ruby in the pool who winked as her cerise swimming cap disappeared below the waterline.

'Doctor Stuart-MacKenzie?' The man's English was straight out of Oxbridge.

I nodded, incapable of speech and pulled my bath-towel around my frame.

He bowed flamboyantly. 'Prince Vijay Kumar Singh II at your service, Ma'am.'

'Your Highness,' I stuttered, feeling distinctly at a disadvantage and wishing I were more suitably dressed.

'May I?' He pointed to Ruby's empty steamer chair next to mine and without waiting for a reply, pushed her towel aside, lowered himself into the seat and relaxed back, his hand in the air. A steward was by his side in seconds. 'Two nimbu-panis.' Removing his sunglasses, his deep-brown eyes locked onto mine. 'Unless you prefer something stronger?'

I hadn't a clue what nimbu-panis was but being temporarily struck dumb all I could do was smile and lower my eyelids. I could sense fellow bathers hovering, intrigued like myself by this dapper male with his broad smile, sculptured physique and impeccable manners. I tried again, lowering my voice to a semi-whisper. 'Your Highness, I . . . I trust your wife is rested and feeling better?'

'She is, Doctor, and following your instructions to the letter. Her uncle is overseeing the herbal infusions which you prescribed earlier, and both send their most sincere gratitude for your professional and caring concern especially when you should have been in Giza and Cairo.'

'Prince Kapoor Dhawan?'

'Yes.' He rotated a large ruby ring on his forefinger. 'We are all indebted to you for saving my son's life.'

I wanted to correct his assumption on the baby's gender but couldn't find the right words. Ruby, pulling off her swimming cap and shaking her short blonde hair, walked up behind him giving me the opportunity to change the subject. She looked as if she was walking out of the pages of some glossy women's magazine in her cerise one-piece suit, matching nail vanish and long, toned and all-over tanned body. As usual, I felt like the poor relation. 'Your Highness, may I introduce Miss Ruby Tavener?'

'Ruby,' acknowledged the Prince removing himself from the chair. 'We have already met, Doctor.' Laughter lines creased his temples as he replaced her towel, took her hand and steadied her as she sat.

The steward arrived with a tray of drinks. The Prince turned away to order a third glass giving me the opportunity to catch Ruby's attention, covertly sniffing my wrist and pointing to him with my chin, my eyebrows raised. Her head dropped to her chest and she covered the move by brushing her fingers through her damp locks, the corners of her mouth lifting. I had no idea what the protocol was for thanking a Prince for a present which probably cost more than my passage to Bombay, accepted my glass of nimbu-panis and left any conversation to Ruby. While they talked about their travels ashore, I enjoyed the sensation of lime soda over crushed ice with what I thought was a hint of mango.

'I understand from Miss Tavener, Doctor, that it is your intention to study the virology of tropical diseases at the CSTM.'

'Yes, that's the plan. However, this depends on my interview with the school's Director and Governors before an official offer can be made. Protocol, apparently.'

'Very laudable, if I may say so.'

'I couldn't agree more, Your Highness,' agreed Tom, smiling as he approached our chairs. 'It's a pity we don't have more dedicated females like Doctor MacKenzie in medicine.' He shook the Princes hand then smiled at Ruby. 'How was the Sahara Desert?'

'Exciting, hot and amazing,' announced my roommate, accepting her drink from the Prince. 'Tell me Doctor Wallace, how is Reverend Pillsbury progressing after his little mishap?'

Little mishap, I thought with derision. The poor man had three teeth shattered.

'He's resting, Miss Tavener, with regular doses of pain-killers and a mouth full of padding.' He turned to me. 'I had to remove the stumps and then stitch his gum. He won't be playing cricket again for a few weeks.'

'Who was bowling?' enquired the Prince.

Tom had the discomfort of looking ashamed. 'Our ship's chaplain, I'm afraid. He's known around the fleet as a rather useful fast bowler.'

'It's a pity poor Reverend Pillsbury was not aware of this at the time,' I suggested. 'He must be in considerable pain, the gums are a most sensitive area.'

'Would you excuse us, Miss Tavener, Your Highness? I've promised Doctor MacKenzie that I would teach her some Hindi medical terms and I seem to have an hour free before my next surgery.'

'Really,' muttered Ruby, her reply soaked in scepticism.

Tom helped me rise and draped my bathrobe around my shoulders. I saw Ruby lower her sunglasses and peer over the frame. She didn't have to say it, we were both wondering if Tom Wallace would appreciate my rose-coloured chemise. Prince Vijay Kumar Singh II certainly would, I thought. Blood rushed up my neck as he raised my fingers to his lips, his warm breath on my skin sending subliminal impulses of danger to my brain. My hand retracted as if burned and, for a split-second I could have sworn I was back in the company of Duncan Fitzpatrick. I backed away wanting to put as much distance as possible between us, Pa's words, *there are no Ten Commandments east of the Suez,*' concentrating my mind.

Ruby was lying on her bed, scantily clad in lace undies and silk stockings, as I put the finishing touches to my make-up at the bulkhead mirror before dinner.

'What do you think of Vijay?'

The question came out of the blue and I stalled, not sure how to respond. I looked at her reflection through the glass. 'VJ?'

She rolled onto her stomach. 'Prince Vijay Kumar Singh II. Son and heir to the Maharaja of Jhalanpur.'

'I think he's a charmer,' I replied. My true opinion of this flirtatious husband who abandoned his wife in her time of need was less complimentary and kept strictly to myself. 'He joined the ship in Marseille, didn't he?'

'Yes, don't you remember, we were standing by the boat deck rail watching the world go by when his entourage boarded.'

An image of sari-clad women, their faces half-covered in silk veils, entering the ship while a mass of luggage piled-up on the quay surfaced along with Tom's later explanation that many Indian Princes owned villas on the French Riviera and held court there throughout the Mediterranean summer, returning to their Indian palaces for a winter of playing polo, hunting and shooting. Vijay Kumar Singh II was no exception. As the heir to the Jhalanpur throne he had carte-blanche to go wherever he chose and, using his family's enormous wealth, he did this in great style. Jealousy coursed through my blood stream like jaundice. Being educated at Winchester and Oxford and, no doubt, having a circle of high-ranking friends within King George VI's court, the Prince was able to enjoy the best of all worlds.

It was obvious that Ruby was impressed, and I didn't want to be a wet blanket. 'Yes, definitely a charmer, and very attractive in an Indian sort of way. Did he travel to Giza with you?'

'No, he had meetings in Ismailia with the Egyptian royal family and joined us at Shepherds Hotel.'

I was surprised Ruby knew so much about his movements and questioned her further. 'Was his physician with him?'

'Oh, yes. He never travels anywhere without his physician.'
I grunted under my breath.

'I told him that we were sharing a cabin and was amazed when he asked me to suggest a gift for you while we were in Cairo. You are a dark horse, Mac, I had no idea that you knew him. I take it you like the gift.'

Probably paid for out of small-change, I thought, refusing to be drawn. 'Ruby, not only is the perfume wonderful, but there is enough of it to last me a life-time.'

'Then enjoy it.' She stood and checked the seams on her stockings. 'It's not every day you get to impress a prince.'

Chapter Seven

Sunday dawned hot and muggy. Frances nodded to a chair by her side as I entered the packed saloon. I was pleasantly surprised to see that her severe bun had been replaced by a tortoiseshell clasp holding her thick burnished copper hair at her collar, her long tresses flowing down her spine. I squeezed past a group of fresh-faced young women of the Fishing Fleet and took in the long table at the front draped in the Union flag and Red Ensign, the Book of Common Prayer resting on a wooden lectern to one side and an ornately carved hymn-board swinging gently from a brass hook above the pianoforte.

This was our third Sunday aboard and as the ss Narkunda cruised at fourteen knots through the murky waters of the Red Sea the passengers and off-duty crew were gathered together for the Sunday morning church service, presided over by the ship's chaplain.

The Captain and his off-duty uniformed officers, sat, straight-backed, on the starboard side while the Anglican passengers in their sedate attire occupied the rows to port, the overflow standing shoulder-to-shoulder around the perimeter bulkheads.

I caught Tom's eye across the aisle and thought how distinguished he looked in his 'all-whites'. He nodded then turned to say something to the Navigation Officer sitting alongside who looked at Frances and smiled. She tried to keep her expression bland, but I dug her in the ribs and her lips cracked.

Gaining her composure, she whispered in my ear, 'Lady Wetherington wondered if you'd join her for a sherry in the lounge bar after the service.'

'I'd be delighted,' I muttered in reply. 'I take it she's now much better?'

Frances nodded in agreement as the chaplain brushed past my shoulder, advanced down the aisle and settled himself at the lectern. In devotional tones he cast his voice above the congregation's head announcing hymn 386. A solemn-faced lady with pinched-features and a crumpled straw hat that looked as if it had seen better days waited, hands hovering above the keys, her eyes locked onto the chaplain's chin as a rustle of skirts and the clearing of throats brought the assembled group to its feet.

A disturbance at the saloon door made me turn and I caught sight of Reverend Pillsbury struggling into the room, one hand over his swollen mouth the other gesticulating to the chaplain that the service should proceed forthwith as his stout frame came to rest against the rear wall. The chaplain stared at this late-comer with some disquiet at having caused his discomfort, pushing his forefinger down the inside of his dog-collar and stretching his neck from side-to-side.

Seeing his obvious embarrassment, the pianist made a unilateral decision to play the opening bars of the hymn and with one collective intake of breath the congregation burst into song.

'Lead us, heavenly Father, lead us
o'er the world's tempestuous sea;
Guard us, guide us, keep us, feed us,

for we have no help but thee;
Yet possessing every blessing,
if our God our Father be.'

Frances held the hymn book at close quarters but after years occupying the chilly pews of my father's church in Riveldene, I was already word perfect.

'Saviour, breathe forgiveness o'er us:
all our weakness thou dost know;
Thou didst tread this earth before us,
thou didst feel its keenest woe;
Lone and dreary, faint and weary,
through the desert thou didst go.'

Very apt, I thought, looking out at an unrelenting horizon of sand and wondering what on earth I was doing standing before a 'man of the cloth' when I had denounced God as being irrelevant weeks earlier. Like the chaplain, I too was beginning to feel hot and agitated.

'Spirit of our God, descending,
fill our hearts with heavenly joy,
Love with every passion blending,
pleasure that can never cloy:
Thus provided, pardoned, guided,
nothing can our peace destroy.'

Well, I concluded, as the last notes drifted out beyond the hull, my world was anything but peaceful. In addition to having no firm idea what my future held regarding the Calcutta School of Tropical Medicine, I was also indulging in exotic dreams about the ship's surgeon and accepting expensive bottles of perfume from a married prince. I shuffled back into my chair and tried to still my mind but Christian prayer and Paul's Letters to the Corinthians were no match for my over-active brain. The chaplain looked as if he was in for the long-haul, so I sighed and began to count heads as if counting sheep.

My eyes scanned the eight rows of heads in front of me then tracked around the walls before gazing out beyond the glass panelling. I caught sight of Salvador D'Souza standing on deck surrounded by other darker-skinned brethren, all intent on participating in the church service from afar. He sensed me looking at him and puffed out his chest. I realised that he, like the majority of Goanese, would be a practising Roman Catholic.

As the Captain got to his feet to read the second lesson, I studied the external group and recognised several more faces. There was the pretty ayah in her bright blue sari who spent her days trying to keep two impish colonial infants in order, and Lady Cottesmore's maid with her dark hair under a mop cap above a very English face, her black, calf-length dress and starched white apron rather sombre in the morning light. It occurred to me that this small floating congregation had a purpose beyond paying homage to their Lord. Like me, they were participating in a maritime tradition which British naval vessels and merchant ships had practised for centuries. Like our seaborne forebears, we were a very long way from home, cut off from family and all that was familiar and it felt reassuring to be praying together with fellow passengers and crew for our own safety and the peace and welfare of our King and country of which we were a distant part. With my spirits uplifted I attacked '*Fight the good fight*' with gusto, my voice reaching the rafters, and looked forward to my schooner of sherry with Lady Wetherington.

The decks were buzzing with people as Frances and I made our way to the second-class lounge.

'Ruby obviously doesn't do church,' commented Frances pulling open the lounge/bar door. Lady Wetherington was seated on a brown leather armchair in the corner, an occasional table in front of her with three schooners of deep amber liquid standing ready and waiting.

'No, I'm afraid Ruby and religion don't appear to mix,' I said, coming to rest by the table. I recalled my roommate's expression resembling that of a child being made to eat its greens when I had invited her to join me before breakfast. 'I believe she was planning to spend the time communing with her bath-tub. Good morning Lady Wetherington. I must say you look very rosy this morning.'

'I feel rosy, dear. Now sit, both of you and tell me all about the ship's gossip. What have I missed?'

Frances cleared her throat. 'I have a sneaky suspicion that Sybil has got wind of your emerald dress, Mac. Why don't you fill her in on the details?'

'Oh, do, Doctor MacKenzie, right from the moment you disembarked in Port Said with Miss Tavener. I do love a bit of romance.'

My face matched the colour of my sherry. 'I wouldn't know anything about romance, Lady Wetherington . . .' There must have been a question mark hovering over my head as I glared at Frances. She was busy wiping spilled sherry off the base of her glass.

'Do call me Sybil, dear. No need to be so formal, after all, you have seen parts of me that even my dear Archie would baulk at.'

'. . . Sybil, but without Frances coming to my rescue with her sewing skills I'm not sure what I would have done.' I spent the next few minutes expounding on Frances's abilities as a seamstress and the events of my birthday, glossing over the more intimate moments. 'I meant to ask, Frances, are you still sleeping on deck at night or has the ship's speed helped ventilate the cabin?'

Frances's hand appeared to shake as more sherry dripped down the outside of the glass.

'She's such a dear,' said Sybil, tapping Frances on the hand. 'After checking that I'm comfortable with my nightly glass of hot milk she beds down outside until the Serang and his lascars start hosing down the decks at dawn.'

'You should try it, Mac,' said Frances, regaining her composure. 'The cool desert air makes for a good night's sleep, believe me.'

'Perhaps I will,' I announced. Are you coming in for lunch, Sybil?'

'I don't think so, dear. Maybe a lightly boiled egg will do me right now. Perhaps you would send the steward over as you leave.'

I polished off the rest of my sherry and rose.

Making our way to the buffet table, we found Ruby helping herself to poached salmon salad and a glass of pomegranate juice, her tailored cream slacks and sleeveless taupe body-hugging top accentuating her figure. 'Hi, girls, how was JC?'

'JC?' whispered Frances from behind.

'Our Saviour is missing you, Ruby. Christ loves a convert, doesn't he Frances?'

'Oh. Indeed.'

'Though what Mary Magdalene would make of your feather boa I'm not too sure.' I helped myself to a Waldorf salad and topped a glass of tomato juice with drops of Worcester Sauce.

'She'd be green with envy,' announced Ruby leading us towards a table, 'and as for that business about the Immaculate Conception,' she looked over her shoulder at Frances and I bringing up the rear, 'even my dad wouldn't have been fooled and he's two bob short of a pound.'

'Will you keep your voice down. Ruby. Frances and I have reputations to maintain.'

'Sorry, girls, no offence intended.' She pushed aside a couple of chairs to ease our passage. 'Now Frances Trotter, what's all this I hear about you and the Navigation Officer watching the sunrise on the fore-deck?'

I stood stock still and Frances nearly tripped over my feet. 'What?'

Ruby dropped into the furthest chair and placed her poached salmon salad down on the blindingly white linen tablecloth and took a large gulp of pomegranate juice.

'Frances, what does Ruby know that I don't?' I sounded like Lady Wetherington.

'I . . .'

'Cat got your tongue?' mocked Ruby.

'I think you've got the wrong end of the stick, Ruby.' Frances appeared to have ants in her pants. 'Officer Hamilton simply thought I would enjoy seeing the sunrise over the Horn of Africa.'

'Is that what he called it?'

I kicked Ruby under the table. 'Was it wonderful?' I asked.

'What, the sunrise or Officer Hamilton's Horn of Africa?'

'Ruby, do shut-up and let Frances explain.'

'There's nothing to explain.' Frances's eyes were oscillating between our faces, her angelic expression fooling no-one. 'I simply didn't want to disturb Sybil at that hour of the morning, so I agreed.' She scratched her head. 'Don't get me wrong, he's really very nice, but I'm sure he was only trying to be kind.' She retreated into her lemonade, intent on avoiding further comment.

Ruby tapped the tablecloth with her fork. 'In my experience, Frances, men are only after one thing and it isn't kindness.'

'Will you be quiet,' I placed an arm on the back of Frances's chair and attempted an older sister approach. 'I'm sure he was the perfect gentleman, Frances.' I could feel her shoulders relax and she leant back against my arm convinced the conversation was over. She was wrong.

'So, when will you be seeing him again, socially?' I nonchalantly asked and felt her tense once more.

'Oh, goodness, Mac, can't a girl have any privacy on this ship?'

'With Lady Wetherington onboard?'

We all burst out laughing.

'You know,' I mused, picking up my knife and fork and tackling my Waldorf-salad, 'if we're not careful, the Fishing

Fleet will be keel-hauling us for getting in the way of their future prospects.'

'Oh, I don't think so, Mac, not with the ship's officers anyway,' replied Frances, checking the dining room for any budding colonial wives. 'After all, the Fishing Fleet are looking for permanent partners, not attractive sailors with a girl in every port.'

I thought of Tom and hoped he didn't fall into this category.

'I knew it,' announced Ruby, going for the jugular. 'She does fancy him,'

Poona's future headmistress slowly lowered her cutlery, sighed deeply and stared at the silver-plated condiment set. 'Ruby, let's just say I'm not ready to become a nun quite yet.' She undid the top button of her blouse and wafted air onto her chest.

'Then I'd better update Lady Wetherington on your early morning goings on, Miss Trotter. She is under the misguided impression that you are a saint,' I declared, winking at Ruby.

Frances looked as if she had been shot. 'Don't you dare, Mac. Sybil would have it around the ship in seconds. I'm to be a sanctimonious headmistress in Poona for goodness sake. I'd never live it down.'

'Then we'd better make a pact to keep your dubious nocturnal trysts strictly to ourselves,' said Ruby, placing her right hand on the tablecloth, fingers spread. 'All for one and one for all,' she announced with conviction.

I looked from one to the other and covered Ruby's hand with mine. 'United we stand.'

Frances didn't hesitate. 'and divided we fall,' she announced, and her hand smacked onto mine.

Major Stokes passed by at this juncture, his plate piled high with curry. 'My, my, lassies, 'ye looks like a coven of witches.'

I looked up and smiled as our hands untangled. 'There's only one problem with that, Major. My fly-swat makes a very poor broomstick.' His guffaw shadowed him across the dining saloon as he made his way to join the two tea-planters from Assam. He appeared to be recounting my words as the other two looked our way and smirked.

'Ruby, what do you know about Major Stokes's companions?'

Ruby seemed reluctant to answer. 'Nothing, really. One's a Scot and the other one's from Manchester as far as I know.'

'Have they been in India long?'

'I've no idea. Probably.' Ruby concentrated on eating her lunch.

'They look like remittance men to me,' suggested Frances, still watching them closely.

'What's a remittance man?' asked Ruby, following her gaze.

'Someone supported financially by their family on the understanding that they never come home.'

'Well, that can't be right,' said Ruby, scratching her head. 'Cyril told me the other day that his tea business is booming.'

'Did they fight in the war?' I couldn't understand what Major Stokes saw in them. To me, they looked rather shady.

'Christ knows, Mac.' Ruby seemed irritated by my questioning. 'Why are you so interested anyway?'

'No reason.' I decided to ask Major Stokes more about them when I got the chance and changed the subject. 'So, what is the plan for this afternoon?'

Chapter Eight

Prince Vijay Kumar Singh II was standing looking out through the cabin porthole as I entered the Jhalanpur suite. He appeared to be watching the ss Narkunda's approach into Aden's Steamer Point and turned as I entered, his casual western dress now replaced with a deep-green thigh-length angarkha jacket buttoned down the front and white trousers tapering at the ankle. His hair was covered in a traditional dark green pagri turban with a diamond-encrusted aigrette of white feathers pinned to one side and looped around his neck, six long strings of pearls glimmered in the sun's rays from the cabin window. He looked magnificent.

My heart beat a tattoo as I tried in vain to gain some composure, annoyed that I could not feel at ease in his presence.

'Doctor Mackenzie, what a pleasant surprise. I assume you are here to see my wife?'

I nodded, trying to keep my distance.

'Then don't let me detain you.'

You're being ridiculous, Elizabeth, I thought, he's merely a male for goodness sake. Do get a grip. I paused.

'Your Highness, I must thank you for your very generous gift from Cairo.' I lifted my chin and met his gaze head-on. 'However, in my profession such gifts are deemed quite unnecessary. Your wife and child needed my help and I was only too happy to give it.' I could feel my Mackenzie spirit rising to the fore. 'I hope you'll not be offended, but, in all conscience, I cannot accept this gift.'

The Prince looked out over Aden's Crater District, a wry smile on his face. 'Perhaps, having checked on my wife and son, we could enjoy a cool drink together and discuss this matter further.'

I let his words merge into the heavy fabrics of the room as I formulated a reply. 'Thank you, but sadly I must refuse. Immediately after examining the Princess I'll be going ashore with friends. Perhaps another time.' I stepped back into the corridor and closed the door behind me cutting off any further comment. Vijay Singh was getting under my skin and I didn't like it one little bit.

On entering the zenana, his wife was reclining on a heavily brocaded chaise longue below an open porthole. I pointed to the bed and helped her up, wondering why her husband could not be satisfied with just one wife. Thankfully Princess Darshwanabai couldn't read my mind and lay back gently onto her massive pillows, pulled her intricately embroidered ghagra skirt above her waist and waited for the now familiar metal horn to connect with her skin.

The baby seemed very content in its amniotic sac, it's tiny heart pulsing rhythmically at one-hundred-and-eighty beats per minute. I smiled reassuringly and began massaging her abdomen, wishing we could communicate in Hindi. I must get Tom to teach me some assuring sentences, I thought, as a zephyr of warm air brushed by my cheek and I heard shouts from the below decks announcing our arrival in port. The Princess's head turned towards the sound and her expression of longing ripped through my heart. This young pregnant girl had been cooped up in her gilded suite since boarding in

Marseille and the injustice of this fact irritated me beyond words. I lowered her skirt and called for her aunt.

'The Princess and baby are both well.'

The aunt clasped her palms to her chest and mumbled something incomprehensible to her charge, who rose from the bed, stretched out her hand for mine and squeezed my fingers in gratitude. They felt damp against mine and I noticed beads of sweat on her brow. The temperature in the harbour was in the hundreds, the high jagged sides of Aden's volcano radiating heat like a furnace onto the conurbation below. My patient needed some air and a change of scenery. By the time I had settled her onto the chaise longue once more, my mind was made up and I was determined to get my own way.

Vijay Singh was sitting at his roll-topped desk reading some documents as I was announced by the chaprassi. I paused, waiting for him to acknowledge me. He remained focused on his papers but spoke, his deep timbered voice clearly cutting through the noise and mayhem outside. 'How is Princess Dashwanabai?'

'I'm delighted to say your wife and baby are both fine, Your Highness.' I moved a couple of steps closer and saw a tug manoeuvring the ship's bow to starboard. 'However, this constant need for her to be coop…' I gritted my teeth and tried again. '. . . to remain continually in this suite does nothing to improve her complexion or give her any mental stimulus.' My fingers crossed in the folds of my skirt.

The Prince placed the papers on his desk and swivelled around in his chair. 'And what do you suggest we do about this, Doctor?'

Was his reply edged with sarcasm? I couldn't tell.

'Is there any way she could spend time ashore during our stay in Aden?' The shrill sounds of life in this hectic British settlement now obscured the whirl of the ceiling fan above my head as ship's officers boomed their orders to deckhands and the engines shook the ship from stem to stern, the massive propellers biting into the churning harbour water rotating sixteen-thousand-tons of floating metal into position between two huge buoys. 'Surely there is some way the Princess can enjoy the ambience of the city for a change?' I didn't remember moving but I was now standing looking over his shoulder at a barren landscape, not a blade of grass in sight, the air visibly shimmering above the roof tops. It instantly reminding me of Pa's oil-painting of Hades hanging in the vestry at home and I was beginning to have second thoughts.

'Forgive me, Doctor Mackenzie, but I understood you to say my wife needed constant bed-rest and no stress.'

'That I did,' I replied, looking down into his bronzed face, 'and I am not suggesting that she undertakes a three mile hike up the volcano. However, sitting in a pleasant, shaded garden somewhere ashore drinking a cool lemonade will be far more beneficial to her recovery than enduring the sounds and smells associated with bunkering this ship.' I relaxed my throat muscles and felt my chin drop.

'I see.' He stood, invading my space, a nuance of lavender from his body invading my nostrils. 'You're quite right, Doctor, and thank you for showing me the error of my ways. I will arrange matters accordingly. In fact, I am to pay my respects to the British Resident here in Aden as soon as we have docked, and I am sure his wife will be only too delighted to entertain yourself and my wife during my visit.'

I held my ground, determined not to be dominated. 'I hardly think the British Resident's wife will need the services of a doctor, Your Highness.'

'She may not, but my wife certainly does, and I know she will refuse to leave her quarters unless you are by her side.'

He had a point, I thought, but knew this would go down like a lead balloon with Ruby. She was hell-bent on taking Frances and I to see the Sira Fort followed by lunch at the Crescent Hotel and had already instructed Stanley to organise it.

The Prince moved closer, his Adam's Apple in line with my nose. His words when they came were soft and intimate. 'I have no right to ask you to give up your plans for Aden, Doctor Mackenzie, especially after missing the shore-trip to Cairo, but I beg you, please do this for Princess Dashwanabai and our son. I would be forever in your debt.'

My hands found themselves clasped in his, gold rings pressing into Scottish flesh and for a moment I could neither respond nor retract. Finally, I acquiesced. 'Very well, Your Highness, if you insist.'

'I do, Doctor. I do. And please, call me Vijay. All my friends do.'

Enough was enough. Like my patient, I needed some fresh air and a change of scenery. Gently extracting my hands, I backed to the exit hoping Ruby and Frances would understand.

Vijay followed, reached behind me to open the door and placed his hand on my shoulder. 'Perhaps we could have that drink together before dinner? We still need to discuss the little matter of my gift.'

'You never give up do you, Vijay?'

'I come from a long line of Rajput warriors, Doctor, and Rajput men are famous for never giving up.'

'Indeed. But I doubt any Rajput warrior has ever come up against the intransigence of a Highland woman.' For the first time since entering the royal apartments I was actually enjoying myself and my lips cracked open. 'Perhaps this time, Your Highness, you have met your match.'

'Then let battle commence, Doctor MacKenzie, and may the best man win.' He bowed his head, confidence oozing from every pore.

'Woman, actually,' I replied, equally assertive, 'but I won't split hairs.' This sparring was all very well but if I was going to meet the British Resident and his wife I needed to attend to my attire. 'Namaste,' I said, showing due reverence. 'and please call me Mac.'

'I'm sorry?'

'To friend or foe alike, Vijay, I'm referred to as Mac and as my foe, you qualify.'

His amused chuckle followed me out of the suite.

Chapter Nine

The limousines meandered along the dusty streets of the Crater District with no greenery to break the monotony of the sand-coloured brick buildings, stark jagged skyline and oppressive cliffs of volcanic rock. I was becoming concerned that our excursion ashore was anything but the pleasant change I had envisaged onboard and could only hope that my patient was faring better in the car ahead than myself. I was damp, my body odour already overpowered my perfumed skin and I was gasping for air in the fetid atmosphere of my vehicle's interior.

Turning into an imposing entrance framed by rusted wrought-iron gates our small convoy drew alongside a stone staircase edged with terracotta planters, the raised path beyond leading to the colonnaded portico of the Resident's house.

I waited while Vijay and his wife stepped from their vehicle to be met by the British Resident, Lieutenant Colonel Sir George Stewart-Symes, who descended the steps to greet his royal guests clad in full dress uniform.

Vijay, still resplendent in his green and white apparel, strode forward leaving Princess Dashwanabai to hover at the rear. She stood alongside her uncle, her red full skirt intertwined with gold and silver thread shimmering in the sunlight, her matching top edged around the collar with mother-of-pearl beads glinting through yards of red and gold silk voile which cascaded over her shoulder and around her neck, face and head. Her fingers, ankles and ears were adorned with gold and silver jewellery and a gold nose-ring pierced the skin of her right nostril.

An Aide-de-Camp assisted me out of my car and I moved to her side and took her right arm. Her aunt, appearing from the other passenger door edged round to her niece's left, offered her arm and we slowly followed the Resident, Vijay and her uncle up the eight wide stone steps and along the sandstone path flanked on both sides by a guard of honour.

Beads of sweat covered my upper lip and forehead while my damp hair brushed the back of my neck and stained my cotton collar as Lady Stewart-Symes, resplendent in an amber-silk kaftan, moved around her husband from the shade of the portico and came to pay homage to the Princess. She bowed low, hands praying, in true Hindu style, then indicated to us to follow her up the remaining stairs and out of the burning sun.

I checked the Princess's pulse as we entered the dark marble entrance hall and became alarmed at the result. The Resident's wife caught my eye and my lips puckered, my eyebrows hitting my hairline. The message was immediately understood, and our hostess instantly took control. Orders were issued to various Residency staff and we were ushered through to a covered rear verandah overlooking a pleasant landscaped garden with fountains playing and Koi Carp lazily swimming in the waters below. I expelled hot air, relieved at the sight.

This was more like it, I thought as I assisted Princess Darshwanabai into a heavily cushioned wicker bath-chair and raised her legs onto a matching wicker pouf. Lady Symes clapped her hands and two sari-clad Indian girls appeared carrying silver trays with jugs of iced lemonade and sweet-meats of every shape and size which they placed on the glass-topped wicker coffee table. Rolled, cool, towelling facecloths from a bamboo box were handed to us to remove the grime of the journey from our hands and face and Lady Symes personally supervised my attempt at laying one such roll across the back of my patient's neck beneath her hair and dupatta scarf. She then walked to the balustrade and beckoned me to her side.

'Perhaps we should leave the Princess to rest and have a walk in the grounds.'

I turned and nodded to my charge who smiled. 'Lead on, Lady Stewart-Symes. I'm sure the Princess will be fine now that she is out of the sun and has refreshments to hand. Her aunt can tend to her needs.'

Lady Symes addressed the Princess in Hindi, taking me rather by surprise, then ushered me into the garden and headed for a sheltered arbour covered in a profusion of cream floribunda roses.

'Now, Doctor Stuart-MacKenzie,' she said, pausing by a trellis of climbing roses. 'Please enlighten me on this unexpected visit by Princess Darshwanabai? I'm intrigued.'

Obviously, my hostess was not in the mood for social chit-chat and I played for time by leaning into an opening rosebud and breathing deeply. 'What a wonderful perfume. How do you manage it in such a stark environment?'

Lady Symes examined me from head to toe, a glimmer of a smile parting her ruby red lips. 'We have staff, dear, and water is delivered daily to irrigate the plants.'

I tried to imagine how many gallons of water it took to keep this barren acreage green and fertile but failed. 'The

Princess is pregnant with her first child, Lady Symes, and has found our passage through Suez and the Red Sea a little trying. I thought a change of scenery . . .'

'No need to explain further, dear. I know just how she feels having produced my own brood in the tropics. Rest and plenty of liquids, that's what's called for in this heat. Not that men would have a clue.' She was now through the arbour and making for a copse of trees. 'Left to them, the British Empire would have fizzled out years ago due to constant infant mortality.' She looked as if she had a bad smell under her nose.

'I couldn't have put it better myself,' I said, joining her on a wooden bench under a Cinnabari tree. 'I mean, about the rest and liquids, of course.'

'So, you're her personnel physician, then?'

'No, Lady Symes . . .'

'Oh, do call me Geraldine. All this Lady business is fine in its place but far too formal out here in the garden, don't you think?' She reminded me of Lady Wetherington.

'Very well, Geraldine, but no, I'm not the Princess's personal physician. In fact, I'm also a passenger on the ss Narkunda and had never even met the young woman until we reached the Eastern Mediterranean.' Geraldine's eyes were on stalks. 'It was as we arrived in Port Said that the ship's surgeon commandeered my services . . .' I gave her a potted history of events, steering clear of the true reasons for the Princess's ailment. My listener hung onto my every word.

'Well, my dear, all I can say is, jolly good show. We need more doctors like you around these parts. So, what takes you to Bombay?'

My reply took her completely by surprise.

'In Calcutta?'

'That's right.'

'Researching viral diseases?'

'Yes.'

'Well, I never. Who's sponsoring you?'

'Sponsoring me?' My mouth suddenly felt dry.

'Yes, dear, sponsoring you.' She could see that further explanation was required. 'Doctor Stuart-MacKenzie, India is not London. We are at least fifty years behind the times out here in the Colonies and women are expected to look after their menfolk and offsprings, not compete in the world of industry, politics or medical research. Not the done thing at all.'

'Really?' I licked my lips and wandered what she would say if she knew my appointment was still subject to a face-to-face interview. My thumbs rotated nervously in my lap.

Her well-manicured hand patted my knee. 'Take my advice, dear, get one of those scientific societies back in Blighty to sponsor your research. That way the puffed-up Calcutta Board of Governors will have no choice but to welcome you with open arms. There's nothing like a large donation to opens doors in the old boys' network, believe me.'

Oh, I do, I thought, trying to recall where such societies had their headquarters.

'Would Edinburgh University offer you a research stipend?'

'I'm not sure.' Duncan Fitzpatrick with his Irish brogue dropped into my thoughts, his excitement at being granted a sabbatical from Ashworth Laboratories triggering some long-forgotten wounds. 'They might.'

'Then make it your priority to write to them without delay. In fact, why don't you get your steward to deliver the letter to me this afternoon and I will include it in our diplomatic bag. That way, it will be in Scotland shortly after you arrive in Calcutta.'

'That's very generous of you. As soon as I'm back on-board I'll get right to it.'

'Excellent. And if there's any other organisation or society who could help you, write to them as well.'

'I really don't know what to say, Geraldine.'

Her hand was back patting my knee. 'Nothing to say, my dear. Just make sure the letters are ashore before you set sail.'

'Oh, believe me, I will.' I silently thanked Vijay for giving me the opportunity to meet with Lady Stewart-Symes. I was not going to let such an opportunity slip through my fingers. I looked at my watch without thinking.

'Now, enough of this,' she announced, standing, 'We should return to my other guests or I'll have Sir George chastising me for failing in my duty as a hostess.'

My mind raced through the compendium of scientific Who's Who as we retraced our steps through the arbour. Princess Darshwanabai and her aunt were being wafted with a huge ostrich-feathered fan hanging above their heads on our arrival, and I noticed a blind punkah-wallah operating the fan's pulley from his position cross-legged in an alcove, his milky-white corneas tugging at my professional heartstrings.

'He's also deaf and dumb,' whispered Geraldine as we settled ourselves down and more refreshments appeared from the interior.

The next hour was full of conversation about life in India with Lady Symes translating from Hindi to English throughout. Her knowledge of the language was extensive and Princess Darshwanabai became quite animated as the dialogue progressed. I learned that she had spent her childhood in Mewar State, the second daughter of the Maharaja of Rajsamand. She had been betrothed to Vijay at the tender age of eight, both dynasties negotiating the marital contract to enhance the prestige of their joint families. She was sixteen before she saw Vijay for the first time, that occasion being her wedding day. I couldn't help thinking that there were worse husbands to invite into a marital bed than the Maharajah of Jhalanpur's son and had it on the tip of my tongue to say when discretion zapped it from my thoughts.

The Princess looked so vulnerable sitting in her bathchair chatting away to us all, her eyes darting between our faces, her words exposing her innocence of the world. She was now nineteen and looking forward to presenting her husband with a son and heir after three barren years trying and failing to become pregnant. She had spent hours praying to Shiva, the Indian God of fertility who finally answered her prayers while she was enjoying the sub-tropical atmosphere in the South of France. I now understood why the family were so concerned for her and the baby's welfare and why she was still clinging to me like a limpet.

I heard the word *Garbhāśaya* pass the aunt's lips and knew that Lady Symes was learning the truth about events in Port Said. Her expression, when she turned to me, left no doubt that I had suddenly risen in her estimation and I shrugged, pretending it was nothing, and quickly handed round the sweetmeats. Geraldine was not to be ignored and insisted on knowing every aspect of my treatment for the Princess, who interjected whenever she felt my explanation lacked sufficient detail.

Her aunt was anxious to know all about me. Where I lived, the size of my family and what my plans were in India. Geraldine asked permission to divulge this personal information and I gave it willingly, delighted to be cementing my relationship with these new-found friends which, until this day, had been impossible.

We moved into a small dining-room off the verandah where a vegetarian light lunch was served. The Princess deferred to me every time she reached for a dish, some of which I approved, the others I rejected and throughout the meal it was a pleasure to see this young mother's face alight with joy, laughter lines at her temples, her colour heightened. This excursion ashore was proving to be a tonic for us both, but time was passing, and I needed to get back to the ship.

Sir George and Lady Stewart-Symes waved us from their porticoed entrance in the mid-afternoon, my hostess assuring me that their Aide-de-Camp would be waiting at the dockside for my letters an hour before sunset. She squeezed my hands, wished me well in my endeavours and told me to keep her abreast of developments. All I could hope was that the developments would be positive.

I was alone in the writing-room onboard deep in thought when Tom found me an hour later. I quickly explained all that had transpired ashore and he immediately concurred with

Geraldine's comments, told me he had an idea, then left. I returned to my letters and didn't notice when Tom returned minutes later accompanied by Vijay, back in casual attire.

'Mac, His Highness would like you to repeat what you have just told me.'

Vijay paced the polished wooden floor as I explained yet again what had happened in the Resident's grounds, his hands clasped behind his back, remaining silent until I had finished speaking.

'Doctor Mac, if you will allow me, I believe I can assist you. I have contacts in Calcutta who could be very beneficial to your cause.'

Tom and I exchanged glances, Tom nodding his approval. I failed to answer, my vocal cords in knots. It had been quite a day and it appeared to be getting even better. Vijay, meanwhile, appeared to interpret my silence as an example of female Scottish intransigence and drove home his point.

'Really, it's the least I can do.' I was still mute. 'And even a Scot wouldn't reject this form of gratitude, surely? After all, Mary, Queen of Scots never rejected help from France and she was a woman, I think.'

I stiffened at that slur while Tom gripped the chair-back desperately trying not to laugh. 'Your Highness,' he said, coming to my aid. 'I think Doctor Mac is experiencing a sudden attack of Dysphonia. In short, she appears to have lost her voice.'

'No, I haven't, you Loon,' I announced, standing. 'I just don't know what to say.'

'What's a Loon?' asked Vijay.

'Don't ask,' replied Tom, pressing my shoulders to make me sit back down. 'Allow me to answer for the young lady. Doctor Elizabeth Stuart-MacKenzie would be delighted to accept your generous offer of help in achieving a PhD research post at the Calcutta School of Tropical Medicine.'

'Excellent,' Vijay moved towards the salon door. 'Perhaps, when her Dysphonia has abated, she could also tell me if she is going to accept the bottle of perfume given on behalf of my wife.' He winked, turned on his heels and was out the door before I could respond.

'The man is a walking cannon-ball,' I said as Tom came to sit by my side, 'and makes my attempts at obtaining sponsorship look rather pathetic.' I ran my eyes down the thin list of potential patrons who were about to receive my pleas for financial help.

'Then, use his name when introducing yourself. Having one of India's most illustrious Princes as a reference will do wonders for your prestige in the hallowed halls of Britain's medical research establishments.'

'But, Tom . . .'

'Just do it, Mac. It's not every day you get such an offer of help.' Tom checked his watch. 'I must dash, I have a surgery in ten minutes. I'll see you in the bar for a pre-dinner drink?'

I nodded, my head down over ss Narkunda headed stationary, my pen hovering above a crisp blank Basildon Bond sheet, my tongue locked firmly between my teeth. Like the ship's captain, I had a tide to catch.

Ruby and Frances stepped from the tender, which was bobbing around at the waterline, as my letters disappeared in the opposite direction, delivered to the boat's duty officer by Stanley, balancing precariously on the bottom rung. I watched the small craft reverse from the ship's side and prayed that my missives would reach the diplomatic bag in good time.

Ruby grabbed some of the parcels from Frances's piled arms and made her way to my side looking the picture of health. Frances looked as if she had been flattened by a steam roller.

'Had a good day?' I enquired, peeling France's fingers from around the handles of four heavy packages. She rubbed the red wheals left behind trying to improve the circulation in her capillaries.

'Wonderful, Mac, haven't we Frances?'

'Yes, wonderful,' she replied, her response devoid of enthusiasm.

I patted Frances's arm. 'You've had the Tavener personal shopper treatment, haven't you?'

'And, about time too,' insisted Ruby, lighting a cigarette and blowing tobacco smoke into my face. 'You are both beyond the pale when it comes to clothing. Someone should have taken you in hand years ago.'

A coughing fit hampered any retort on my part, but Frances was not going to let that comment pass. 'If I've told you once today, Ruby, I've told you a thousand times. A girl's school is hardly the place for lace knickers, silk stockings and satin shoes.'

'But, Frances, dear, it certainly is the place for tripping the light fantastic with a certain Navigation Officer at the ship's ball tomorrow night.'

An army officer standing close by chuckled causing Frances
to gasp in horror, grab her bags and scuttle off in the direction
of the stairs, resembling a novice nun late for Vespers.

'Oops!' said Ruby as I gritted my teeth. 'Shall we?' She
pointed to the bow with her cigarette holder and plodded off,
cigarette smoke trailing in her wake.

A Windmill Girl from Soho will never understand someone
as reserved as Frances, I thought, and returned my attention to
the tender now berthing by the harbour steps, a uniformed
gentleman waiting patiently for the ship's lascars to make it
fast. He stretched forwards, took a small package from the duty
officer and strode off down the quay. I recognised the Aide-de-
Camp from his swagger and felt relief like releasing the stays on
a too-tight corset.

'Hello, Doctor Mackenzie.'

I couldn't see who had spoken until I looked down and
found two little English imps standing side-by-side, their hands
clasped together, their ayah hovering in the rear.

'Good Afternoon, Charlotte, William. And what have you
been up to in Aden?'

'Oh, we've had a lovely time,' said William, nudging his
sister in the ribs. 'Haven't we, Charlotte?'

He sounded like Ruby. 'I'm going to be Sinbad-the-Sailor
tomorrow night and Charlotte's got a costume of a . . .' he
paused and frowned at his ayah.

'A gypsy,' she assisted.

'What are you going as?' His wide eyes scanned my features.

'William, that's very rude.' The ayah stepped forward
grabbed him by his collar, bowed to me and dragged him away.

Charlotte stood her ground and pulled on my skirt. 'What are you going to be?'

I knelt to be on her level, her blonde curls framing a peaches and cream face. 'I don't know yet, Charlotte, but I promise, when I've decided you'll be the first to know.'

'Oh, goody.' With that she hop-scotched off down the deck in the wake of her brother. I remained where I was trying to think of anything in my trunk which would convert into a suitable costume. I was not known for being creative and fancy dress had never been my idea of a fun thing to do even as a child. I decided I would pass on the Gala Ball and retire to bed early with a good book rather than let the side down. After all, I mused, Ruby would be a very hard act to follow.

Chapter Ten

The Gulf of Aden shimmered in the morning light as the ss Narkunda's mooring lines snaked aboard and the ship moved out of Steamer Point on its way to Bombay and the start of a new chapter in my life. I lowered myself into a steamer-chair on the starboard deck hoping to get a few minutes peace away from the excitement permeating the ship from bow to stern and bridge to bilge.

Tonight, was to be the highlight of the cruise - the Gala Ball - its fancy-dress theme of "East Meets West" testing the imagination of passengers from First Class to steerage, everyone mingling together and dancing the night away, clad in all manner of costumes. For such a spectacular event the ship could not be found wanting and the lascars had started early, winding fairy-lights around the deck's side-rails as stewards busied themselves covering tables with ornately embroidered cloths of every hue, some with small metal discs sewn into the material which acted like miniature mirrors reflecting the hectic activity all about.

I wished the whole idea would go away and was attempting to block it out by studying my notebook of Hindi words and phrases when I was respectfully asked by the Serang if I would move to allow the lascars to attach brass lanterns to the underside of the super-structure. I looked up and noticed a metal ring welded into the deck-head above me, pulled myself out of the chair and decided to adjourn to the bow. Here, a huge Bedouin tent was being erected, supervised by Jim, the Navigation Officer, who waved on seeing me and suggested I vacated the area if I didn't want to become part of the scenery. Tutting to myself and stubbing my toe on a pile of hookahs lying by the life-jacket stowage box, I made my way to the writing-room where I finally found some solitude and closed my mind to the activity on deck.

'Great minds think alike,' said Frances as she dropped into a chair next to me, her hands clasping a large white cotton handkerchief and a length of frilled white lace, a pincushion on ribbon hanging round her neck. 'It's bedlam out there.'

'Tell me about it?' I replied, sarcasm tainting my response. 'Anyone would think there was a major event taking place.'

Frances eyed me from over her half-rimmed spectacles which she wore for close work. 'Not your cup of tea then, fancy dress?'

'With what I have in my wardrobe, Frances, the only fancy dress I could cobble together would be that of a missionary nun!'

'Oh, come on, it can't be that bad.'

'Worse. Anyway, what are you doing with that handkerchief?' I looked down at her fingers fiddling with the edge of the material, attaching lace to it with pins.

She sighed and paused. 'Sybil has decided to become Queen Victoria for the night, and I've been commandeered to make her a royal bonnet with ringlets and long ribbons.' She pulled some ringlets of horsehair out of her pocket and held them aloft. 'I dread to think where these have come from.'

'Probably the Bombay Amateur Operatic Society,' I suggested, 'The Pirates of Penzance, perhaps?'

Frances stuffed them back in her pocket. 'More like Widow Twanky's cast-offs from Aladdin and his Lamp, if you ask me.'

When she wanted to, Frances had a wicked sense of humour. 'Never mind Sybil, what about you? What are you planning to go as?'

Frances continued pinning. 'Me? Oh, that's easy, I'm to be Florence Nightingale, the lady with the lamp . . .'

My expression stopped her in her tracks.

'What's so amusing?'

'Nothing, Frances. Well nothing to do with your choice of costume, which I think is excellent. It's just that Florence is the very reason I'm sitting here in the middle of the Indian Ocean.' I stared at the horizon and cobalt blue sea. Total recall took me back to my childhood bedroom and nights spent reading Florence Nightingale's biography by candlelight. I related the story to Frances. '. . . so, you see, if it weren't for Florence I would never have gone into medicine.'

'Then I'm pleased I've been of service to you, Mistress Elizabeth.'

I nodded with due deference and picked up my notebook. We sat in companionable silence for some minutes, Frances busy pinning and sewing and me mouthing Hindi phrases. 'I saw the Navigation Officer erecting a Bedouin tent at the bow earlier,' I commented, losing concentration, 'so, it could be your lucky night.'

Frances nearly swallowed a mouth full of pins. 'Really, Mac.' She reached down to collect some which had fallen on the floor. 'There are times when you and Ruby are quite trying.

I'm sure Jim has more on his mind right now than feathering his own nest.'

'Oh, it's Jim now, is it? Well, he'll certainly have to be creative if he's to woo the likes of Florence Nightingale tonight. According to her biography, she was pretty strait-laced.'

Frances paused mid-pinning and held my attention. 'Outward appearances can be deceptive, Mac.'

My index finger came off the page and pierced the air. 'Ah, so yesterday's purchases in Aden WILL be making an appearance tonight then?'

Frances blushed and remained silent.

'Come on, Frances, what was in all those packages. I'm intrigued.'

She placed the bonnet on the table and sat back in her chair. 'Well, apart from a beautiful midnight blue silk night-dress, which I adore, I'm now the proud owner of two buttermilk silk chemises, a pale blue satin camisole, three pairs of lace knickers and two pairs of fine seamed stockings. All very decadent and totally unsuitable for Poona.'

'But perfect for a Bedouin tent.'

She accidentally stuck the needle in her thumb and sucked it vigorously, berating me at the same time. 'Elizabeth Stuart-Mackenzie, whatever happened to your Presbyterian principles?' She examined her thumb for permanent damage, but none was evident. 'Come to think of it, though,' she added, rubbing the puncture wound with her forefinger, 'with a pair of finger-symbols and seven veils I could probably make a certain Navigation Officer's day.'

'Assuming Queen Victoria didn't clap you in irons first!' We both burst out laughing as Major Stokes walked in.

'Eyup, lassies, you seem perky this mornin'. It's like Clapham Junction out there.' He turned and pointed to the deck. 'I was intendin' to practise some tunes on the old Joanna for later but the bar looks like somat out of t'Arabian Nights, so a rendition of Danny Boy didn't seem quite appropriate.'

I pulled out a chair and gestured for him to sit.

'Thank ye kindly, Doctor Mac, me old pins aren't what they used to be. Now, what was you both laughin' at when I came in?'

'We were imagining Lady Wetherington clad in seven veils,' I quipped, as Frances disappeared into her hanky.

'It'd take more than seven veils to cover that frame,' he quipped, 'and that's a fact.'

I quickly changed the subject. 'And which well-known character will you be imitating tonight, Major? Just so that we recognise you during the Gay Gordons, you understand.'

The Major lit up a cheroot and aimed smoke-rings at the ceiling. 'Happen I'll appear as Old Nosey, seein' as we both served King and Country in India.' He looked at his dumbfounded audience of two and pointed the cheroot in our direction. 'I'm talkin' about Major General Wellesley, lassies, Lord Wellington to you and the Frogs. He was called Old Nosey by his troops 'cos of his rather long hooter.'

'I had no idea Wellington fought in India,' I said, surprised. 'Did you, Frances?'

'Oh yes,' she replied before the Major could respond. 'His brother was the Governor General of India at that time and

Wellesley always considered the Indian Battle of Assaye to be his greatest campaign, even though we all associate him with Waterloo.'

The Major slapped his thigh. 'Well said, Missy, I can see you knows your military history.'

'I should do, Major. My mother's family hails from County Meath. The Wellesleys were our landed gentry.'

'Is that so? Well I'll be.' He rubbed his hooter and returned to his cheroot. 'You're in good company tonight then, lassie, as I intend to strut me stuff as the great man 'imself and if any Indian Tipoo gets in me way, 'ed better watch out.'

'I didn't know you had Irish blood in your veins, Frances.'

'You know what they say, Mac, still waters run deep.' She raised her eyebrows and stuck her tongue in her cheek.

'Enough of this bletherin', ladies, it must be time for elevenses so what's your tipple?'

'Not for me, Major, I have a house-call to make.' I stood and placed a hand on France's shoulder. 'See you later, Florence, with or without your lamp.'

'Eh?' queried the Major.

'Tonight, Major, Frances, or should I say Florence, will be on hand to tend to all your wounded soldiers.' I walked towards the door. 'She's just been getting some tips from me on silk tourniquets and satin dressings.' With that I stepped out into the chaos which was the deck and elbowed my way to First-Class.

To my surprise, the Jhalanpur Suite was as chaotic as the deck, with the zenana drowning in Eastern paraphernalia in the form of shoes, bangles, ghagras, kauchlis, paggars and shawls all littering the suite's cushions and Persian carpets.

As I entered, Princess Dashwanabai, dressed in puckered trousers and a cropped top was sitting cross-legged on the floor encircled by her female relatives who were all chattering like a flock of starlings.

'What are you doing on the floor?' I enquired, tiptoeing across the mounds of fabric and baubles and easing my patient to her feet. I pointed sternly at the couch, trying to retain an air of authority, but failing miserably as the excitement in the room became infectious and the corners of my mouth tilted upwards.

The Princess looked suitably ashamed, biting her lower lip and flickering her eyelashes at me which only amused me more. 'Now lie there, you little minx and don't move,' I said, my index finger pointing at her sternum. Her aunt appeared behind me holding a beaten copper tray supporting a glass of chilled Nimbu Panis. I took it and nodded. 'Perhaps you could tell me what is happening here today.'

'We make stories, Doctor, for tonight.' She could tell I was confused, clapped her hands and spoke quickly to one of the younger women. Seconds later Prince Kapoor Dhawan came through the door and sat by his niece while his wife explained her dilemma. Suddenly, he held up his hand to stop her in mid-flow and turned to face me.

'I understand from my wife that you would like to know what is happening in the zenana today, Doctor Mackenzie, and why Princess Dashwanabai was not resting as she should.' He waved his finger at his niece who blew him a kiss. The aunt

ushered me to a large cushion by the couch and made me sit
and enjoy my drink. It tasted like nectar.

'My family,' said the Princess's uncle, encompassing the
ladies surrounding me with his left hand, 'are putting on a play
for Prince Vijay Kumar Singh II and myself tonight while the
rest of the ship's passengers enjoy the Gala Ball.'

Obviously, the Jhalanpur women were to be excluded from
the jollity of the fancy-dress party on board, I thought, and had
therefore decided to organise a party of their own. It occurred
to me that this was not so different from the Royal household
of Queen Victoria and Prince Albert. Their children would
organise private plays and pantomimes for their parents'
delectation during the holidays within the confines of Osborne
House.

'They have been debating which of the many poems from
the Thousand Nights they wish too . . . how do you say? . . .
present, and who is to play which part.'

I raised my glass to the ladies who all nodded
enthusiastically. 'The Thousand Nights, Prince Kapoor
Dhawan? Would this be the famous Tales from the Arabian
Nights, known in Great Britain as One Thousand and One
Nights, depicted in the wonderful symphony by Rimsky
Korsakov.'

'Exactly so, and it pleases me to know that you are familiar
with the stories. They have been passed down through the ages
in our land and are greatly admired.' He then translated our
conversation to his family who all became very vocal, asking
questions from all directions. 'As you can see, my relatives are

also delighted and want to know which of the many characters is your favourite.'

I didn't hesitate. 'Scheherazade, of course.' This brought rapturous applause from the group, the name clearly needing no translation. 'For me, any Queen who can avoid having her head chopped off by telling a thousand and one stories has to be admired.' Princess Dashwanabai shook her uncle's arm and looked at me as she spoke.

'My niece thinks Scheherazade would have been very like you, Doctor Mackenzie.'

'I hardly think so, Your Highnesses.' My cheeks were burning.

'On the contrary,' he replied, tapping his niece's hand, 'it took single-minded vision and a determination to succeed where others had failed, which, you must agree, bear some similarity to your own characteristics.'

Obviously, Prince Kapoor Dhawan had been in conversation with Vijay, I thought. I looked from one to the other of the Rajputan women reclining by my feet, each clad in the finest textiles of the East, their nose-rings and jewellery jangling as they moved their heads. We were so different, our backgrounds so diametrically opposed. My patient, meanwhile, beckoned to her uncle and whispered in his ear. His expression reminded me of a rather stern hospital matron I had known in Edinburgh. Undeterred, the Princess dug her fingers into his wrist, her eyes pleading, her head on one side like a puppy waiting for its master to throw a ball.

'What is it the Princess wishes to know?' I asked, my curiosity getting the better of me.

He coughed, rotated his ruby ring on his little finger and took a deep breath. 'I must apologise in advance, Doctor MacKenzie, for my niece's impertinence, but she believes that you should attend the Gala Ball tonight as Scheherazade. I have pointed out that this is not her concern, but she insists.'

I scratched my hairline trying to think of a suitable response then turned to my patient whose eyes were firmly fixed on my face. 'Much as I do not wish to disappoint your Highness, I'm afraid I have nothing in my baggage which is remotely similar to that worn by the famous Moghul Queen.' I allowed my eyes to wander across the whole group. 'I'm afraid silks and satins are hardly ideal in the cold climate of Northern England.' I brushed my hand over my long cream pleated skirt as my words were translated. Before the Prince had even finished speaking the room erupted into something resembling a cattle auction, each female talking over the next trying to be heard. Finally, he raised his hands and demanded silence.

'As you have probably guessed, Doctor MacKenzie, my niece and her relatives consider it their duty to dress you from what we have here.' He peered at the feminine detritus laid out before us and shook his head. 'The decision is entirely yours, of course.'

I didn't know what to say. All eyes were on me, making me feel like a patient about to be dissected on the operating table and, at that moment, I wasn't sure which would be preferable. 'Where's your sense of adventure, Mac?' I whispered under my breath. I returned the Prince's stare, then, knowing Aunt Karr would be proud of my MacKenzie spirit, bowed to the ladies, my hands placed firmly together in front of my nose and willingly went to my fate.

'I do hope you know what you're submitting yourself to,' said Prince Kapoor Dhawan as he was ushered unceremoniously towards the door. 'I'll leave you in the capable hands of my first wife and pray that you survive the experience.'

The door closed firmly behind him and I was left encircled by a cluster of enthusiastic women all desperate to get their hands on me. I felt like a crippled impala surrounded by baying jackals and needed to take back control. Remembering the real reason for my visit to the Jhalanpur suite I held up my hands and bellowed 'Silence!' bringing the room to a standstill. 'First, I must check on my patient and her baby.'

Lunch came and went with offerings of fresh fruit and sweet-meats and more chilled refreshment while long discussions took place on how Scheherazade should be presented to the passengers and crew of the ss Narkunda. I felt like one of my sister's rag dolls as the women twisted my hair this way and that, experimenting with various styles which were then discussed in length and rejected. I was dressed and undressed repeatedly and bangles, strings of beads, long dangling earrings and various nose-rings were attached to my person time and again as the room's conversation grew louder and louder.

By mid-afternoon it was agreed that a stunning peacock blue, gold and pale green ensemble made up of tapered trousers, a cropped tight-fitting short-sleeved top, wide knee-length skirt and a long gold-edged shawl that was so fine it could have been pulled through a syringe, I was then handed a floor-length cotton Egyptian kaftan and instructed to return to the zenana two hours before the evening's activities began.

I arrived back at the cabin feeling as if I had been plucked and oiled like an oven-prepared chicken and collapsed on my bed with exhaustion. I could only hope as I drifted off to sleep that I'd manage a moonlight-saunter with Tom without tripping over in Scheherazade's raised wooden platform slippers with turned-up sequinned toes.

Ruby woke me with a cup of Earl Grey tea at five o'clock demanding to know where I had been all day. As I rose from the horizontal I noticed a stunning Cleopatra outfit hanging from a peg on the back of the door.

'Oh, Ruby, that's gorgeous. Wherever did it come from?'

'The Windmill Theatre,' she said, sitting on the end of her bed painting her toenails. 'I purloined it as I left.'

'Ruby, you didn't?'

'Of course I did. Where d'you think it came from, Simon Arzt Departmental Store?'

'Well, no. Even Simon Arzt would struggle to produce Cleopatra without notice but, even so.'

'Don't be so prissy, Mac. The Windmill wouldn't have missed it, they had another fifteen just like it in the wardrobe department.' She changed position and started on her other foot. 'Anyway, enough about my costume, what is cabin 20's Cinderella going to wear to the ball.' Her eyes met mine and I quickly turned away.

'Scheherazade,' I muttered.

'Sheery who?'

'Scheherazade,' I repeated grabbing my towel, toilet bag and kaftan.

'Who's she, then?' asked Ruby, grabbing one of her toes and painting the nail with one wine-red flourish.

'Oh, just some Moghul serving wench. No-one special.' I needed to get away before I was pinned to the bulkhead. I mumbled something about taking a bath and disappeared down the corridor as Ruby's head poked out from the cabin waving my bathrobe in her hand.

Salvador was sitting patiently outside the bathing cubicle waiting for me to appear.

'Sorry, Salvador, I fell asleep.'

'No problem, Memsahib. Water still warm. Enjoy your washing.' He wandered off leaving me to my ablutions which I realised needed to be rapid if I were to be back in the Jhalanpur Suite on time. I could hear the Major singing *Danny Boy* at the top of his voice in a cubicle close by and tried to imagine Lord Wellington's reaction to an elderly Yorkshire impersonator sporting a potbelly and smoking a cheroot. I concluded that Wellesley's rather large hooter would have been well and truly put out, to say nothing of Queen Victoria's reaction to Sybil's attempt at royalty. No doubt, I thought, as I soaped myself all over, our late Monarch would not have been amused.

Scrubbing my back with the loofah, I wondered who Tom Wallace would be and how he would react to seeing me in full regal, Eastern attire. My goose-bumps tingled with anticipation as I poured fresh water over my head, patted myself dry and rushed from the cubicle dressed only in a pair of lace panties and the borrowed kaftan.

Chapter Eleven

Prince Kapoor Dhawan escorted me along the First-Class deck towards a Bedouin dressed officer standing to attention alongside our ship's Captain disguised as Lord Nelson.

I kept my eyes firmly fixed on my gold and silver curled wedges and remained two steps behind my chaperone as he confirmed our names.

'Ali Baba and Queen Scheherazade,' bellowed the Bedouin, his voice that of a Sergeant Major screaming orders to his troops. Every head turned towards us and a collective intake of breath halted conversation. Lord Nelson, his right empty jacket sleeve pinned across his chest and an eye-patch covering one eye, bowed low to welcome us.

A steward in white uniform and red fez held out a silver tray full of crystal flutes of champagne or fresh juice and my escort lifted one of each from the tray and handed me the champagne. My hand came up exposing an intricate deep-red henna tattoo of swirls and loops covering my skin from wrist to knuckle, my fingers adorned with beaten gold, silver and amber rings. I looked at them shimmering in the lantern light and thought how useful they would be as knuckle-dusters to some Northumbria docker and sipped my drink.

We moved forwards, pausing by a table which bulged with canapes, savoury biscuits and various dips making my stomach rumble. I hadn't eaten anything substantial since breakfast, but on reaching for a savoury bite-sized samosa I found that the brass medallions attached to a gold thread between my nose and earlobe hampered any chance of sustenance and gave up. No wonder Moghul women were so slim, I thought, as I placed it back on the platter.

Prince Kapoor Dhawan leant in and whispered in my ear, his pointed turban brushing the top of my head. 'You appear to be causing quite a stir, my dear.'

I looked up to find numerous costume-clad passengers staring at me from afar and enjoyed every nudge and sigh from the crowd as we progressed towards the deck-rail. I was especially pleased to see Miss High-and-Mighty from the departure shed in Tilbury Docks, dressed as a belly dancer, standing, open-mouthed, as I passed by. It was clear she hadn't recognised me, which was no surprise as even I didn't recognise myself. I hid my smile behind my veil and savoured my moment of feline one-upmanship.

Four dhoti-clad musicians sat crossed-legged on a raised platform covered in camel-bag cushions playing sitars, their safa-turbans in varying tones of burnt-orange bobbing to the rhythms created by their twelve-stringed instruments as fairy lights, draped between wooden poles, created a canopy above their heads. It was all so magical, and, I thought, if it hadn't been for Princess Darshwanabai's insistence, I would have missed it all by having an early night!

A familiar voice made me turn. Standing alongside Ali Baba insisting on an introduction was a life-sized version of Saladin.

'Your Highness,' said Prince Kapoor Dhawan, looking in my direction, 'allow me to present his most illustrious Excellency, Salah ud Din . . .'

'Such a pleasure, Queen Scheherazade,' interrupted Vijay, his jet-black beard, gold turban, heavily embroidered tunic and flowing robe filling my vision.

I lowered my eyes to the floor. 'Your Excellency, I am honoured to be in your exalted presence.'

He raised one eyebrow to Ali Baba who shrugged and sipped his pomegranate juice. 'The honour is all mine, Your Majesty,' he countered. 'Could I interest you in some light refreshment in my humble tent?'

'Indeed you could.' The thought of spiced lamb or chicken made me salivate. 'Ali Baba tells me that sheep's eyes are quite a delicacy in these parts, although haggis is more my style.'

Vijay's head rolled back and a loud guffaw rent the air before he slapped my consort on the back, causing him to choke. 'Well, Ali Baba, you're certainly a dark horse. Perhaps we could do a trade. My army for your Queen?'

Prince Kapoor Dhawan rubbed his hands together imitating a money shark from an Arab Souk. 'There is no price in the land to compare with the beauty of Scheherazade, Your Eminence.'

'Then we should retire below and continue this discussion over a hookah.' His hand cupped my elbow, the gesture rather possessive. 'Your Highness.'

I was glad my raised colour was hidden but our eyes met, and his lopsided smile confirmed my worst fears. Vijay Kumar Singh II could read my mind from one hundred paces, veil or no veil. Thankfully, the moment was broken by the Bedouin Officer's voice bellowing out across the deck once more.

'Cleopatra, Queen of the Nile.'

Saved by the bell, I thought, as my fifteen minutes of fame instantly evaporated and Ruby appeared at Lord Nelson's side looking every inch the Egyptian Goddess. She was magnificent and she knew it. From head to toe she was encased in gold sequins, her midriff bare, an emerald gem lodged in her belly button and her blond hair hidden under a straight, black, shoulder-length wig, the wide, gold band stretching across her forehead sprouting a rising asp with piercing emerald eyes which hovered menacingly above her heavily black-lined eyelids. Teetering on four-inch mules, she towered over the assembled group like Mount Everest above the Himalayas. Her eyelids barely closed in greeting then she glided across the deck towards us as the mass of costumed passengers spontaneously applauded.

In two strides Vijay was blocking her path. 'Salaam Alaikum, Cleopatra,' he announced, raising his hand to his hairline and rotating it in exaggerated fashion before placing it against his heart, his turbaned head lowered. 'Dinner awaits you.' He swung his robe in an arc across his chest, stepped sideways to give Ruby room then pointed towards the companionway steps. Remaining in character, my roommate sashayed across the deck as if born to the role with Vijay following in her wake.

'Her Most Royal Majesty, Queen Victoria, the Empress of India and Major-General Sir Arthur Wellesley,' bellowed the officer as our party exited the upper deck, Saladin and Cleopatra ahead, both majestic in height and magnificence, parting the revellers with regal domination.

We arrived with due ceremony at the Bedouin tent, where the Navigation Officer, in his T. E. Lawrence outfit of desert uniform and kaffiyeh head-dress, stood by the entrance. He welcomed us warmly and indicated to a long table in the tent's interior, laden with an abundance of hot and cold cuisine from both Europe, the Middle East, and the Indian sub-continent. A miniature Moghul Palace complete with turreted walls, all made from palm sugar, stood at the centre of this amazing banquet and the aromas were intoxicating.

Ruby moved closer and dug me in the ribs. 'You tell fibs, Elizabeth Stuart-Mackenzie. Big white ones.'

I fluttered my eyelashes in a Princess Darshwanabai sort of way. 'I have no idea what you mean, Cleo.'

She tossed her Asp-clad head upwards causing her black tresses to sway from side to side. 'If you're a Moghul serving wench, Sherri, I'm the Queen of the May.' She studied me with a critical eye like a farmer inspecting a prize bull. 'Now, own-up, where did you get that outfit?'

'Simon Arzt,' I replied, 'while your back was turned.' I caught my own reflection in a polished brass salver and enjoyed the sight of Scheherazade melding into the elaborate Eastern surroundings as I lied shamelessly.

We moved slowly along the table inspecting the many dishes on display. Ruby plucked a paprika and lemon chicken kebab from a platter, wafting it under my nose. My hand gripped her arm and the kebab disappeared under my veil while no one was looking. Ruby tutted and moved on.

'King Richard,' shouted Saladin, striding over to the corner of the tent where a tall knight sporting a St George's Cross surcoat over chainmail and wearing a gold crenelated crown stood by the bar, a pewter beer tankard in his hand.

'Saladin, my boy,' replied King Richard, 'good to see you in this part of the realm.'

Vijay, never one for ignoring a pretty face, bowed to King Richard's companion. 'And who is this fair maiden hovering in your shadow?'

'This,' announced Tom with due reverence, 'is Florence of Crimea, an angel to every battle-weary warrior who ever lived to tell the tale.'

Frances, swathed in an ankle-length grey contoured skirt, a white lace-collared blouse, a crisp white linen pinafore and starched nurses cap curtsied demurely to Vijay and placed her Tilly lamp firmly on the bar-top. I caught a glimpse of sheer silk stocking as her rear leg was exposed and had difficulty remaining in character.

Ruby couldn't resist commenting. 'King Richard, you rake, I see your companion's stockinged ankle is all that is needed to keep you from your Crusade.'

If looks could kill Frances would have been arrested for murder. Tom, meanwhile, had no idea what she was talking about. Vijay obviously did.

'I take exception to that comment, Cleopatra. We are mere mortals when it comes to the wiles of you ladies, especially when you pamper to our egos.'

Frances was now apoplectic and searching the tent for an escape.

Tom was being ignored so decided to go on the offensive. 'And who is this Ali Baba escorts to the gathering?'

'This, my Lord,' announced Prince Kapoor Dhawan, taking my left hand and delivering me before the King of England, 'is Scheherazade, Arabia's most famous Queen and story-teller.'

My henna tattoo merged with Tom's lips. 'You are truly the beauty of the desert, My Lady,' he said, 'and you have forever stolen my heart.'

I turned to Ali Baba who was having difficulty keeping a straight face. 'Are all English Knights so free with their favours or do we consider their words to be merely hot air?'

'It is not good to believe the words of the infidel, Your Highness,' replied my chaperone, 'particularly one so far from home.'

'Shame,' I replied, descending onto a fat leather pouf, 'perhaps Saladin should run him through with his scimitar for being so insolent.'

'Touché! King Richard,' quipped Vijay. 'Like a certain female Doctor I met recently, Scheherazade appears to take no prisoners.' He moved around a stubby carved ebony table and stretched out opposite me on a long couch.

Tom bent to my level, lifted my chin with his gloved hand and stared into my eyes. 'Perhaps, Your Highness, you have distant Jacobite relatives?'

My cutting response was curtailed by the steward hovering, waiting to take our order. 'A panis for myself and Ali Baba and champagne for the ladies,' announced Vijay, as Tom retrieved his beer. Minutes later our table was filled with small pots of delicacies, a large tray of spiced succulent lamb, a bowl of wild rice and a dish of leavened bread.

Saladin and Ali Baba were now deep in conversation whilst drawing on hookahs bubbling by the table while Ruby and Frances traded impressions of the tent, one so prim and the other so exotic. Tom took the opportunity to lean in and whisper complimentary words through my gauze veil.

'You look stunning, Mac. Can I assume your alto-ego is full of Eastern promise?'

'That depends on your sexual inclinations, King Richard. From what I recall, Sire, you have a predilection for young boys and nurses.'

Tom stepped back, hand on heart. 'You shouldn't believe all you read in dispatches, Ma'am. I'm merely acting as escort to a fellow officer's maiden while he's off inspecting the watch.' He moved his scabbard to one side with a flourish and descended onto a couch close by ensuring our thighs came into contact.

Ruby dropped onto a leather pouf and stretched over for a piece of leaven bread before scooping up some minted lamb. I couldn't wait any longer, starvation was beginning to set in. Unclipping the string of medallions from my nose, my veil fell away and I filled my mouth with the aromatic lamb, paying scant attention to anything other than satisfying my hunger.

'You appear to relish our cuisine, Scheherazade, haggis or no haggis?' commented Vijay. Tom lifted a second morsel to my lips and deliberately left his forefinger on my tongue. In the dim lantern light of the Bedouin tent I sucked on the appendage with total abandonment.

'You're a jezebel, Elizabeth Stuart-MacKenzie,' he whispered and ran his hand along the contours of my arm.

Flushed with too much male admiration, a surfeit of sexual innuendo and a heady mix of champagne bubbles, I gave Scheherazade's Eastern promise full rein and the adage, *once bitten, twice shy* was mentally tossed into the Indian Ocean.

We all ate, drank and made merry as the hours ticked by until Lawrence of Arabia appeared by Frances's side, encircled her waist, placed another flute of champagne in her hand, whispered something in her ear and whisked her away. Ali Baba, using the interruption to remind Saladin of their expected attendance in the Jhalanpur Suite, rose from his couch, bowed and apologised for breaking up our gathering. Saladin followed, apologising for abandoning us to the uncouth ways of the Crusader, Richard, threw his long robe over his shoulder and strode from the tent as if on his way into battle.

Ruby's eyes followed Vijay across the tent then lay back on the couch, stretched for the hookah and bubbled away while Tom and I finished the saffron and cardamom rice pudding with candied fruit. As our glasses were refilled for the umpteenth time a stocky Mark Anthony, dressed in full Roman Centurion uniform approached Ruby, extended his hand and invited her to take the night air in a Glaswegian accent.

'Who was that?' enquired Tom watching them go.

'One of the Assam tea-planters,' I replied, re-attaching my string of medallions to my nose.

'Shall we go too?' Tom took my arm and lead me out of the tent. I could hear the resident band tuning up as a group of costumed youngsters pushed past heading towards the sound. I caught sight of William and Charlotte somewhere in the middle and wondered what had happened to their ayah.

We arrived at the stern-rail which I clung to for support, blinking to keep things in focus. 'Riveldene seems a lifetime away,' I said, conscious of Tom standing behind me. 'Never, in a million years could I have imagined this night back in Northumbria.'

'Maybe your father's words had hidden meaning, Mac.' Tom's fingers were now playing with the medallions hanging from my right ear.

'Which words are those?' I whispered, leaning onto his broad chest.

He sucked my earlobe as his hand cupped my right breast. 'There are no ten commandments east of the Suez.'

Chapter Twelve

Tom's arm rested across my right hip as we lay, side-on, in his single berth, our perspiration mingling where our naked bodies touched, a damp salty footprint of our outline staining the sheet below as the ceiling fan cast a cool zephyr breeze across my skin.

In the shadowy stillness I could just make out a mound of silks, satins and chain mail jumbled together in pools across the wooden floor and a sword propped awkwardly against the wash-hand basin, each abandoned in pursuit of more sensual pleasures.

I eased my foot from under Tom's calf and heard him sigh; a deep masculine sigh of contentment at a conquest successfully executed. He had played me like a well strung Stradivarius, his prolonged, meandering caresses of foreplay stimulating sexual desire in me so intense that I lost all inhibition, my spine arching to his touch like a feline on heat. Penetration, when it came, was deep, fluid and powerful, my hips matching his, thrust for thrust, a primeval display of copulation, climax and collapse, like nothing I had ever experienced before. As my blood pressure slowly descended and my breathing returned to normality, I lay back against the cabin bulkhead and felt my vagina throbbing. I had been in the hands of a very experienced lover and felt sweetly liberated. This reserved Englishman had taught me a very salutary lesson. Never again would I judge a book by its cover.

The refrain of a foxtrot was playing somewhere above me, the Gala Ball still in full swing as the ss Narkunda cruised on through the night and, like the revellers on deck, I wanted it all to go on forever. Rotating on a sixpence, I gently ran my fingers down Tom's sternum until they reached his groin. Reacting, his hand made contact with the flesh of my buttock and he pulled me across his thighs.

'Are all Northumbrian doctors so demanding?' he whispered, hovering between sleep and sexual proclivity, 'or is it your wild Highland ways that keeps me from my beauty sleep?'

My knees and hands took my weight as the tip of my tongue traced a line so recently inscribed by my fingers, coming to rest amongst his pubic hair.

'Just the sight of your manhood,' I said, resting my chin on his groin and coyly meeting his gaze, 'and a lack of anything better to play with out here on the ocean.'

'Well, far be it from me to . . . oh . . . put any obstacles in your way . . . Oh God! . . . just remember what you're playing with . . . ummmh! . . . is needed for other matters in the morning . . .OH, LORD, Mac, DON'T STOP!'

By three o'clock Tom was snoring contentedly. I eased myself off the bed and tried in vain to carefully disentangle Scheherazade's ensemble from King Richard's chainmail without tearing the fine material in the dark. I gave up, reached below the bed for my panties, and hopped around the floor trying to find the correct opening. Fingering the bulkhead, I located Tom's wardrobe and pulled a uniform shirt off a hanger, pushed my arms through the sleeves, buttoned the garment to the collar and checked that I was decently covered before creeping out of the cabin.

All was quiet. I tiptoed down the corridor and up the metal stairs to the boat-deck in bare feet, halted to check if the way was clear then legged it to cabin 8, bashing my tibia on the life-jacket stowage before arriving at my cabin door furiously rubbing the damaged skin.

In the semi-darkness of the cabin, Ruby lay in a stupor, her Cleopatra outfit slung across my bed. I drew in a breath. The air in the room was rather fetid. As I struggled to quietly open the porthole I coughed, then coughed again, the back of my throat suddenly irritated. My breathing was now coming in gasps, my nasal passages were beginning to tingle, and my throat was now burning. Something was very wrong.

'Jesus,' I choked and dropped to the floor trying to get my befuddled brain to work. Instinctively I crawled towards the door, my tear ducts working overtime, my lungs on fire. I slid my hands up the hot cabin bulkhead in the dark, searching for the light switch.

The cabin illuminated and I scanned the room in horror as the deckhead slowly blistered fore to aft, flecks of cream paint falling like snowflakes onto the cabin floor, charring the linoleum where it landed.

'Ruby,' I shouted, and shook her, but she didn't respond. 'Ruby, wake up!' She was out cold, and a chill went down my spine as I recognised that this wasn't due to alcohol. I squealed as the lamp bulb exploded, shards of glass coating my head and arms, the hairs fizzing as they burned. With adrenalin pumping through my veins, I dragged Ruby bodily off the bed and out through the cabin door, my feet searing on the suddenly hot metal doorframe, then heaved her dead weight along the smoke-filled corridor, my cracked voice screaming as I went.

'Help! Help me! FIRE! FIRE!'

An officer appeared from nowhere as we reached the warm deck.

'Over there,' I yelled. 'Fire above cabin 8.'

I rolled Ruby onto her stomach, pushed both of her hands under her forehead and knelt by her crown. Placing both my hands flat on her back either side of her spine, I rocked forwards pushing down on her ribcage before rocking back and lifting her elbows into the air, repeating the process once, twice, three times as Ruby remained dead to the world.

'Jesus!' I cried, continuing on, oblivious to Tom's shirt sliding above my hips as my hands kneaded Ruby's back before pulling her arms almost out of their sockets and praying in vain for movement, any movement from my cabin companion.

A team of lascars in protective clothing, some dragging fire hoses, rushed by, orders ripping the air as a fire bell rang out and I lurched with the deck as the ship made a sudden correction in heading, chaos and confusion escalating all around me.

'Come on, Ruby, for God sake, breath,' I yelled, tense with pent-up frustration, but she lay limp under my hands. Blaspheming like a Newcastle docker I began again, pressing her ribcage like a human piston, crushing her bones then pulling her elbows into the air.

'For fuck's sake, Ruby, breath damn you.' I was beginning to think the unthinkable. My shoulders ached from all the pushing and pulling and Ruby's lips were turning blue when suddenly she gasped, her head shot up from her hands, and her chest exploded into a raucous, guttural coughing fit.

'Oh, thank God,' I cried, pulling her into a sitting position and resting her spine against my chest, her head flopping forwards as I raised her arms to expand her chest. 'Water,' I screamed to a steward running past with wet blankets dripping from his arms. 'I need water, drinking water.' He dropped a blanket from the pile and rushed on. I grabbed Ruby by her hair, turning her head to one side and squeezed the end of the blanket into her mouth knowing the salt-water would make her sick as she spluttered and gagged but that was better than her dying from carbon-monoxide poisoning. My eyes were swimming in toxic tears and black smoke was billowing around my head as wailing from every direction added to the pandemonium on deck.

'MAC.' Tom was above me, trying to drag me off Ruby, but I was welded to her spine, refusing to believe that she was breathing alone, the wet blanket tented around both of us for protection from the heat.

'Get up, damn you.'

I ignored him and continued to pump Ruby's arms up and down as if she were learning to fly.

'MAC, STOP! She's breathing. We've got to move. The fire could ignite this deck at any time. Steward, over here.'

Masculine arms bodily lifted me over someone's shoulder, and I was bundled unceremoniously towards the stern, my rear-end and panties now totally exposed to the elements. I looked back through the gloom as my body bounced up and down and I could just make out Tom following with Ruby lying limp in his arms, then my world suddenly imploded as my head hit something solid above me.

I woke in the sick bay, with a gash across my cranium and a wet flannel over my face.

'Tom,' I whimpered, my voice rasping and my throat full of sharp knives.

'I'm here,' called a familiar voice from some way off. I pushed the flannel away and I blinked twice before bringing a fuzzy image of Tom's face into view.

'Where's Ruby, is she alive?

'Hush, Mac, she's safe. You kept her alive. Now rest. You've had a major crack on the head causing concussion and your own breathing is still laboured.'

'What about the others? How are Frances and Lady Worthing . . .' I coughed up black soot into the flannel and was immediately given a glass of water to sooth the burning sensation. 'Lady . . . Worthington? . . . and have you seen little Charlotte and William. Are they OK?'

'Mac, for God's sake, stop asking questions. Everything is under control. I have to go but I'll be back as soon as I can.'

'But what about Major . . .'

'Mac!' Tom disappeared through the door his insistent words left hanging in the air. I lay back on the pillow and concentrated on breathing, checking my pulse rate until it dropped below eighty beats a minute then closed my eyes as exhaustion kicked in. A sound close by interrupted my stupor, a sound of someone struggling to say my name. It was Ruby and the doctor in me reacted immediately. I dragged myself off my bed wanting to check her vital signs and collapsed onto the floor, my legs giving way from under me, a sharp pain from my left arm shooting through my shoulder blade and my head exploding like the Krakatoa volcano.

'Oh, Christ,' I groaned, trying to hold my brain together as my stomach contents shot up my oesophagus and I spewed yellow bile and black slime all over the floor.

'Don't mov …e. I'll … get … help,' Ruby croaked. I could hear her staggering to the door and attempting to call out but all that she produced was a coughing fit. As a thousand flashing lights rotated across my retina, a violent metallic clanging noise split my eardrums. I had no idea what she had done but it worked.

'It's . . . Dr . . .Mac, she's . . . collap. . .sed.'

'Memsahib, I go find doctor.' I stared into Salvador's concerned face. 'You need Doctor.'

I shook my head and spewed up more bile all over his feet. 'No, Salvador,' I whimpered, wiping my mouth on the back of my hand. 'I'm OK.' My eyeballs erupted in another kaleidoscope of colour.

'Really, Memsahib? You really OK?'

My eyelids blinked a response. 'Water . . . please.'

Ruby staggered to her bed and slumped on the mattress, her body bent double, her ribcage encased in white bandage, tears streaming down her cheeks. I stretched out my hand and touched her knee. It was beyond me to do more. 'Breathe . . . Ruby . . . breathe.'

Frances found us like this, her clothes covered in soot, her hair singed around her fringe, eyebrows and eyelashes, her eyes sunken in their sockets. She looked as if she had come straight from the battlefield, but of the three of us, at least she was standing.

'What happened?' I asked, as Ruby coughed up black phlegm into a sterile dish held under her chin.

'I don't know exactly, Mac. No-one's saying very much right now.'

'But what . . . started . . .it?' mumbled Ruby holding onto her throat.

Frances cradled Ruby around the waist and eased her into a half-sitting position. 'I . . . I've no idea. It's mayhem up there and everyone has been sent to the hurricane deck, well those who are not injured, that is.'

My head felt like a ten-pound cannon ball. 'Are we afloat?' I asked, but Frances's attention was now on dabbing my brow with a fresh wet flannel.

'Christ! Do you two ever do what you're told?' Tom's voice was ice cold. He elbowed Frances out of the way, bodily picked me up and lay me back on the bed. 'Now, stay there.'

My eyelid was unceremoniously lifted to my eyebrow and a sharp white light was shone into my iris.

'Ow, that hurts.'

'Quiet.'

Tom was obviously not amused and peered into the other iris then removed the light and stuck his index finger in front of my right eye. 'Now, follow my finger.'

I dutifully followed the digit as it slowly moved from side to side. My left eye would not focus properly but I didn't say anything, blinking repeatedly as my tear ducts gushed liquid. 'OK?'

Tom grunted, prised open my mouth and aimed the torch at my tonsils. 'It's not a pretty sight but I think you'll live.'

'My feet hurt.' A burning sensation had finally reached my brain.

'Your soles are charred from touching hot metal as you pulled Ruby out of danger. They're superficial, but badly blistered. What were you doing in bare feet? Where were your shoes?'

'In your cabin,' I croaked, and coughed up more soot. Red blotches appeared across Tom's neck and earlobes as he nodded to Frances who made herself scarce, then turned his attention to Ruby. 'Now Ruby Tavener, are you going to do as you're told, or should I crack another two ribs?'

I lay back, knowing my cabin mate was in good hands and drifted off to sleep, realising for the first time that my left arm was also in a sling.

Chapter Thirteen

The only sound was that of the sea lapping against the still hull and the haunting refrain of Sergeant Major Wilson's bagpipes playing a familiar tribute to fallen soldiers in war. The melody of 'Going Home' ripped into my guts as I remembered hearing it at so many services in churchyards around Berwick-on-Tweed after the Great War.

I closed my eyes, willing time to reverse, eager to return to the normality of shipboard life before the night of the Gala Ball.

"God, intervene," I begged hopelessly, knowing that this type of miracle could never be granted. It never was.

My sobs felt like tiny explosions from a dying gas fire, the red glow of toxic fumes still burning my throat and lungs as I forced myself to take in the scene before me.

In full dress uniform, the crew of the ss Narkunda stood in line abreast, their peaked caps held stiffly against their right thighs, their bare heads erect, eyes staring out across the Indian Ocean, each face devoid of expression. At right-angles to the crew stood the ship's Chaplain, cassock hanging limply in the still air, the ship's Bible in his hands. Alongside him, the ship's Captain. Behind them stood Tom and his assistant, the Chief Engineer, the Purser, Reverend Pillsbury, Lady Cottesmore and Prince Vijay Kumar Sing II with Prince Kapoor Dhawan one pace behind that.

On the opposite side, Ruby and I had front row seats, both sitting erect in steamer-chairs with Frances standing between, her hands gripping the chair backs, the whites of her knuckles clearly visible. The rest of the passengers either formed lines to our sides and rear or watched from the Promenade deck above. The silence was intense everyone waited, their eyes fixed on a flat board balanced horizontally across the ship's gunwhale, a shroud covered in a Union flag lying on top. I shuddered.

Four junior officers stood to attention, two at the centre and two at the rear, waiting patiently to do their duty. The pipes fell silent and the ship's Chaplain stepped forward, Bible in hand and recited Psalm 130.

Out of the deep have I called unto thee, O Lord,
Lord hear my voice . . .

I mouthed every familiar word, every line, every inflection as I sobbed silently.

Ruby's hand rose from her lap and she placed it on my right shoulder. I reached up to cover hers and Frances closed both with her own as, together, we uttered the Lord's prayer.

Our Father which art in heaven . . .

As one, the junior officers made ready while the Chaplain raised his voice to the heavens and began the committal.

Unto Almighty God we commend the soul of our brother departed, Major Archibald Clarence Stokes and commit his body to the deep in sure and certain hope of the Resurrection unto eternal life.

A tight steel band crushed my ribcage and my breathing laboured. My head was spinning, my mind reliving the day I had stood next to this larger than life ex-soldier watching the statue of Ferdinand de Lesseps slip past our hull as the ss Narkunda manoeuvred into the Suez Canal. I could hear his jocular Yorkshire quips about Napoleon's useless engineers as if he were still standing next to me. Did he have a wife and family somewhere who were still to learn of his demise, I wondered?

With a nod from the Captain, the board was raised to a forty-five-degree angle. Slowly, very slowly at first, but gathering momentum, Major Stokes's charred remains, hidden by the shroud, slid from under the Union flag, and vertically dived into the deep ocean below. The splash reverberated around the quiet ship, the finality of the moment stark under a blistering sun.

'Goodbye, Major,' I muttered as he sank to the ocean bed.

The First Officer stepped in front of Lady Cottesmore and handed her a large wreath. As a three-gun rifle salute from the Bombay Lancers blasted into the air above our heads she stepped to the gunwhale and threw the wreath onto the water. Sergeant Major Wilson lifted his bagpipes, a low growl irritating my eardrums as the bag filled with air and then the soulful rendition of Lord Lovat's Lament filled the void. A chill ran down my spine.

My knees were shaking, my vision blurred and my sorrow deeper than the ocean itself. I had seen a great deal of death in my young life, but this felt so personal, so tragic, so unnecessary. If only Major Stokes hadn't fallen into an alcohol infused sleep still holding onto his burning cheroot that night, this grotesque scene would never have happened. Why hadn't I noticed smoke seeping under his cabin door as I crept back to my bed at three o'clock in the morning? Why hadn't I arrived earlier? No amount of counter argument from Tom had been capable of assuaging my guilt. No-one had been there to put out his damned burning cheroot and all I could do was demand answers from God. Why did he have to die? As always, God was silent.

The young officers dropped their arms, placed their peaked caps back onto their heads, pulled the board off the gunwhale and turned as one to march off through the lines. The reluctant congregation moved away.

Vijay and Kapoor Dhawan walked across to where we were sitting and with the help of Salvador and Tom assisted us back to the First-Class lounge, the only public room aboard the ss Narkunda that hadn't been affected by smoke damage. Lady Wetherington had gone ahead and now stood before a table of bubbling champagne flutes and fresh lemonade, waiting for us to join her. We quietly stood in a circle and raised our glasses.

Tom spoke for us all. 'To Major Archibald Clarence Stokes. A loyal soldier of the Crown and a son of the White Rose of York. May he rest in peace.'

'Major Stokes,' we echoed and drank deeply.

A little later I sat across from Tom in his office, my arm resting on his desktop and my foot raised on a stool, staring at the blank bulkhead above his head, all thoughts of our intimate hours together forgotten. 'How much damage is there from the fire?'

'A lot, but thanks to your early intervention and the First Officer turning the ship away from the wind and reducing the ship's speed, the fire crews were able to confine the flames to the forward section of the boat-deck.'

'So, it didn't travel upwards onto the Promenade deck?'

'No, it couldn't get through the metal sheeting between decks, although it certainly tried.'

'I don't understand.' My head still hurt, and I was having difficulty concentrating. 'Why was it burning the ceiling of our cabin?'

'All the cabin bulkheads are wood, Mac, not metal. The fire burned through Major Stokes deckhead and into the service ducting above. Once there, the ventilation fans and forward motion of the ship forced the flames backwards, melting the paint and giving off toxic fumes. Ruby is lucky to be alive.'

'I thought I'd lost her, you know?'

'But you didn't, Mac.' He grabbed my hands and squeezed hard, his voice fracturing. 'You dragged her out and kept her breathing without any thought for your own safety.'

'And pulled the muscles in my shoulder, to boot.' I groaned, rubbing my arm inside the sling.

'Exactly. Ruby is no lightweight for someone your size. What with that, breathing carbon-monoxide fumes, smacking your head on the deckhead D-ring and burning your feet on the metal door frame, it's a wonder you are sitting here at all.'

'So, what happens now?' I wiggled my toes. There was a burning sensation in the ball of my left foot.

'We wait. Another ship in the fleet is being re-routed to us and will take some of the passengers off while our chippies do some temporary repairs. Meanwhile, you will have my cabin.'

'Where will you sleep?' I sounded like my mother.

'I will put a mattress in the sickbay and sleep there so I can keep an eye on the injured.'

'And Frances?'

'The lascars and stewards were making up beds on the hurricane deck as I passed earlier so she will probably be sleeping in the open from now on, under an awning.'

I grimaced, imagining Sybil Wetherington camping on deck and moved my arm into an easier position. 'Frances won't mind, Tom, she's used to it.' I smiled slightly, recalling our teasing conversation about her watching a sunrise over the Horn of Africa. It all seemed so long ago.

Tom handed me a glass of water and some aspirin. 'Do you feel up to visiting the Jhalanpur suite? The Princess and her family are desperate to see you. Apparently, they don't believe Vijay or Kapoor Dhawan and want to see you with their own eyes.'

In all the chaos I had completely forgotten about my patient. 'Yes, of course. I should take my costume back to them as well.'

'How are you going to explain the fact that it survived the fire?' Tom's forehead wrinkled.

'I'm not sure. If they ask, I'll tell them it was in my metal trunk which didn't get damaged, but I don't believe they will.'

'Before you go, Mac, there's something you should know. Vijay told me this morning that the Princess was involved in a palace fire when she was a child. She suffered third degree burns to her back and her brother was asphyxiated and died. Apparently, when she heard that the boat deck had caught fire, she had a panic attack.'

My good hand shot to my mouth. 'Oh, Christ, Tom, what about the baby?'

'Vijay didn't say, but he certainly didn't seem . . .' A commotion in the corridor stopped Tom in his tracks.

'Doctor. . .where is Doctor?' A woman's hysterical voice shattered my thoughts. Without thinking I threw myself into the corridor and crashed into a sari-clad female, her face covered.

'What is it? What's wrong?'

'Princess. Please. You come,' stammered her aunt. 'She in much pain.'

Chapter Fourteen

The foetus was no bigger than the palm of my hand. I stood by the washbasin, the gold taps glinting in the lamplight and thought how peaceful the little boy looked, his tiny fingers resting on his chest, his fine veins, like threads of silk, clearly visible through his translucent skin. He lay there, 5 inches long, a miniature future Maharajah of Jhalanpur, now no more.

Nothing in my medical training had prepared me for what to do next. I just stood there, motionless, trying to maintain a professional air while the Princess's blood dripped from my hands staining the bandage at my wrist. This was the second needless tragedy on board, another life lost before I could intervene. I felt utterly useless.

I sensed a presence by my left shoulder and looked up into the deep-set, rheumy eyes of Vijay's physician.

'Doctor, the Princess, she needs you. I will take care of her child.'

He gently lifted the foetus from my protective palm and placed it in a small, lined gold casket. My mind recoiled at the sight. Where had that come from? I tried to speak but no words would come. What could I say? What was there to say? Another miscarriage, like thousands of others, but one so significant to the Jhalanpur dynasty. A boy, a son, an heir to a princely fortune. Would there be others? I hoped so, but that was not going to bring solace to this young wife who so longed to give her prince what he desired. Hindu culture was still very new to me but one thing I knew instinctively. Princess

Darshwanabai needed to get pregnant again quickly or Vijay would replace her with a more fertile version.

I walked across to her bedside. Colourless, ghostly, her eyes stared into oblivion, not a sound emanating from her body. Yet she breathed, her heart pumped, her organs functioned, despite resembling an ethereal vision. Hovering between life and death, she took no part in me or my administrations. I brought a cup to her lips, a draught of laudanum to counter the mental anguish now threatening her sanity. She was my patient, but the only medicine for her bereavement was time, and time was something I could not give her.

I backed away, into the equally sombre reception room. The Prince was gripping the back of a chair, his chin extended forwards, fighting any sign of emotion. Such a proud man, standing upright, rigidly so, but quietly grief-stricken inside. I wanted to give solace but, in his world, such acts of benevolence were not sought, so I hid behind my own professional barrier and reported medically on the loss of his son.

'There was nothing we could do, Your Highness. Your wife's fear of fire created enormous anxiety in her physically. This affected the stability of the foetus . . . your son . . . who, at only seventeen weeks gestation, had no defence.'

My words chilled the atmosphere like a north wind across the Scottish moors. Vijay straightened as he pulled himself out of his trance and began to speak, but I had reached my own emotional threshold. My knees trembled, my vision faltered, and I went into free fall. From far off I could hear his voice; something about his concern for his wife's sanity, but my knees now buckled. All I remembered were strong arms grabbing me before everything went black.

Chapter Fifteen

We wallowed about in the Indian Ocean for another two days, the ship's forward boat deck resembling a sight from Dante's Inferno. Five of the second-class cabin bulkheads on the starboard side were buckled and sodden, the companionway's paint blistered and charred, the superstructure, all the way up to the hurricane deck, streaked with plumes of black soot and tainting the air with acrid fumes. The area was roped off and from where I stood alongside the second-class lounge, its windows smudged and tainted dark brown, the ss Narkunda resembled a derelict coal bulk-carrier rather than a smart P&O passenger liner. I shivered as I realised again how lucky I was still to be alive. Amazingly, there had been no other fatalities, my warning cries having given the passengers time to escape danger. Some minor burns and lacerations were treated in the sickbay but only William and Charlotte's ayah suffered a broken femur from tripping over the life-jacket stowage in her rush to get the children to safety.

My hands shook as I leant on a scorched steamer-chair lying abandoned by the ship's rail. A teardrop traced a dark line on the distressed teak below my fingertips as I pictured Major Stokes, his coattails flapping in the breeze, the obligatory cheroot between his lips.

'Memsahib?' I nodded as footsteps invaded my privacy. 'The Doctor, he need you to come below.'

Tom had asked me to sign Vijay's son's death in the medical log before he could officially release the body. 'I'll be there shortly, Salvador.'

'Yes, Memsahib. Do you want I stay?'

'No, thank you. That will be all.'

I wondered what would happen to the tiny Rajputan foetus and suddenly could not rest until I knew. Leaving the charred scene behind, I gingerly climbed the rear companionway steps to the Jhalanpur Suite and tapped on the door.

The chaprassi greeted me, bowing low, his impeccably tailored Hindu uniform and pagari headdress a sharp contrast to the grimy shambles of the lower boat-deck.

'Prince Kapoor Dhawan, please.'

He stepped back allowing me to enter and indicated to a gilt-edged chair by the door.

I nodded and sat, feet crossed at the ankles, my left hand supporting the sling covering my right shoulder and arm and waited patiently. I didn't have to wait long.

'Doctor MacKenzie, you should be resting.' The Prince strode across to my chair, bowing ceremoniously on arrival, then clapped his hands and demanded refreshments for his guest. The chaprassi disappeared as I was led to a wine-red chaise longue where we both settled, our eyes mirroring each other's pain.

'I . . .' My vocal cords seemed to have snapped.

'Take your time, my dear.'

The chaprassi laid a silver salver on the table close by then backed away, fingers pressed to his forehead. I accepted a frosted glass and felt the cool liquid lubricate my throat.

'Before I sign the surgeon's official log . . . I wanted to know how . . . when the infant will be. . .' I couldn't go on. My desire to understand Hindu custom was only adding to the distress in this first-class suite. The Prince's neck muscles were taut as he lowered his gaze, a throbbing vein pulsing in his wrist. His stress level was intense, and I wasn't helping.

'I'm so sorry, I should not have bothered you.' I rose, about to make a rapid exit but his hand barred my way, his head shaking as he pulled me back down.

'Doctor Mackenzie, your interest in our customs is perfectly natural in the circumstances, so allow me to explain what will happen to my niece's child.' He paused, a thin smile relaxing the tension around his lips and eyes. 'Normally, we cremate our loved ones within twenty-four hours of their passing, placing the body on a funeral pyre, close to a sacred river or water. The eldest son or male mourner then has the duty of lighting the pyre and the ashes are scattered in that sacred spot.' He paused and stared into the distance. 'However, we believe that babies, children and saints are pure and unattached to their bodies, so they are buried, not cremated.' His words brought solace to my tortured thoughts as he continued. 'Prince Vijay Kumar Singh's unborn son will be buried, without ceremony, in sacred ground, directly after we arrive in Bombay.'

'Thank you, Prince Kapoor Dhawan. I needed to know. I needed to understand.'

'Your question is perfectly reasonable, Doctor MacKenzie. I hope my answer has set your mind at rest.'

'It has, Your Highness, and I will pray for both mother and child. Please tell Princess Darshwanabai that I will never forget her and that I will not rest until I hear that she has made a complete recovery and is blessed with another child to give her joy.'

We parted as friends not knowing when or if we would ever meet again. As I made my way to the sick bay, I had a premonition that our paths would indeed cross again, though how or why I had no clue.

Tom was checking on Ruby's progress as I came through the door, her verbal complaints confirming that she was on the mend.

'Ow! For God's sake, Tom, if that bandage gets any tighter, I'll die of asphyxiation.'

'You nearly did,' I pointed out as I propped myself against her bed. 'And, don't take the Lord's name in vain, he might be listening.'

'Then you tell this sadistic bugger to give me some room to breathe.'

'As you can hear, Mac, Miss Tavener appears to be finding her voice, though why she is giving me grief when it was you who cracked two of her ribs, I'll never know.'

Tom tucked the ends of the bandage out of sight, pulled Ruby's jaw down, pressed a wooden spatula onto her tongue and peered into her mouth with a light. Irritated guttural noises came from his patient followed by a coughing fit once he'd finished his inspection.

'You'll do,' he said, handing her a glass of water. Now drink this, lie back and rest your larynx. That's an order.'

As he ushered me to the door, I caught sight of Ruby holding two fingers in the air and rediscovered my smile. Life goes on, I thought, and plopped down onto the chair by Tom's desk.

'Are you OK?' Tom sounded very like my father showing concern for my welfare after a particularly trying day at the Riveldene surgery.

'Yes, I think so. Where do I sign?'

He pulled the log across the desk and pointed to the relevant section. 'I have put the cause of death as a spontaneous abortion due to excessive stress on the mother during a shipboard fire. Do you agree?'

I rubbed my left hand across my forehead trying to remove the image of the foetus lying dead in my hands. 'Yes, Tom, I do. Is there anything else?'

'Well, yes there is, but this is not the time or place, so I suggest you get some rest and we can meet in the first-class lounge this evening and have that conversation over a drink.'

With that he opened the door to his cabin, helped me to undress and left me lying on his bed covered in a sheet with only the rotating ceiling fan for company. Despite my state of mind, the drone of the fan-blades was soporific, and I gave in to my exhaustion.

Chapter Sixteen

Bombay?' I said, sounding like a cracked record.

'Yes, Mac, Bombay,' repeated Tom, sitting opposite me in the first-class lounge with a tankard of beer at his lips, about to imbibe. 'The fire has changed everything in the short term. With substantial repairs needed, the ship won't be going anywhere for quite a while.'

'Well, obviously,' I said, sipping a schooner of sherry. 'How long do you think the ss Narkunda will be out of action?'

'I have no idea, but that's not the point.' He sat closer, keeping his voice low. 'When do you have to be in Calcutta?'

I hesitated. 'That depends on a response from the CSTM. I imagine they'll want to interview me as soon as possible.'

Tom's shoulders sagged. 'Why?'

'P&O won't need me for some time, unless I am allocated another ship, which I very much doubt, so, it's likely I'll be seconded to the Surgeon General, Bombay and I will end up temporarily working with the IMS.'

'IMS?' My frown touched the bridge of my nose.

'Indian Medical Services.' He sat back, relishing his beer, waiting for me to catch on.

'And you're wondering if we can spend some time together in Bombay before I leave for Calcutta.'

'Exactly. Think about it, Mac, a week of R&R while you mend both mentally and physically before taking up your research post is just what your doctor would prescribe. And I can't think of anyone better to administer to your medical needs than me.'

My look of disdain was pure, Aunt Karr. 'I bet you say that to all the girls.'

Tom hesitated, pressing his fingers together, his eyes lowered, and failed to answer.

'I'm joking, Tom,' I quickly added, sensing I had hit a nerve. 'Tom?'

'There's something you ...'

'Another drink, Memsahib?' asked the steward leaning over and taking my empty glass.

'No. No thank you.' I waited for Tom to continue.

'Forgive me, Mac, I'm being selfish. I just wanted to spend more time with you, that's all.' His words sounded flat.

I sat in silence trying to work out why he had suddenly changed his mind.

'I would like that too, Tom, but I've come a long way to work at the CSTM and I don't want to jeopardise that by delaying my arrival.'

He pointed to my sling. 'I know. I just thought the college would understand once they heard of what had happened here. I have no right to ask you anyway. Of course you must go straight to Calcutta. Forget I ever mentioned it.'

That was easier said than done. The thought of a forty-hour train journey to Calcutta with luggage, a sprained shoulder, singed lungs, blistered feet, and a gash on my head, instead of spending days in the lap of luxury in some Bombay upmarket hotel made his offer of rest and recuperation very appealing. I was torn, knowing that Arthur and Elsie Thornton were expecting me and would be mightily put-out by another change of plan, to say nothing of the schools Board of Governors.

What I needed was space to put things into perspective. 'I'm going on deck to clear my head. Tom.' He was half out of his chair. 'No, you stay here, I won't be long.'

'Mac, I'm so sorry, I didn't mean to upset you.'

'You haven't, Tom. Really.'

I paced the promenade deck, torn between staying or going, and becoming more frustrated by the minute.

'Penny for them?' asked Frances, coming to stand alongside.

'I've been invited to stay in Bombay for a week while I mend.'

'All expenses paid in a luxury hotel with a certain ship's surgeon?'

'Is it that obvious?' I replied, longing for a plush bathroom with a lion's-foot bath.

'You know what Ruby would say?'

I smiled. 'Yes, I do, but Ruby isn't risking a career in viral research, is she?'

'No, but in my opinion nor are you. One week is not going to make any difference to your career, Mac, and Tom's offer makes logical sense.'

'Frances Trotter, I'm surprised at you. Whatever would your colleagues in Poona say if they could hear you now?'

Frances had the grace to look ashamed. 'They'd probably put me on the first ship back home, Mac, but that's not the point. We are talking about you, not me and, after all you've done on this trip, it's time you put yourself first.'

'But . . .'

'No buts, Elizabeth Stuart-MacKenzie, this is India not Edinburgh and you deserve some good old-fashioned male nurturing right now. If the Board of Governors in Calcutta do object, you'll just have to join me on that passage back to Tilbury.'

I could feel my resolve crumbling like an East Coast cliff-face pounded by a North Sea gale as Frances's words sank in. Tom had not been part of the plan back in Riveldene, but now that he was, it seemed crazy not to grab some happiness while I still had the chance. I knew I was in no fit shape to face whatever was ahead of me and baulked at arriving in anything other than perfect order.

'I guess a delay would give any potential sponsors more time to reply,' I argued.

'Indeed,' confirmed Frances, clasping my hands in hers. 'Go for it, Mac. What can you lose?'

'Only my livelihood, my reputation and my self-respect, Frances.'

'Oh, is that all? Then, frankly, I wouldn't hang around a minute longer. Tom will be waiting for your answer.'

I rushed back to the lounge expecting to find Tom where I had left him, but he was gone.

The steward turned as I walked up to the bar. 'Excuse me, did Doctor Wallace leave any message for me?'

'No, Memsahib. The Doctor, he buy a bottle of whisky and say he no want to be disturbed.'

That sounded a bit odd. Tom didn't like whisky. I checked his cabin, the sickbay, and the dining room without success, so

I returned to his surgery and wrote a quick note, hoping to meet up with him later.

Dear Tom,

Life is too short to miss out on happiness. Calcutta will just have to wait for another seven days.

Love

Mac

X

Later, turned out to be the next morning when Tom popped his head around the cabin door, his eyes rather bloodshot.

'Did you get my note?' I asked, watching his expression very closely.

'I did. What changed your mind?'

'The thought of a large lions-foot bath,' I quipped, trying to keep the atmosphere light.

'Then, I'd better book us a suite at the Taj Mahal Hotel,' he said and disappeared back into the sickbay.

There was great excitement aboard when the ss Mulbera arrived to offer assistance. This British India Lines ship was up-wind of the ss Narkunda when I came on deck, moving ahead at a steady five knots on the same heading and preparing to take on passengers. She had been on passage between Mombasa and Bombay and had diverted to help us at the request of P&O.

Lady Wetherington and Reverend Pillsbury were among the second-class passengers who had opted to transfer mid-ocean in the hope of greater comfort and less delay, and we watched with some trepidation as the ships' crews ferried one and all, clad in ss Narkunda lifejackets, across the choppy divide. Sybil waved her large flower-brimmed hat for all it was worth, causing the launch to rock alarmingly. We were sad to see them go, and the ship felt empty and abandoned without them, but Sybil had my mail which she promised to post immediately on arrival in Bombay. This would guarantee that Elsie Thornton and the CSTM would have prior knowledge of my injuries and my revised arrival date in Calcutta before I even reached dry land.

I was particularly sad to see Prince Kapoor Dhawan depart. He was going ahead to make arrangements for the Jhalanpur funeral, and his departure left me bereft and full of remorse, the little Prince haunting my hours like some spectral shadow.

The ss Narkunda cruised slowly towards Bombay with the forward boat-deck resembling a building site. It was mayhem trying to avoid the ship's chippy and crew stripping out the burned cabins and jettisoning charred bulkheads and fixtures overboard, while lascars swung from precarious gantries scrubbing and scraping the blackened super-structure and guard-rails.

'I imagine resting in a combat zone is a bit like this,' remarked Frances, as we sunbathed on the hurricane deck trying to make the best of the situation.

'Stanley is not too impressed either,' said Ruby, grimacing as she re-adjusted her position in the steamer-chair. 'He is being inundated with complaints from first-class and would willingly throw them all overboard with the debris.'

'I can't imagine Miss High-and-Mighty is happy sharing her dining-room with the likes of us.' I grabbed a cushion from another chair and eased it behind Ruby's back.

'Thanks, Mac, my ribs are giving me hell this morning. As for Miss High-and-Mighty, she is now dining with a sanitary inspector and his wife from Birmingham and I don't think she can understand a word they say.'

'Well,' I replied, thinking of Arthur Thornton, 'that's justice for you.' I got up and walked to the bow. 'What's that smell?'

Standing with the ship's black funnels at my rear, I filled my lungs with sea air and caught a whiff of tropical flowers, oriental spices, human ordure, and rotting vegetation.

'Hey, girls,' I shouted, 'I think I can smell India.' From a clear blue sky, screeching gannets and gliding shearwaters circled the ship, their noisy arrival quickening my pulse-rate and loosening my bowels. I gripped the rail and tried to steady my nerves. Somewhere out there, I thought, just below the horizon, Bombay was waiting with its strange cultural traditions, shrouded in a haze of polluted air. I frowned as I realised that I was far from ready for my new life.

Chapter Seventeen

We stood at the starboard rail watching the shambles below as two tugs with lines fore and aft nudged the ss Narkunda towards Ballard Pier. Steamer trunks swayed to the motion as they were stacked by the gangway door, the lascars and stewards moving in one continuous loop like an army of ants, while Stanley scratched his head and directed operations.

Constant orders were bellowed from the bridge to crews manning the lines while Indian stevedores clad in drab, discoloured dhotis and pleated turbans hovered on shore ready to clear the liner of her passengers and belongings. My eardrums ached from three sharp blasts sounded from ss Narkunda's steam whistle, then the ship shuddered, her engines went astern, and she was expertly manoeuvred alongside.

It was ten-forty-five on a dusty, crowded Tuesday morning, and we had finally arrived, three weeks and four days after leaving Tilbury Docks. I recalled the Elizabeth Stuart-MacKenzie of that damp and grey October day and compared her with the woman standing above this chaotic, sultry dockside in Bombay. The contrast was stark. After all the highs and lows of the passage and the many and varied experiences I had faced along the way, any resemblance between my two selves was merely skin deep and as tenuous as comparing Nimbu Panis with Newcastle Brown Ale. I chuckled silently.

Sweat was trickling down my neck and back from the humidity, my eyes swivelling left and right trying to take in all the unfamiliar sights of this bustling harbour.

'Doesn't look much, does it?' commented Ruby frowning down at the grubby façade of the harbourside buildings.

I leant out to get a better view between the girders of a giant, rusty shoreside crane with its chain and hook dangling precariously above my head. 'Crikey, look at those police officers manhandling the beggars off the dock using truncheons.' I winced as one poor down-and-out was smacked sharply against his legs and dragged bodily backwards.

'It's like Wembley Stadium on Cup-Final day,' remarked Frances, borrowing Ruby's fly-swat and making figure of eight movements above her head. 'How we are to find our way out of here between all these crowds is beyond me.'

The sea of humanity began to part, and a canvass-sided sloping gangway rolled towards the ship's side. Stanley took control of proceedings and the first-class passengers began to disembark, their exit blocked by stevedores and local agents all keen to make headway in the opposite direction.

'It's total mayhem,' sighed Frances, holding her nose with a lace hankie. 'And the smell!'

'Get used to it, Miss Trotter,' croaked Ruby, retrieving her fly-swat and decapitating a large blue-bottle against the rail.

'To think, we paid good money to experience all this,' I groaned. It was an understatement to say I was not impressed, and I was more than ready to turn around and head straight back to Riveldene.

'Come back Soho, all is forgiven,' was Ruby's derogatory comment on the scene. 'I suggest we get out of this dust and get a drink.'

'OK,' agreed Frances looking at her watch, 'but I have to catch the Bombay to Poona Mail in two hours if I'm to arrive at my new school tonight, so I haven't got long.'

Getting to the first-class lounge was a challenge as we pushed and shoved others out of the way, Frances gamely trying to protect my right arm with her body. With relief, we flopped into chairs by the bar and ordered drinks.

'Now Mac,' announced Frances, 'what's your address in Calcutta?'

I pulled a rather crumpled letter from Elsie Thornton out of my skirt pocket and handed it over. While she scribbled away in her address book, I eyeballed Ruby. 'So, are you finally going to tell us what happens to you now?'

Ruby played with her cocktail stick, the ice cubes clinking in her glass. 'To be frank, Mac, I'm not sure. I'm waiting for an agent from the Indian Civil Service to arrive with a train ticket to Delhi where I shall be met by some official who will take me to my hotel.'

'Exactly what will you be doing in Delhi?' asked Frances, putting her address book back in her bag and handing me the letter.

'Oh, didn't I say?'

I exchanged weary glances with Frances and we both shook our heads.

'I will be the rich mistress of one of our British Empire's wealthier aristocrats.'

'Great Scot!' My lemonade fizzed up my nostril. 'Which wealthy aristocrat is that, then? Just so I don't put my foot in it with his very wealthy wife at some future social function.'

'The same one who bought me the Cartier watch and got me fired from the Windmill Theatre, Mac. And no, this time I am not lying.'

'Well, I'll be damned,' announced Frances, too shocked to realise that she had sworn.

Tom popped his head around the bar door at this juncture. 'Time to go, Mac. Our transport will be here shortly.'

'Right. Just give me five minutes, I need to find Salvador.' I turned to the girls. 'Well, this is it. Thanks a million for your friendship over the past weeks. I can't imagine what I would have done without you both.' I downed the rest of my drink and grabbed my handbag. 'Don't forget to keep in touch,' I pointed at Ruby, 'wherever you happen to be and, both of you, stay safe.' With tearful hugs all round we parted company and I headed for the boat deck where our Goan steward was lugging my smoke-stained trunk away from the companionway steps. 'Salvador,' I called.

His head came up as the end of my trunk scraped the top metal step and thumped onto the teak deck. 'Yes. Memsahib.'

I handed him a small white envelope with what I hoped was the appropriate tip, plus written details of my room number at Bombay's Taj Mahal Hotel, so he could organise the transfer of my baggage. 'My medical bag is still in Doctor Wallace's office. Please be sure to keep it safe until it reaches the hotel and thank you for everything you have done for me during the voyage.'

'It is my honour, Memsahib. Safe on-going.' He bowed and bent to lift my trunk once more as I headed towards the exit.

'Doctor MacKenzie, Doctor Mackenzie, do stop.'

I turned and found Lady Wetherington pushing through the crowds waving a piece of paper aloft. 'There you are, my dear. I have been looking all over the ship for you.'

'Goodness, Sybil, whatever are you doing back onboard?'

'I'm here to retrieve all my main luggage before those dilatory stevedores put it on a train to some God-forsaken corner of the sub-continent.' She glared at the dock. 'In the rush to get onto the SS Mulbera the other day I forgot to give you my address. Now, here it is.' She stuffed it into my hand. 'When you get to Calcutta make sure those stuffy Governors write to Lord Wetherington asking for a reference and do keep in touch.'

She held on tightly to her rather large straw hat decorated with a mass of voile froth and ribbons as Salvador staggered past dragging all my worldly goods towards the gangway. 'If you're back in Bombay at any time please come and stay. We have plenty of room and I know my Archie will be fascinated to learn of your exploits. Now take care, dear, and don't get dysentery.'

With that she was on her way, gliding down the gangway like a stately galleon on its way to sea, her lace-edged umbrella swaying from side to side as she spotted dear Archie in full dress uniform standing, head and shoulders above the indigenous population, on the dock.

I handed some letters to Stanley who was waiting patiently by the rail.

'Have a good stay in Bombay, Doctor Mac,' he said, a wry smile on his lips. 'I'll make sure these are on the Imperial Mail with today's post. They'll be in Calcutta by Sunday mornin', mark my words.'

'Thank you, Stanley.'

'Your most welcome Ma'am.' He tipped his hat, shook hands with Tom and moved away.

'Who's collecting Ruby?' asked Tom, helping me negotiate the wobbly gangway.

'Some chap from the ICS, apparently. She's on her way to Delhi and a life of luxury.'

'Who with?'

I could see Frances at the bottom of the ramp in deep conversation with Jim Hamilton. 'I'll tell you later.' Jim's hang-dog expression spoke volumes and I wondered if our future Headmistress was also having second thoughts, but she seemed composed as Tom and I arrived on terra firma. She came over to give Tom a peck on the cheek, then another hug for me.

'Don't forget, Mac, I expect a letter a week from now on, and, if you need anything altering, you know where I am.' Jim looked at his watch and took her arm. Her back stiffened and her chin lifted as he nodded to Tom then eased her into the throng of dhoti's, turbans, baggage and dust, intent on hailing a vacant rickshaw to take her to the Victoria Terminus and her train.

'There goes the best headmistress India could ever wish for,' I said, as Tom raised his hand and waved at a short, uniformed Indian by the entrance. The man rushed forward and bowed. 'Namaste, Sahib. I have vehicle outside,' he said, his head swaying from side-to-side like a highly-strung parrot.

'Mac, this is the concierge from the Taj Mahal Hotel. Mustafa, this is Doctor Stuart-Mackenzie from England.'

The concierge's eyes were so far out of their sockets in surprise, I would have diagnosed a thyroid problem. Another bow, deeper and with greater reverence followed. 'Namaste, Doctor Memsahib. A great honour you give us to come to our humble city.' I was convinced his spinal cord would rupture if his head rocked any harder. 'Please to follow. Come, come.'

He shouted some incomprehensible instruction at the rabble, pushed any obstacles out of our path with his flailing arms and ushered us forward, his neck resembling that of a demented owl as his head rotated on its axis, trying to keep an eye on proceedings. We eventually made it to the hotel's black sedan, parked by the entrance, where a rotund Indian chauffeur sat, puffing on a roll-your-own cigarette, his derriere trying vainly to remain within the confines of the driver's seat. Mustafa grandly opened the rear passenger door, exposing plush cream leather seating and freshly swept floor mats.

'Doctor Memsahib, you sit, please.'

I dropped onto sprung upholstery, my body dripping with sweat, my head mimicking Mustafa's as I thanked him. For goodness sake, Mac, get a grip, I thought, as I rummaged around in my skirt pocket for a hankie.

'Is it far?' I asked Tom, as the car engine burst into life and our concierge leapt into the front seat.

'Not far, Doctor Memsahib,' interrupted Mustafa. 'Very short time.'

Tom laughed and pointed at a very imposing, red brick, six-storey, domed building ahead.'

'Good Lord, is that it?' Tom nodded, once. 'It looks like St Pancras Station on steroids.'

'Wait till you see the interior, Mac. This hotel is as legendry as Raffles in Singapore, according to Mustafa.'

'Yes, Doctor Memsahib. We very notorious. We service famous guests many times.'

I giggled into my hankie, my eyes watering with amusement. 'Good job I'm not famous then,' I whispered into Tom's ear and stuck my left fist firmly against my lips as another giggle threatened.

We had only gone five-hundred yards when we drew to a standstill. Through the front window I could see a large bullock, resting in the centre of the road, impersonating a roundabout. This was causing mass confusion amongst the cyclists, rickshaws, handcarts and the myriad of pedestrians. Our chauffeur leant out of his driver's door shouting obscenities and pressing the horn for all it was worth. No-one took a blind bit of notice! At this point, Mustafa, whistle in hand, jumped from the car and waved his hands around wildly, causing even more chaos. By now my sides were splitting from suppressed laughter, I had hiccoughs, and was in danger of wetting myself.

'Hold your breath for five seconds,' suggested Tom chuckling and slapping me on the back.

The car lurched forward, stopped, lurched forward again and moved off, leaving Mustafa attempting a new four-hundred-yard running record as we circumnavigated the bullock at speed and made it to the hotel entrance in a cloud of dust.

Hiccoughing my way into the lobby, I was drawn to a huge floral display of purple gladioli and white delphiniums. They formed an enormous centrepiece around which four curved gilded velvet settees invited customers to rest their weary legs. I collapsed and took in my surroundings. They were magnificent.

The domed ceiling above my head was the size of that in St Paul's Cathedral, and around its perimeter crystal chandeliers hung from circular ceiling recesses, the huge expanse supported on marbled, tapered pillars which in turn rested on an immense marble floor. An exquisite round Persian silk carpet mirrored the dome and the whole room was illuminated by heavy brass table lamps adorned with cream and gold shot-silk shades. I was captivated by the luxury.

'It's like something out of the Arabian Nights,' I muttered, as a flustered Mustafa, his pleated turban at a twenty-five-degree angle appeared at the entrance, his chest bellowing alarmingly.

I did think he might need artificial respiration and was relieved to see Tom walk through the swing doors and pause by his side to check all was well before moving on to the receptionist standing patiently at his post.

'Chai, Memsahib?' said a pretty, uniformed staff member holding a brass tray.

'I'm sorry, what?'

'Chai, Memsahib. Black tea.'

'Oh, yes, thank you.' I took one of the small glasses from the tray and sipped the contents. It was hot and bitter but helped rid me of my hiccoughs. I was still sipping it when Tom beckoned to me from across the lobby, pointing to a grand marble staircase on my left. I placed my glass on the side table, quietly thanking Frances for persuading me to stay on in Bombay and I moved towards the stairs to join Tom by the lift.

'Let's hope my injuries don't put a damper on proceedings,' I said, as we waited for the lift doors to open.

'As your Doctor, Mac, I prescribe some gentle exercise to strengthen your shoulder muscles and I know just which ones will do the trick.'

'Perhaps I should have retained my Scheherazade costume to give my exercises a little Oriental flavour,' I suggested.

'Don't worry, I'll get Mustafa to buy you seven veils and some finger-cymbals at the local bazaar tomorrow.'

An image of our turbaned concierge gyrating around the bazaar clad from head to toe in seven veils and finger-cymbals triggered another coughing fit, resulting in more hiccoughs.

'Hold your breath for five seconds,' repeated Tom as the lift doors closed and we were whisked to the fifth floor.

'Is that the sum total of your professional advice?' I asked, following him along the hotel corridor. 'Hic!'

'Only to those with a myoclonic jerk of the diaphragm, Mac.'

We entered a plush Oriental suite with views over the harbour and a king-sized bed, raised on a carpeted plinth, draped in mosquito netting.

'A myoclonic jerk of the diaphragm sounds like something from the pages of the Kamasutra,' I declared, dropping my bag by the heavily carved armoire and kicking off my shoes. Tom was occupied tipping the porter and the bed looked so inviting, so I headed straight for it intent on checking the springs and, with one last jerk of my diaphragm, I collapsed head-first onto the eiderdown and promptly fell asleep.

Chapter Eighteen

So much for the Kamasutra,' commented Tom, naked
except for a hotel bath towel wrapped around his hips and
tucked in at the waist. He bent to kiss my forehead and handed
me a glass of chilled buck's fizz.

'What time is it?' I rolled the champagne around my mouth
to clean my teeth and eased my way into an upright position.
Looking down I noticed I was bare chested and pulled the
sheet up, self-consciously.

'Eight-thirty-five, to be precise and don't bother with the
sheet. I have spent the last seventeen hours fondling those
beautiful breasts while their owner gave a very good impression
of Sleeping Beauty.' He moved to the window and threw back
the curtains letting in a shaft of bright sunlight.

'Oh, Tom, I'm so sorry. Why didn't you wake me?'

'Well, I did think about it, but your breasts were quite
happy moulding with the palm of my hands, so we agreed to let
sleeping dogs lie. As for your writhing buttocks, well.'

I aimed a pillow at his bare chest and missed.

'You'll never make a cricketer with a throw like that,' he
joked, picking up the offending item and placing it on a chair.

'Just you wait until I'm out of this bloody sling, Doctor
Wallace. Then, watch out!'

'Promises, promises, Doctor Stuart-MacKenzie.'

An apple in a fruit bowl on my bedside table took flight and
caught him 'twixt knee and thigh.

'Ouch!' Both hands protecting his groin, he headed for the
bed and lifted me bodily from beneath the sheet. I was

unceremoniously carried into the bathroom and lowered into a warm, perfumed bathtub standing on ornate, cast-iron feet. 'Now you minx, get washed so we can go to breakfast.' He handed me a bar of sandalwood soap then gently removed the dripping sling from my right arm.

I sank below the waterline and wallowed in sheer luxury as three weeks of shipboard life faded along with any residual grime trapped in my pores, nails and Mackenzie locks. I emerged like a set of sterilized theatre instruments, invigorated and ready to savour the delights of Bombay.

We spent the next four days seeing the sights, sampling the cuisine and recapturing the sexual pleasures of our one night aboard ship, each act of intercourse deepening our feelings of satisfaction and contentment.

I could get used to this lifestyle, I thought, as I touched the gash on my head. It was knitting together nicely, the soles of my feet were on the mend and my right arm less painful as my personal physiotherapist applied his medical skills with almond oil to manipulate my shoulder whenever there was a pause in proceedings.

A knock on our bedroom door early on the fourth day brought news from P&O. Tom was to visit the Surgeon General of Bombay that morning for pre-lunch drinks at his residence in Malabar Point while I remained behind having a full body massage in the hotel spa. He left, assuring me he would be back for lunch and I went in search of my masseuse. Duly pummelled, oiled and smelling of jasmine, I was crossing the lobby on my way back to our suite when a receptionist called my name.

'Doctor Memsahib. I have a letter for you.' He handed me a Taj Mahal embossed white envelope. 'It very important.'

I pulled the letter from inside and quickly scanned down the page. 'Has Prince Kumar Singh II been staying here at the hotel?' I asked, my mind racing.

'Yes, Doctor Memsahib. He left for Rajputan this morning in his private train along with his entourage.'

Damn, I thought, wishing I had known. 'Was there anything else left for me?'

'Yes, this.'

He moved to the end of the desk and pointed to a large brown leather trunk with metal corner protectors, my initials stamped with gold-lettering into the top.

'Goodness,' I gasped, rubbing my fingers over the surface.

'And this,' added the receptionist holding up a matching medical bag, also monogrammed.

'Please have the trunk brought to my room. I'll take the bag.' As I ascended in the lift, I read the letter more slowly.

Dear Doctor Mac,

It is with great sadness that I have missed you this morning as I had wanted to present you with my small gifts before I left Bombay for Jhalanpur. However, I am confident that you will find good use for them over the coming years and I know your contribution to medical science here in my country will be fruitful and of benefit to all.

I have written to a close colleague in Calcutta explaining your desire to do research at the CSTM and have asked for his intervention with the Board of Governors. Surgeon-General Sir Peter Bonham-Cavendish is the Head of Immunisation for the IMS, based in Calcutta. Like you, he hails

from north of the border so he will be delighted to assist a fellow Scot. Do
not hesitate to contact him on your arrival, he is expecting you.

    Yours

    Vijay Kumar Singh II

I met Tom for lunch on the hotel terrace at two o'clock. Over
samosas and a mouth-watering lamb tagine, he explained what
he would be doing for the next month and I agreed to
accompany him to St George's Hospital that afternoon where
he was to meet the IMS clinicians.

    'It will be good for you to see the setup here in Bombay,
Mac. You may be pleasantly surprised.'

    I handed over Vijay's letter and took a mouthful of fennel
and ginger ice-cream.

    Tom's eyebrows slowly rose as he took in the contents.
'Well, who said miracles couldn't happen?'

    I stretched across the linen tablecloth and placed a dessert
spoon of ice-cream into his mouth. 'Delicious, isn't it?'

    He nodded, re-reading Vijay's words. 'With a
recommendation from Sir Peter Bonham-Cavendish, Mac,
you'll probably be offered the post as Lord Irwin's personal
physician.'

    'What, our current Viceroy? I think not,' I said, wiping my
mouth on a matching serviette. 'Still, Vijay was as good as his
word and you should see the gifts that he has left me.' I
explained the trunk and medical bag as we ordered coffee.

    'He didn't, by chance, leave me anything?' Tom resembled a
petulant child.

'Having a Cinderella moment, are we?' I quipped. 'You're never satisfied, Doctor Wallace. What do you think I've been giving you for the past three days?'

His eyes scanned the dining-room checking no-one had overhead our conversation. 'True, but you'll be gone next week, then what am I supposed to do?'

'Take bromide,' I replied grinning, and dropped two sugar lumps into my coffee cup.

Walking through the portals of St George's Hospital that afternoon brought me down to earth with a thud. The smell of carbolic soap, antiseptic cream and that metallic iron aroma of human blood filled my nostrils and I was back in Riveldene surgery. Suddenly, life had become real again.

A missionary nurse, in starched white from head to toe, her uniform simply adorned with a large wooden crucifix hanging around her neck asked if she could help us. We were directed to the second floor where a Colonel Grafton-Young met us and gave us a tour of the building. He held the post of Surgeon to the Governor of Bombay at Government House and was responsible for clinical staff appointments throughout the Maharashtra district. As we moved from ward to ward, I took in the peeling paint, the iron bedsteads and the whirring ceiling fans as patient after patient passed by on what seemed to be a conveyer belt of tropical illnesses. The hospital even had an isolation ward for sailors and was known throughout Maharashtra as the European General Hospital as it had initially catered only for European patients and military personnel. Tom was to be based here for the next few weeks, assisting in both the dispensary and theatres as and when required.

Over a pot of Earl Grey tea in the clinicians' quiet room, the Colonel began questioning me as to my reason for being in India.

'It was whilst dealing with an epidemic of smallpox in the Berwick area and watching so many of my patients die that I decided my future lay in the research of infectious diseases and their cause.' I sounded rather pompous, but I was a little irritated by his cross-examination. Tom was over by the metal-framed window deep in conversation with a Doctor Watts, so I ploughed on. 'I have chosen to follow in Sir Roland Ross's footsteps by joining the CSTM. It seems a very good place to undertake my research.'

'You appear to be very confident of success, Miss Mackenzie.' The epithet was quite deliberate on his part. 'Let us hope your journey to our shores does not prove to have been in vain.' He glanced at his watch and stood. 'Forgive me, but more important matters are pressing.'

I was being dismissed in a very misogynistic manner and I didn't like it one little bit. I was still gritting my teeth as we headed back to the hotel in a rickshaw.

'So, Mac, what did you think of the hospital?'

'It certainly needed a lick of paint, but it was spotlessly clean, and the staff were very caring.'

'What about Colonel Grafton-Young?'

I hesitated. 'Interesting and very old-school. Actually, I found him rather pompous. He insisted on calling me Miss

MacKenzie and made it quite clear that female clinicians were rather beneath him.'

'Surely not?' argued Tom, helping me out of the rickshaw.

'Afraid so,' I replied, walking towards the hotel entrance. Mustafa leapt to the door to welcome me back.

'You train ticket, Doctor Memsahib. The train it leave Monday at three o'clock.'

'Thank you, Mustafa.' I pocketed the ticket and headed across the lobby my mind still locked on the Colonel. I recalled Geraldine Smythe's words in Aden about the attitude of our male, British, ruling classes here in India and realised that I had just experienced a foretaste of things to come.

'You look miles away,' remarked Tom, as he followed me into the suite.

'Sorry, I can't get your temporary boss off my mind. If he is anything to go by, I'm going to have a fight on my hands in Calcutta and I'm not sure how to deal with it.'

Tom's arms encircled my waist, his face nuzzled into my neck. 'Forewarned, is fore-armed, Mac, and I'm sure your Highland spirit will put paid to the likes of Colonel Grafton-Young. Now, why don't I take your mind of it with some therapeutic body contact?'

I was still mulling over the problem at dawn after a restless night turning my side of the bed linen into a ward sister's nightmare. I stroked Tom's back as he lay on his side. He groaned in his sleep as his muscles twitched at my touch, making me smile. I was falling in love with this quiet Englishman, I thought, and this emotion was severely complicating my life. How were we to continue a long-distance love affair with me in Calcutta and Tom on the high seas? Impossible to imagine but the obvious alternative was unthinkable, unreasonable and out of the question. Our feelings for each other ran deep, but I was not one of the Fishing Fleet, no matter what my heart was saying.

Abandoning sleep, I tiptoed to the bathroom and stood under a cold shower to clear my head, then dressed and went for a walk along the seafront.

It was eerily quiet at dawn, the only humans in evidence being the sweepers on the street with their brooms and shovels removing litter, animal waste and filth which had accumulated from the day before. I paused by the harbour steps in front of the 'Gateway to India' arch and stared out across the basin to the shimmering Arabian Sea beyond, trying to quell the battle between my head and my heart. In frustration, I picked up a stone, lobbed it into the water and vented my spleen.

'Bloody hell, Mac, what did you think you were doing having a ship-board romance?'

Parakeets exploded from the cracks in the archway walls at this sudden commotion then circled overhead, screeching like banshees, before settling back on to various precipitous ledges. I looked at my watch and knew Tom would be wondering where I was. If only I was like Ruby, I thought, making my way across the parade ground on my way back to the hotel. "Love them and leave them" was her motto in life and one that would have put my heart firmly back in its box. There was only one problem, as always. I was not Ruby.

Cutting through a tree-lined park, I passed a bullock harnessed to a lawnmower, its long halter attached to a central post, slowly plodding in ever decreasing circles across a large lawn. I immediately thought of Pa and his constant battle with our rusty old lawnmower back at the Vicarage which constantly put him at risk of a hernia. Here was the solution. I smiled. The idea was so simple and effective. With each rotation the lawnmower discharged grass cuttings in lines resembling railway tracks which the beast then munched as it wandered past. Duly manicured, the lawn was then fertilised from the bullock's back end.

'Well, Pa,' I said, continuing on, 'this would certainly reduce your stress levels.' Whether Pa could or would want to acquire a bullock was beyond me, but at least the idea had lightened my mood and given me another amusing anecdote for my next letter home.

Chapter Nineteen

It was Sunday in the hills above Bombay. We were sitting on a blanket enjoying a hotel picnic at the Karnala Fort overlooking the Bhor Pass. We had left our car and driver six-hundred-feet below, then continued on foot to the Pandu's Tower, a massive basalt pillar which, in ancient times, had been used as a watchtower. The views into the valley below were stunning. Tom handed me a slice of mango dripping in honey and cinnamon, the flavours merging as they slipped down my throat. I picked up my glass of Pimms and leant back on my left elbow, looking into a clear blue sky.

'Tom, this is heaven.'

He leant over and covered my mouth with his own. 'Remember today when you are up to your eyes in laboratory test tubes.'

'Ugh, don't remind me,' I said and carefully turned onto my front to let my bare feet waft in the breeze.

'Happy?'

I nodded, sensing that Tom had an ulterior motive to this question and that this idyllic setting, which he had chosen as a surprise, was about to take on greater significance. I needed to steer the conversation away from a possible marriage proposal if I were to avoid rejecting the very person who had captured my heart. 'Tom, I was wondering . . .'

'No, me first.' He stretched full length on the blanket and protected his eyes from the sun with his forearm. 'I'm not sure what you're about to say, but it's important I say something first.'

I held my breath. Every sinew on high alert, my heart willing Tom on while my head refused to listen.

'Elizabeth, I think I'm falling in love with you.'

I clenched my jaw, knowing I was about to ruin his day.

He stretched across the divide and took my hand. 'Believe me, I didn't intend this to happen, and I am sorry if it puts any pressure on you, but you must know that I could never stand in your way.'

'What?'

'Please, let me finish. I would do anything to hold you back right now, but you have a career ahead of you, Mac, and you must follow your ambitions.' He paused sorrow deeply etched across his features. 'Apart from which, my hands are tied.'

I turned slowly and came upright, my Pimms drenching the grassy knoll. 'Tied? Tied in what way?' My heart was in danger of going into cardiac arrest.

'I'm so sorry, Mac, I did try to tell you onboard ship after the fire, but I was interrupted and then you walked out on some pretext that you wanted some space to think. I assumed you had guessed what I was about to say.'

'No, Tom. What were you going to tell me?'

'The fact that I'm married, Mac.'

I didn't know whether to laugh or cry. Tom had, in one sentence, let me off the hook. My head was cock-a-hoop but my heart was now checking into intensive care, bleeding profusely from being rejected for the second time in my life. All I could do was remain still while I tracked back over the past four weeks. Stanley's smirk as we left the ship. The crew probably knowing the truth and seeing me as an easy conquest.

No doubt I had been the talk of the lower deck; that loose woman with airs and graces; the ship's bike, another notch on Tom Wallace's bedpost. A prize fool.

'Mac, you've gone white. God, what have I done?'

Blind anger was now coursing through my veins, but I was determined not to need my aunt's cream sherry and rich Dundee cake to pull me through this time. If I was this doctor's courtesan, then I would play it for all it was worth.

'No, you haven't done anything,' I stalled, giving my brain time to get on-side. 'You were right, of course. I rather thought that might be the case. You couldn't get to your age and still be single unless you had a preference for your own gender.' I looked down into his horrified face. 'You don't, do you?'

'Christ, no.' He was upright, distaste written across his features. 'No, of course not.'

'That's alright then.' I brushed my skirt for something to do with my hands. 'Did you think I'd be upset?' Tom's eyes needed morphine. 'Well, you can relax, because I'm not. I may be a country bumpkin from Northumbria, but we're not completely naive up north.' I could feel my pulse rate pounding under my fingers. It was through the roof.

'Please, Mac, just let me explain.'

'There's nothing to explain, Tom.'

'But it's complicated.'

'It always is.'

'For goodness sake. This is not easy for me.'

'Look, Tom, if your wife doesn't understand you or she won't give you a divorce, that's your problem. Please don't worry about me, I have heard it all before.' My heart was firmly in isolation and my head back in control. I pulled Tom's face towards me and kissed him, long and hard, my tongue massaging his tonsils. 'Don't let's spoil a beautiful friendship,' I whispered. I looked at my watch. 'We only have hours left so let's make the most of it then part with no bad feelings.'

I was on my feet packing the picnic hamper with rather less care than the hotel had done. Tom shook his head, trying to get a grip on the situation as he helped me gather our bits together, his actions resembling some automaton. We walked back down the slope hand in hand, mine holding his as if I were dragging a child away from a sweet stall. By the time we reached the car my teeth were welded together but I was determined to see the night through without giving away my disgust at being used. If Tom wanted a whore, he was going to get one and I was going to give him a night he would never forget. After all, I concluded, bile rising from my stomach, he had paid enough for it.

Soft music was playing from the hotel terrace as we sat by our bedroom window having dinner, both looking out over the bay. I had requested room service as I knew I would never get through dinner in the hotel dining-room, so Tom had ordered while I went for a shower. I heard the waiter wheel in the trolley, the rattle of ice on glass and muted words as the door closed, while I was putting the finishing touches to my lipstick.

In the reflection of the bathroom mirror the rose lace camisole from Cairo complemented my tanned skin perfectly, as did my hair, hanging loosely across my bare shoulders in soft curls, adding to the sensuous look of a femme fatal.

Vijay's bottle of perfume stood on the marble shelf, saved from the fire by one of the lascars, the amber liquid glinting in the lamplight. I dabbed some on my cleavage, earlobes, knees and ankles, then took a deep breath and opened the door. Tom was by the window lost in thought, a crystal brandy balloon in his hand. He turned and watched as I walked to the edge of the bed, sat with my ankles crossed and tapped the gold silk coverlet by my side.

'Mac, you look beautiful.'

'I aim to please, Doctor.'

He handed me a chilled glass of Kir Royale and bent to kiss my damaged shoulder. 'How is it?'

'On the mend,' I replied, 'like the rest of me.' If only he knew, I thought. My finger traced the buttons on his trousers, and I felt him harden below the beige cotton twill. 'This time tomorrow I'll be halfway across India and this will all be a dream,' I announced, rubbing my thighs against his.

I stood and ran my fingers through the hair at the nape of his neck. His head moved in a figure of eight, gleaning maximum pleasure from my touch and he ran his hand down my spine, where it came to rest on the mound of my right buttock. The tip of my tongue made wet circles around the sensitive skin below his left ear and my hips pushed forward, my groin rubbing against the bulge between his legs, then I sighed. 'I'm starving,' I whispered, taking his hand and drawing him across to the candlelit dining-table, resplendent in pure white linen, a single rose in a silver vase being the only decoration.

'So, here we are,' I proclaimed, raising my glass and toasting my host. 'Our last night in Bombay.'

'Mac, about today.'

I placed two fingers against his lips. 'Don't spoil tonight, Tom. We're both adults and I went into this with my eyes wide open. Let's leave it like that, shall we?' My heart was under sedation and outwardly I was calmer than a cadaver. 'Now what delight have you ordered for our first course?'

We ate, drank and made merry as if this was the most natural thing in the world and I played my part like a professional, never dropping my guard for an instant. The band stopped playing, the tree frogs fell asleep and the moon climbed to its zenith as we reminisced about our time aboard the ss Narkunda. Finally, I set my coffee cup on its saucer and ran my fingers across my lips. 'Shall we?'

Tom didn't need asking twice. He moved from his chair and gently lifted me into his arms and carried me to the bed. I lay back against the feather pillows, my arms outstretched, and watched as Tom divested himself of his clothing then crawled on all fours until he was directly above me, his manhood throbbing in expectation.

He slipped the thin straps of my camisole over my shoulders and untied the satin ribbon holding it in place. Silk and lace slipped sideways, exposing my breasts, my nipples hard from his touch. His hand sank to my stomach then slid between my thighs, his thumb and forefinger releasing the hooks and eyes holding the silk gusset in place and pulling the flimsy barrier away as I opened my legs and drew him down onto my body.

His mouth met mine and our teeth grated together, enamel against enamel as his penis, powered by his hips, slid south towards my thighs and thrust into my vagina like a burnished sword driving into my core.

I gasped, then groaned, then rubbed my nipples against his chest.

We began to move, matching each other stroke for stroke, locked in a sexual act of self-gratification, each without a care, without responsibility, without control. We gave in to all our base desires, like conspirators in an act of treachery before the reckoning, our cries of passion anaesthetising my shattered emotions. We were like animals, doing what animals do. Desire, anger and frustration driving us on.

Around three o'clock, we collapsed, exhausted, sucked dry. All that was left were memories.

I woke to the sound of the tree frogs, my muscles complaining as I staggered to the lavatory. My skin burned as I emptied my bladder and, for once, I felt sympathy for the world's prostitutes who experienced this for a living.

'Was it all worth it?' I asked, as I lowered myself into a warm bath, the water acting as a balm to my aching limbs. I lay there, wondering why I had needed vengeance. I was not a whore, I never would be, and, if I allowed my feminine side to rule my life, I would continually have problems with the opposite sex. Their self-serving, privileged and deceitful attitude to women would be a constant hurdle to my career and if I wanted to compete on their terms, I had to toughen up.

I climbed from the tub and rubbed myself down then stared at my dishevelled self in the steamy bathroom mirror.

Peering at my blood-shot eyes I finally accepted that I was unusual and ahead of my time. Changing this masculine-ruled medical profession and dragging those pompous, self-righteous clinicians into the modern world would mean pushing the boundaries, whatever the cost. It was a tall order, but I was determined to succeed, starting with consigning Tom Wallace to history alongside Duncan Fitzgerald. As for my emotions, they had to remain firmly imprisoned behind a wall of cynicism.

Chapter Twenty

It was mid-afternoon and the platform at Mole Station was buzzing with activity. Tom and I made our way through the crowds in front of my new leather baggage which rocked precariously on a squeaky sack-barrow pushed by a dhoti-clad railway worker.

The train, in its olive grey and blue livery, stood waiting, each of the seven carriages emblazoned with the coat of arms of the Great Indian Peninsula Railway picked out in gold. I was reminded of the advertising posters for the Orient Express Boat Train from Victoria Station to Calais and felt a twinge of homesickness.

Mustafa was standing by an open carriage door. 'This way, Doctor Memsahib,' he shouted, some distance from where we were. The porter nodded to Tom and passed ahead as we halted in the shelter of the station buildings, Tom's hands resting gently around my waist. He turned me to face him and ran his finger across my cheek.

'Mac, I love you more than life. I know you don't believe me, but it's true.' He pulled a small box from his pocket and offered it to me, pushing it into my reluctant hands. 'Please, take it.' He paused, searching my face for some glimmer of acceptance.

Every part of me wanted to throw it onto the railway tracks but I remembered Ruby's Cartier watch and curled my fingers around the gift. He undid the clasp, opened the lid and removed a thick Indian bracelet, its semi-circular, ivory arms encasing a large, malachite, oval stone embedded in beaten silver. I pulled the silver rod from the hinged clasp and Tom fastened the bracelet on my wrist.

'It was in the jewellery shop at the hotel. Hopefully, it will remind you of our stay there in the months to come.' His eyes were watering, his hands shaking as he held onto my fingers, desperate for some response.

I smiled and held him close. 'It's beautiful, Tom. You have given me so much in the last month, more than I could ever have imagined.' I kissed his forehead, his eyelids then the tip of his nose. 'Believe me, I'll never forget our time in Bombay.' I pulled back. I was in danger of losing control of my emotions and had to get away, fast.

The station guard's whistle rent the air and we hurried along the platform towards Mustafa, our hands tearing apart as I climbed aboard. The carriage door slammed, the wheels juddered into life and, like my departure from Newcastle, I felt the cold hand of loneliness puncture my resolve. I leant out of the window, my hand raised like the Pope giving absolution and watched Tom cup his hands to his lips.

'I love you,' he mouthed, as the train picked up speed, the distance too great for sound. Moments later, he was gone, slowly fading into the polluted smog of Bombay and assuredly out of my life for ever.

I sank onto the blue leather seating of the carriage and stared at the ivory and malachite bracelet around my wrist, wondering if it was sufficient compensation for a ruined reputation. What would my mother say if she knew I had been in a love affair with a married man? Knowing Ma, I thought, she would accuse me of being a loose woman with no moral values, while Pa would argue that the church took pity on fallen women and would pray for my soul rather than criticise my actions.

Either way, I would have lost my parents' respect, and I shuddered, knowing that they had just cause. Tom's deception had upended my moral compass and left me floundering in a quagmire of guilt. *"Medice, cura te ipsum"* was all very well, but how was I supposed to heal myself when I had no tools in my medical kit to repair the damage?

With the arid countryside of Maharashtra flickering past my train window like some monochrome lantern display in the movies, I gave up trying to fight the inevitable and drifted into an exhausted, tearful sleep.

Sometime later a tap on my compartment door brought me back to reality with a start.

'Memsahib,' said a tall, turbaned steward, standing in the corridor, averting his eyes. 'Dinner, it will be served in the dining-car in short time. You want this dining, yes?'

'Yes. Yes, of course,' I stammered, noting with horror, the dark shadows below my eyes through the compartment mirror. 'I will be there in ten minutes.'

'We wait on you coming, Memsahib. You are table eight.'

Rummaging through my overnight bag, I pulled out my toiletries and stood by the wash-hand basin attempting to make myself presentable. I was not sure what a fallen woman should look like, but Ruby had taught me enough tricks on-board to hide a multitude of facial defects and these now came in very handy. By the time I walked into the dining-car my self-respect was back in place.

I wandered through the carriage searching for my seat, feeling the inquisitive eyes of male diners following my progress. I felt exposed and uncomfortable and my mood darkened further when I realised that I would not be dining alone. I was about to retrace my steps when a steward in black tie and dinner-suit pulled out a chair.

'Good evening, Memsahib. Please, to sit. I bring menu.'

I sat, clenching my fists under the tablecloth and nodding politely to the female sitting opposite. There was a pregnant pause while each of us waited for the other to speak then we both spoke at once creating even more embarrassment. 'I'm sorry, you first,' I said, trying to sound interested.

'Good Evening.' A hand crossed the table, palm outstretched. I shook it and felt her firm grip on my skin. 'My name is Gloria Hodgson and we appear to be dining together.'

I warmed to her soft brown eyes and friendly countenance. 'Elizabeth Stuart-MacKenzie . . . from Northumbria . . . in England,' I replied, trying to place her accent, 'and I suspect you are also a long way from home.'

Her smile was broad and welcoming. 'Charleston to be exact . . . in West Virginia . . . America.'

'Goodness, whatever brings you to these shores?' The steward placed a menu in front of me and asked if I cared for an aperitif. 'Sherry, please.' He handed a Gin and Tonic to my companion and departed. 'I must apologise, Miss Hodgson, my question was very presumptuous.'

'Not at all.' She picked up her glass and sipped the chilled liquid. 'I'll explain shortly, but we should order our meal first, or we could be waiting a long time for our food.' She leant across the white tablecloth, lowered her voice, and kept her eyes fixed on the steward's back. 'The service on this train is excellent, but the kitchen staff are far from organised.'

I caught sight of a gentleman three tables away furiously drumming his fingers on his place setting. 'Good idea.' I picked up my menu and scanned the dishes on offer. 'Do you have any recommendations?' I recalled Tom telling me to douse everything in lemon or lime juice and coughed to hide my sudden intake of breath.

'You can't go wrong with a chicken or vegetable curry, but I would stay well clear of the fish unless you have a strong stomach.'

'Vegetable curry it is then. What about the soup?'

She peered over her menu. 'Thin, but edible.'

We both ordered the same meal then settled back into our velvet-upholstered chairs as I took in my surroundings. The restaurant car was very elegant. Polished teak panelling lined the walls, brass wall lights and window fittings sparkled in the artificial light, and the curtain drapes toned perfectly with the wine-red carpet. A hushed murmur of masculine voices mingled with the clickety-clack of the train's wheels while the stewards tracked back and forth, their silver trays held aloft.

'We seem to be out-numbered, this evening,' I observed, as a rather rotund gentleman with a huge moustache winked in my direction.

'Tonight, and every night. Sadly, India is a very masculine continent where women are supposed to know their place. You and I are in the minority.' She shrugged her broad shoulders and continued. 'Now, you were asking what I was doing here.'

I nodded, eyes now firmly on my fellow diner as my schooner of sherry made an appearance.

'Well, I work for the WMS and I'm on my way to a conference in Calcutta.'

'WMS?'

'Women's Medical Service, India.'

'Oh, right.' I made a mental note of yet another official acronym, feeling irritated by all these confusing initials. 'What is your role there?'

'I'm a doctor.'

My mouth dropped open. 'Really?'

'Really. I came to India after qualifying at the Women's Medical College in Pennsylvania.' Laughter lines appeared at her temples. 'It seems very immature now, but, back then, I was looking for a bit of excitement rather than returning to boring old Charleston, so I persuaded the American Baptist Missionary Society to fund my passage out to India. Fortunately, the Cama Hospital in Bombay was one of the first Indian hospitals to accept qualified female doctors, so I got the job and I've been there ever since.'

'Fascinating,' I said, shaking my head in disbelief. 'What is the conference about?'

'Maternity and Child Welfare. I'm presenting a paper on whether indigenous Dais are worth training.'

The arrival of my soup cut short any response, but my mind was brimming with questions.

'What about yourself?'

My spoon paused halfway to my mouth. 'Perhaps surprisingly, I am also a medic, Dr Hodgson. Small world, isn't it?'

'Sure is. We must compare notes.' She paused. 'Doctor Elizabeth Stuart-MacKenzie.' She rolled my name around her tongue. 'It sounds very Scottish.'

'It is, and rather long-winded, so most people refer to me as Doctor Mac. So much simpler.' My soup was so thin, I could see the company crest on the bottom of the china bowl. 'As for exchanging notes, I doubt I have anything useful to say. I only arrived here a week ago.'

'Nonsense, you must have extensive knowledge of obstetrics and paediatrics working as a female doctor in England.'

'Maybe, but I imagine childbirth in the north of England is a far cry from childbirth out here in the tropics.' I acknowledged the steward as he removed my soup bowl. 'Although, the causes of miscarriage and child mortality are the same the world over, I suppose?' An image of a tiny foetus resting in my hand in the Jhalanpur Suite clouded my vision and I involuntarily shuddered.

Doctor Hodgson's hand touched my fingers as I gripped the table edge. 'Are you feeling alright?'

'Yes. . . Yes, I'm fine.' I poured myself some water and explained. 'We had a pregnant mother onboard ship during my passage from England who suddenly began to miscarry. She was a Hindu, so the ship's surgeon asked me if I would act on his behalf.' My heart was not enjoying this reflection one bit. 'Initially, I managed to save the pregnancy using Black Haw, regular uterine massage and a ban on spicy food.' Dr Hodgson was nodding enthusiastically. 'The treatment was going well until we had a fire onboard ship and the mother's fear caused the foetus to abort. There was nothing I could do.'

'You must have been on the ss Narkunda. I saw it as it docked.'

'Yes. It wasn't the smoothest of passages.' I could feel Tom's presence hovering, threatening to upset my equilibrium so I quickly changed the subject. 'Are you familiar with the Calcutta School of Tropical Medicine?'

'Yes, of course. Why do you ask?'

I bit my lower lip. 'Oh, just curious. I've been offered a post-doctorate position there in viral research and epidemiology.'

'Doctor Mac, that is the best news I have heard in years. The WMS will be absolutely thrilled.' Dr Hodgson was almost salivating.

'Why?

She raised her hand and tapped her watch at the steward. 'The WMS is desperate for in-depth research into all aspects of obstetrics here in India if we are ever to get any decent funding from the ICS and IMS.' She beckoned the steward over and demanded to know where our food was, while I mentally battled trying to recall the Government Departments referred to in the abbreviations. 'Unfortunately, our pompous Civil Servants, Public Health Commissioners and Civil Surgeons are simply not interested in childbirth. It is beneath them. In fact, half of them do not know the first thing about it. Left to them, generations could be wiped out through sheer ignorance.' She sounded like Lady Geraldine Stewart-Symes. You know that in Bombay alone, over forty-two percent of mothers die in childbirth, fifty-three percent of children are stillborn and fifteen percent more die within two weeks of birth.'

I was horrified, the percentages bouncing around my head like electrons in an atom.

'You're shocked, aren't you?' I nodded. 'Well, it's true, and all it would take to improve these statistics is decent funding, good sanitation, basic education and solid research. You could be a very useful addition to our crusade.'

My vegetable curry finally arrived, and I mulled over what I had heard as I ate. 'Doctor Hodgson, you mentioned your lecture on . . . Dais. What are they?'

'Not what, Doctor Mac, but who.' She sighed, wiped her mouth on her linen napkin and sat back, her curry half-eaten. 'In every village and town in India you will find a low-caste birthing attendant; a sort of indigenous midwife, who has no medical knowledge, no idea about the birth-canal and has never heard the word sepsis. Her position in the community is hereditary, passed on from mother to daughter and her practices and religious rituals are neither scientific, hygienic, or safe. In many cases, they are downright barbaric.'

An image of a witch doctor sprang to mind, and I had to remember to breath. 'For example?'

'Dais believe in quick births. It is not uncommon therefore for foetal arms and legs to be pulled off during a forced labour or for the placenta to be manually removed by cutting the mother's naval cord to get at it.'

I was in danger of regurgitating my curry.

'Another example,' she said, her voice full of enthusiasm, 'is the custom of female infanticide . . .'

'Enough, Doctor Hodgson.' I pushed my plate away and drank deeply from my water glass. 'Are you telling me that this is all going on under the noses of our fine British Government Ministers and they are doing nothing about it?'

My companion shook her head. 'Don't misunderstand me, the majority of Indian women give birth naturally, often in mud huts or out in the field, but when there are complications, like a breach-birth or still-birth, the village Dai is the only midwife on hand.'

'What about the Missionary Nurses? They must know what is going on.'

'They do, Doctor Mac. So do our Civil Surgeons and various well-meaning fund-raisers, but, in a country where epidemics kill thousands, child marriage is legal, venereal disease is common and life is cheap, this subject is not a priority.'

We talked long into the night and, as the Imperial India Mail rattled on towards Calcutta, I spent the wee small hours making copious notes about what I had learned. The subject was huge and multi-faceted and would take time to fully understand but, I thought, if Gloria Hodgson was right, Indian women were getting a raw deal from their British rulers and something needed to be done about it.

I was still awake at dawn, watching the sun through my slatted carriage window as it rose into a dust filled sky, the orange pollution hovering above the dry earth like mustard gas over a battlefield. I still had twenty-four hours to go before arriving in Calcutta and I intended to make the very most of my time, learning all I could about women's welfare and the problems female clinicians were facing within their profession.

It had occurred to me while burning the midnight oil that the Women's Medical Service could be a good organisation to have on side when I attended my interview with Dr Chakramachari at the CSTM. Logically, I was the ideal candidate to carry out new research on the effects of tropical diseases on maternal death and infant mortality because I was medically qualified, professionally experienced, and fully conversant with smallpox and obstetrics. Equally, being female, I could gain entry into the zenanas where my male counterparts would never dare to venture.

'Stick that in your pipe and smoke it, Doctor Chakramachari,' I announced, as my reflection smiled at me from across the carriage. If the WMS's work is a crusade, I decided, then I would be their knight in shining armour and fight the good fight like Richard the Lionheart.

Something, like a knife, suddenly cleaved my heart and I dropped onto my bed, head in hands, total recall of Tom's chainmail, lying abandoned on a cabin floor, burning through my emotions like acid on skin. I couldn't breathe; I couldn't see; I couldn't move, and every muscle in my body shook alarmingly. There was nothing I could do. My sudden and violent panic attack was in total control and it was going to run its course, despite me.

I slumped into a foetal position, sweat beading from every pore, and succumbed to the full force of my grief as all the pent-up emotion which I had so successfully kept in check over the days burst like a ruptured artery, crashing over my well-being and threatening my sanity.

When it finally subsided, I felt drained but strangely calm. The attack had been cathartic. I now needed to cauterize the wound before healing could begin, but I was a mess and far from sure I had the mental capacity to carry it out.

'One step at a time,' I whispered, easing myself into a sitting position and thinking about the future. If I concentrated on my career, maybe things would fall into place. Tom would always be somewhere deep in my psyche, but I would not let him ruin my life. I was not a loose woman, and I would not saddle myself with the epithet.

The girl who left Riveldene still had important work to do. That had to be my priority. The past was the past, I could not change it, but, with time, I thought, I could learn to live with the shame.

Chapter Twenty-One

I had always considered the crowded back streets of Newcastle to be Dickensian and a blot on Northumbria's landscape, but the old city of Calcutta was both that and a whole lot more. The degree of dereliction, miasma, depredation, and human suffering took social neglect to a whole new level.

I had only been in the city for eight days and was already familiar with limbless beggars, stunted children and deformed, maimed, or blind women, all living in the gutter with not an ounce of dignity.

The contrast between that and the broad, leafy, bungalow-strewn avenues of the cantonment, where the British military, civil servants and their families lived in pampered splendour, was stark, and anyone with a social conscience could quickly became utterly disillusioned with the jewel in Queen Victoria's crown.

To improve the plight of these poor souls seemed beyond impossible, so the Government in Delhi simply kicked it into the long grass, and nothing was ever done. Nations, cultures, and religions simply muddled along in a melting pot of complicit indifference, while the Indian Army spent most of its energies keeping a tight lid on any social unrest and engaging in constant cross-border skirmishes on behalf of the Empire.

It was a disgrace, of course, but pointing this out to those in power only caused colonial outrage and personal offence, as I found out to my cost . . .

Elsie Thornton had taken me under her wing the moment I crossed her threshold, and the process of integrating me into Calcutta society began in earnest.

Firstly, I needed some personal 'business' cards to distribute to all and sundry before any invitations could come my way. Then, I needed transport, so Elsie accompanied me to the East Indian Railways lost property office where I purchased a second-hand lady's bicycle with the obligatory wicker basket attached to the handlebars for what Elsie assured me was a pittance. Next, I was enrolled into the local riding club, tennis club and Ladies Charity Fund-Raising Club before enduring tea with the Vicar prior to attending Sunday Matins. I was neither impressed with the Vicar nor excited about Matins but decided to keep my views on the church to myself.

My hostess, meanwhile, was in her element, expounding her knowledge of my medical abilities to friends and acquaintances alike and bathing in reflected glory as I winced.

If this were not enough, I was obliged to apply for membership to the illustrious Calcutta Club where one could enjoy watching polo and cricket or play golf, indulge in elegant dining both indoors and on the terrace, and trip the light fantastic with the great and good of Colonial India at their Friday night dances.

I was proposed by Arthur and seconded by one of his subordinates, then subjected to an interview with the club's committee who, to a man, had little experience of what to do about a single female member. It was all so farcical I had to smile.

Elsie's life seemed to be a constant round of pre-breakfast rides, coffee mornings, tea parties, church bazaars, dinner parties and grand balls, all of which were an anathema to me and left me mentally exhausted. I could see why the wives from the Fishing Fleet thought it was a step-up from life in the Home Counties, but, for me this constant socialising within a small, tight-knit community, where gossip was the daily pastime, seemed both shallow and irrelevant. Even Arthur, whose strong socialist, progressive views, honed from growing up amongst the mining communities of the Yorkshire coalfields, baulked at discussing 'business' with a woman, even one with medical letters after her name.

It was so frustrating. After years of burning the midnight oil in Pa's study, arguing the fundamentals of politics, religion and social injustice, this complete disregard for female enhancement really stuck in my craw, as did their attitude to local customs.

They considered the Hindu caste system of Brahmins, Kshatriyas, Vaishyas, Shudras and untouchables as shameful, but thought nothing of filling their homes with cooks, ayahs, derzis, dhobis, punkah-wallahs and sweepers. In fact, the middle and working-class English women of the Raj appeared to morph into supercilious matriarchs with aspirations well above their station.

I was irritated by their stupidity, amazed at their arrogance, and in danger of becoming *persona non grata*.

My letters home were peppered with such opinions and complaints, these missives being the only outlet for my angst. Patience had never been my best virtue and I was afraid it was beginning to show to my detriment, so I gritted my teeth, tried to moderate my opinions, paid lip-service to my peers and kept progress on my future plans to myself.

Not that I had much to report. I had cycled over to Fort William and the residence of Surgeon-General Sir Peter Bonham-Cavendish to introduce myself after Vijay's introduction, only to learn that he was in Delhi and would not be back for three days. I then rang Dr Chakramachari's office regarding my interview, to be told that he was off sick, and I was to ring back the following week.

My funds were getting depressingly low and I needed to earn some money fast if I were to pay my way. Handing out free medical advice to Elsie's lady friends on such subjects as bunions, piles and the best laxative for constipation was not going to cut it. Something had to change.

I was getting ready for dinner before heading out with Elsie and Arthur and their guests to yet another soiree at the Calcutta Club when the family ayah tapped on my bedroom door and entered carrying my freshly laundered and ironed tartan evening dress.

'Namaste,' I said, remembering Frances turning her nose up at this prim and rather staid ensemble and shuddered as I recalled the events of that morning in the Thornton's drawing room.

I had been surrounded by bolts of taffeta, chiffon, satin, velvet and lace cloth while my hostess discussed the latest European fashion with a room full of wives. The family tailor scribbled Indian hieroglyphics onto a grubby pad, nodding like Mustafa at the Taj Mahal Hotel and bowing incessantly whenever an instruction was given. In the middle of this, I stood like a stuffed mannequin having my vital statistics taken by the ayah and wishing I were back aboard the ss Narkunda.

Somewhere in the back streets of the city, sewing machines were now trundling away into the night, creating Parisienne haute couture at a cost my bank balance could have done without.

Stepping into my MacKenzie tartan, I tried not to feel like a fish out of water in a place I did not belong and steeled myself for the evening ahead.

The verandah was full of uniformed officers and their ladies, the Vicar sporting a frayed dog-collar and stained cassock, a rather bilious local Deputy Police-Chief with podgy hands and my hosts, when I finally made my appearance.

'There you are, Elizabeth,' waved Elsie from the other end of the verandah, her voluptuous frame trapping a junior civil servant between a marble jardinière overflowing with cerise bougainvillea and a wicker bath-chair. 'I have told Mr Davies all about you, dear, and he is keen to make your acquaintance.'

My heart sank as I made my way reluctantly through the guests. Elsie's matchmaking attempts were evident for all to see.

'He's one of Arthur's young sanitary inspectors, aren't you, Jonathan?' she said, raising her hand and whispering behind her palm, 'and he's single.'

I felt rather sorry for the poor chap, whose face replicated a boiled prawn, and decided to put him at his ease. 'Good Evening, Mr Davies, no doubt being involved with all things sanitary keeps you very busy in these parts.' I caught Arthur eyeing me over his glass of whisky from the verandah steps and quickly changed the subject.

Jonathan Davies seemed unusually interested in my medical career as we progressed through dinner, paying particular attention when I talked of my wish to do research on pregnancy, childbirth and post-natal mortality. I was just imparting my knowledge of the situation in Bombay which Gloria Hodgson had highlighted when I felt a hand caress my left knee and begin to slide up my thigh.

The Deputy Police-Chief seated to my left was in deep conversation with a Mrs Goodfellow and remained so as I slapped his wrist, tore his fingers from my skirt and swivelled my legs to the right, accidentally knocking my knees against Jonathan's thigh, causing him to resemble a startled chipmunk.

'Oh, I'm so sorry, Jonathan, I had no intention of banging into you, but I had no choice.' My head indicated towards my bilious neighbour as my eyebrows lifted to the chandelier.

'Not a problem. Really,' stammered the junior sanitary inspector, who glared at the back of the police officer's head and tutted rather loudly. 'You were saying, Doctor MacKenzie?'

I nudged my chair closer to Jonathan. 'Only that this research covers so many different causes, including sanitation, but no-one in authority appears to think it matters.' I sighed and looked straight at Arthur who was trying to attract Elsie's attention.

'Well, it matters to me,' replied Jonathan, 'if that is any consolation.'

My smile must have lit up the room. 'Do you mean that?'

'I do. Those statistics from Bombay are disgraceful and we should all be doing something about it.'

Elsie interrupted my response as she stood, indicating to the wives that they should reconvene in the drawing room.

'Perhaps we can continue this discussion at the Calcutta Club,' I suggested, acknowledging Elsie and rising from my chair.

'I would welcome that, Doctor MacKenzie, and perhaps I could have the first dance?'

'Be careful what you wish for, Mr Davies. We northern lassies tend to have two left feet.'

'Then we should be ideally suited, Madam. So do I.'

I was still chuckling as I moved away from the table, snubbing the exaggerated nod from the Deputy Police-Chief as I passed.

By the time I arrived back at the Thornton bungalow it was nearly dawn and I was in a much more positive mood. Jonathan Davies had been the perfect gentleman and had invited me on his next field visit to see for myself the lack of sanitation in the local villages. My feet ached, my toes were a little crumpled from being stepped on during the Viennese Waltz, but otherwise I was in good spirits. Discarding my tartan evening dress, shoes, and undies onto my bedroom chaise-longue, I climbed into bed and had the best night's sleep in weeks.

Chapter Twenty-Two

I was cycling back from the tennis club after playing a mixed-doubles match with Elsie's canasta friends, when a black Rolls Royce passed me going in my direction. I hardly registered it, my mind still mulling over the need to find gainful employment, so was surprised when I turned the corner and found the vehicle parked outside the Thornton's bungalow.

As I pulled up at the gate, a uniformed chaprassi appeared from the passenger seat.

'Can I help you?' I asked, opening the gate and wheeling my cycle through. He hesitated, then placed his palms together, thumbs to his forehead and bowed.

'Namaste, Memsahib. I look for Memsahib Doctor. She live here, yes?'

'Eh, yes. That's right.'

'I have letter for her.' He produced a white envelope from his sleeve, my name visibly written in bold copperplate.

'I am Doctor Stuart-MacKenzie.' I pointed to the addressee. 'The letter is for me.'

'Then I have honour to deliver it.' He passed it over. 'My mistress, she ask for reply. I wait.'

All was quiet as I entered the hall as my hostess was away visiting some local bazaar, so I walked to the drawing-room desk, slit the envelope with Arthur's bone-handled letter-opener and pulled out the contents.

Dear Doctor Stuart-MacKenzie,

I am in need of your professional assistance on a family matter which is rather urgent. Would you be free to have tea with me tomorrow at three o-clock? If so, please tell my chaprassi and I will arrange for a car to collect you at two-thirty.

Yours, sincerely

Lady Cottesmore

I had to read it twice before the words sank in. The last time I had seen Lady Cottesmore she was throwing a wreath into the Indian Ocean at Major Stoke's funeral. We had hardly spoken three words during the whole of the passage, and I had no idea she lived in Calcutta. How she had found me was a mystery and why she wanted my help, intriguing. However, I certainly intended to find out the answer to both questions and told the chaprassi I would be available. He bowed once more, got back into the car and was driven away.

All I could think about as I went for a bath was how I was going to keep this from Elsie Thornton. She would dine out on it for weeks if she knew, so I needed some credible excuse if I were to lay a false trail.

It came in the form of a telephone call that evening from the Bonham-Cavendish residence. Sir Peter was now back from Delhi and happy to make my acquaintance. I said I would ring back on the Sunday morning and returned to my meal.

Elsie was all ears and delighted that I had a meeting with such a distinguished surgeon. I pointed out the necessity for my hosts to keep their counsel and retired early, feigning a headache.

Fortunately, being a Sunday, they were both at the Calcutta Club when the Cottesmore car arrived to collect me. I sat in the rear, my new medical bag by my side and let the Rolls Royce suspension carry me out of the city limits.

We passed the Dhakuria freshwater lakes on our way into Rabindra Sarobar, a peaceful residential area full of migrating birds, banyan trees and a profusion of flowering vegetation. I stared at the manicured lawns edging a long, gravelled drive as we approached the imposing frontage of Benningtons, a large Palladian villa. This was the Cottesmore residence and a far cry from the Thornton's bungalow.

I was led up a curved marble staircase to the first floor and asked to wait in a drawing room facing north, overlooking a substantial meadow bordering one of the lakes. I did not have to wait long. White and gold leaf painted double doors opened and Lady Cottesmore appeared, clapping her hands for tea to be served as she ushered me to a seat.

'Doctor Stuart-MacKenzie, it is a pleasure to see you again. How are you settling into India?'

We made polite conversation as the maid, who could have stepped out of the pages of a P.G Wodehouse play, placed a Spode tea-service on the table alongside a three-tiered cake stand full of bite-sized sandwiches and iced fairy cakes. Once she disappeared, Lady Cottesmore sat back and studied me carefully.

'Doctor, I have asked you to come here in a professional capacity. We have a situation in the family which has recently been brought to my attention and one which cannot be allowed to tarnish my husband's good name.'

I placed my china cup on its saucer and rested my hands in my lap. Who in the family had marred their copy book? 'How can I be of service, Lady Cottesmore?'

'I would like you to carry out an examination here, in the privacy of this house, Doctor, and then inform me of your diagnosis.'

'But, surely, you have a family physician to do this. Why me?'

'A reasonable question, Doctor Stuart-MacKenzie. The answer is that I need to rely on a doctor's confidentiality, which, sadly, I cannot guarantee with your fellow medical professionals in Calcutta.'

I was astonished. 'Surely not. All doctors swear to uphold the Hippocratic Oath and maintain confidentiality for their patients, whatever the pressure.'

'You would hope so, dear, but I'm afraid walls have ears and the Indian Medical Service leaks like a sieve.' She offered me a sandwich and continued. 'You are probably wondering how I found you?'

I nodded my mouth full of cucumber sandwich.

'It was my godson, Jonathan Harrington-Davies. He mentioned you yesterday. He was very impressed with your medical knowledge, particularly in female matters.'

I had to remember to close my mouth. 'Jonathan Davies is your godson?'

'Yes.' She smiled. 'Please, do not be fooled by appearances. Jonathan is destined for high office within the Indian Civil Service. However, he insists on starting on the bottom rung and working his way up. He believes that by removing all signs of his social class, he will get to know the lower ranks more easily and understand their grievances better.'

'Very commendable,' I said, dabbing my mouth with an Egyptian cotton napkin monogrammed with the family crest.

'Do you think so? Personally, I think he is mad, but it is his wish and I have no intention of overruling him, even though the thought of him working in the sanitary department fills me with horror.' She looked as if she had just sucked a lemon and I could not help laughing.

'You remind me so much of my aunt,' I said.

'I imagine your desire to put a medical career before becoming a wife and mother would have caused your aunt and parents some consternation too. Am I right?'

'From my parents, definitely, but from my aunt, well, I think she gave up on me years ago.'

'Exactly. One cannot put an old head on young shoulders. More tea?'

I handed over my cup.

'Let us get back to the matter at hand. Your patient, Doctor, is staying here in Calcutta while her father is in Africa acting as the British Governor of Tanganyika. Sadly, my sister-in-law died in childbirth, so I have taken on the role as guardian in my brother's absence and am trying to bring some discipline into her life.'

'Is it working?'

'No, as you will see for yourself. Please follow me.'

We climbed to the second floor and along a marble corridor framed with oil paintings of historical battles, seascapes, and numerous family portraits until we reached an ornately carved oak door. Lady Cottesmore knocked and entered.

'Henriette, allow me to introduce Doctor Stuart-MacKenzie who is here to examine you.' She then turned to me with a pained expression on her face. 'Doctor, this is my niece, Henriette.'

The young woman sitting at her dressing-table slowly turned. 'Good Lord,' I exclaimed, as I stared at the face of Miss High-and-Mighty from Tilbury Docks.

'I see you recognise my niece, Doctor. You are not the only one. Henrietta made her presence known to many of the passengers and crew on the ss Narkunda, didn't you, dear?'

The short explanation allowed me time to regain my composure. 'We met, very briefly, Lady Cottesmore,' I said, trying to maintain a professional air. 'Now, what seems to be the trouble.'

Henriette burst into tears and rushed over to her bed, dropping face down onto the mattress, her legs spread-eagled.

'I believe my niece is suffering from some type of venereal disease, Doctor.' She walked over to the bed and tapped Henriette on the shoulder. 'I think it is a little late for all these hysterics, Hettie.'

Her words did nothing to lower the volume. I placed my medical bag on the chair and joined Lady Cottesmore by the bed.

'I trust I can rely on your discretion, Doctor Stuart-MacKenzie. It is important to keep the matter firmly within these four walls, as I am sure you understand. God willing, you will also be able to remove this infliction from both my niece and this house.'

'You have my word, Lady Cottesmore, never fear.'

'Good. Now, is there anything you need for the examination?'

Henriette groaned into her pillow.

'Boiling water and some fresh towels.'

'Very well, I will tell Maud. Meanwhile, I will leave you to carry out your examination in peace. When you are finished, please re-join me in the drawing-room.' With that, she turned on her heels and left the room.

I bit my upper lip, trying to imagine what Ruby would do in this situation and decided, after her sarcastic put-down in the departure hall at Tilbury, that she would announce the young girl's plight to the world. Fortunately, I was more forgiving than Ruby. I swallowed any personal animosity I felt and sat on the edge of the bed.

'Right, Henriette, please turn over and stop crying. You are not the first young lady who has found herself in this predicament and you will not be the last. The remedy is not pleasant but then, nor is the disease. However, I am sure it can be cured, and you will come through the experience all in one piece. Do you understand?'

The frightened young woman who gazed into my eyes with a look of horrified supplication was a far cry from the pompous little vixen who I had encountered weeks before and my heart went out to her. This was going to hurt, and the consequences of her dalliance on the ss Narkunda would be imprinted on her psyche for ever. Equally, I was in no position to take the high ground after my behaviour onboard ship and mentally crossed my fingers hoping Lady Cottesmore's niece was not pregnant into the bargain.

The maid delivered the hot water and towels, then retired. While I sterilized the surgical instruments in the bathroom, I instructed Henriette to remove her skirt and her panties and to lie back on the bed on top of one of the towels. When I returned her face was devoid of colour and, on checking her throat, I could see that her glands were swollen. I explained what I was about to do, and she blanched. Fearing she might faint I told her to close her eyes, take deep breathes and try to relax.

Famous last words, I thought, as I greased, then gently eased the stainless-steel speculum into her vagina and began opening the blades. Her stomach muscles went into spasm as she called out in pain, but the villa walls were thick, and no-one was near enough to hear her cries.

Chapter Twenty-Three

Lady Cottesmore was sitting at her desk busily writing when I entered later that afternoon.

'What is your diagnosis, Doctor Stuart-MacKenzie?'

'Perhaps, under the circumstances, Lady Cottesmore, it would be easier to call me Elizabeth or Doctor Mac.'

'Very well, dear, and you may call me Virginia. Now, what have you got to tell me?'

'Well, you were right, it is a venereal disease, but it is not gonorrhoea. However, I need to examine the smears from the lesions under a microscope before I can say for certain if it is merely genital herpes, soft chancre or genital syphilis.'

Virginia's hand shot to a silver cross hanging around her neck. 'And, if it is syphilis?'

'She will be subjected to a course of very painful arsphenamine anti-syphilitic injections and daily vaginal irrigations of potassium permanganate. She will also be highly contagious until the lesions have disappeared, so she must have her own crockery, cutlery, glassware, bed linen and towels until I say otherwise.'

'I think I need a drink. What about you?'

I nodded. 'Whatever you are having will be fine.'

She pulled the bell-cord by the fireplace and came to sit on the sofa. 'How is my niece?'

'Sore. I have given her a mild narcotic and she is sleeping. Has she told you who she caught it from?'

'No, she refuses to talk about it.'

I thought back to the night of the Gala Ball and pictured Henriette, dressed in seven veils, and exposing too much flesh, standing on the promenade deck with one of Ruby's middle-aged Assam tea-planters alongside, his hands firmly clasped to her hips.

Maud took our order and returned with two highball crystal glasses of gin and tonic and placed them on silver coasters. 'Doctor Stuart-MacKenzie will be staying for dinner, Maud.' Virginia looked over the rim of her drink at me, her eyebrows raised questioningly.

'Thank you, that would be lovely,'

'Please inform the cook and set another place at table.' Maud curtsied and left. 'Could there be complications?'

I was thinking of dinner and had to make myself concentrate. 'I'm afraid there could be.' I picked up my glass and ran my finger around the rim trying to find the right words. 'If it is syphilis, the positive news is that we have caught it early so there should be no long-term side-effects for Henriette's health. However, if she is pregnant, then her baby could also contract the disease.'

Virginia's hand shook and her drink spilled onto her dress. 'Whatever am I going to tell her father?' She busily rubbed the stain with a hankie, as if she were trying to erase my words.

'Possibly nothing at all,' I insisted. 'With luck, Henriette will not be pregnant, but, even if she is, the cure is so invasive it could well trigger a spontaneous abortion.'

'You appear to have a great deal of experience in the matter, Elizabeth?'

'I am afraid I have. Venereal diseases are common wherever there are prostitutes and Newcastle is no exception. Married women fall victim to their husbands' sexual proclivities all the time and we medics are expected to pick up the pieces.' I paused, not sure how to broach my next question. 'May I ask how you found out about your niece's condition?' I crossed my fingers under my skirt and hoped I had not overstepped the mark.

'She spoke to Jonathon. Obviously, my niece would never dream of approaching me with such a matter, but she has no other females to confide in, so my godson was her only other choice.'

That explained a lot, I thought, having wondered why he had shown such interest in my career on Friday night. It all now made sense. 'Thank you for telling me, Virginia. As Jonathan knows the situation, I must urgently ask for his help.'

'Please explain.' Virginia was now sitting on the edge of her seat.

'As a new arrival in Calcutta, I have no way of obtaining the drugs I need for Henriette's treatment, nor a laboratory where I can work. My lodgings are not ideal either.' I helped myself to another sandwich and tried to explain. 'Elsie and Arthur Thornton have been very kind in allowing me to stay in their home temporarily, but Elsie loves to gossip and if she saw one of your cars delivering me back and forth, the news would be round the cantonment within minutes.'

'I see.' Virginia ran her fingers through her greying hair. 'How could Jonathan help?'

'Well, for a start, as a Sanitary Inspector whose work covers community vaccination programmes, he may be able to obtain the drugs that I need from the local army barracks. The dispensary there will have plenty of medication for venereal diseases.'

'Good thinking, Elizabeth. VD is certainly the army's Achilles heel. They are sure to have supplies in Fort William.'

'Exactly. And, if I use Jonathan's field trips as a ruse, I can come and go without Elsie Thornton being any the wiser.'

'Then it is fortunate that he will be joining us for dinner. As for somewhere for you to work, we have any number of rooms here which you could use as a temporary laboratory. Allow me show you.'

I could tell that she needed to do something practical, and a guided tour of the house was the perfect solution. We wandered from room to room, Virginia questioning me throughout on what I needed and how she could help. It was decided a small room off the laundry was ideal for my microscope, instruments and medications and we returned to the drawing-room with me feeling rather chipper.

'Elizabeth?' My hostess placed two fairy cakes on a Spode tea-plate and handed it over. 'Would it be more sensible for you to stay here during my niece's treatment, assuming we could think of a reason for you being absent from your lodgings?'

'Well . . .yes . . . I suppose?'

'Good. Then Lord Cottesmore and Jonathan must put their thinking caps on and come up with a suitable excuse.' Her

facial features had lost their hang-dog expression. 'We must
also discuss the matter of your fees.'

'But . . .'

'No buts, Elizabeth, we could not possibly expect you to
work for free. I will ask my husband what the hourly rate is for
the services of a surgeon these days and you can keep a tally of
your time. Now, how about a sherry before dinner? I think we
both deserve one, don't you?'

Having been given the use of a guest bathroom to freshen up
before dinner, I was on my way down the stairs when Jonathan
appeared in the hall. 'Good evening, Doctor Mac, let me
introduce you to my godfather.'

I was a little wobbly on my feet from too much alcohol
before sunset and welcomed his arm as he led me through to
the library where an attractive, elderly gentleman with white
sideburns and a balding pate was attentively listening to his
wife. 'Ah, this must be our young clinician?' he said, looking up
from his position in front of a glowing fire.

'Yes, Sir,' said Jonathan. Allow me to introduce Elizabeth
Stuart-MacKenzie, recently arrived from England on the ss
Narkunda.'

Lord Cottesmore took my hand and shook it
enthusiastically. 'Welcome to India, my dear. We need more
women like you in this God-forsaken country and I understand
this family is indebted to you for your help.'

I instantly warmed to this English statesman who, in one
sentence, had put me at my ease. I had no idea what his
profession was, but assumed it was something important in the
Government and enjoyed the rest of the evening being

entertained, listening to his detailed accounts of life in the colonies.

We were enjoying our lemon syllabub when the conversation turned to the matter of my absence from the Thornton residence. I explained why I was not yet in gainful employment, and the importance of being available at short notice to attend my interview at the CSTM. Scenarios were then batted back and forth across the dining-table like a tennis ball at Wimbledon, while poor Henriette remained in her room, I assumed without an appetite due to the fear of what was ahead. It was Lord Cottesmore who finally came up with a feasible plan.

'Let us keep this simple. You met Henriette on the ship, that is not a lie. So, what would be more natural than you agreeing to come to the aid of one of her closest friends, here in Calcutta, who is heavily pregnant, has complications and needs a qualified midwife to remain with her until the baby is born.' He waited for his wife to comment.

'It certainly sounds plausible, darling. As Elizabeth is presently in need of funds, she would hardly turn down the opportunity to earn some extra fees, even if it were merely as a midwife.'

'Well done, Sir,' enthused Jonathan, already convinced. 'Doctor Mac would be available to attend her interview once this Doctor Chakramachari was back at his desk, so it all makes perfect sense. What do you say, Doctor Mac?'

'She is in complete agreement,' announced Lord Cottesmore with a twinkle in his eye. 'Now, I could do with some coffee.'

Jonathan dropped me back at the bungalow before midnight with a promise to pick me up after lunch the following day and return me to the bosom of the Cottesmore family. This would give me time to pack everything I needed for my stay and for our Sanitary Inspector to requisition my list of drugs from the military dispensary at Fort William.

I had the plan off pat and was sure Elsie and Arthur would believe every word.

Chapter Twenty-Four

B oth the Thorntons saw me off the premises the following day with a cheery wave and my promise to keep them informed of developments. Jonathan had decided not to appear at the house for fear of bumping into his boss, so he organised a pony and trap to collect me from the house and transport me out of the cantonment to a rendezvous point where he was waiting in the Rolls Royce. He paid the driver, transferred my luggage, and we arrived at Benningtons in time for tea. I immediately went to check on Henriette and update her on my findings. It was not good news.

Having burned the midnight oil peering into my microscope, I could not escape the fact that the spiral-shaped bacterium floating on the lens were those of *Treponema Pallidum*. Henriette had syphilis, and the treatment would need to be carefully administered if she were not to suffer major side effects.

I intended to check my findings again once I had my instruments set up in my temporary laboratory, but there was no point in hiding the truth. My patient had to face the facts and it was my job to tell her.

She took it badly, and clung to my arm like a drowning man, begging me not to hurt her.

'Henriette, you have to be brave,' I said, trying to keep my voice steady. 'The injections will be painful, and you will be sore, but they will kill off the bacterium for good and you will recover. Now, lie down and let me take another smear.'

Using the house-phone, I contacted Sir Peter Bonham-Cavendish and arranged to meet him for drinks at the Bengal Club the following afternoon, which brought up the question of transport.

'Do you drive?' asked Virginia, lighting a cigarette. I nodded, thinking of the miles I had covered around the byways of Berwick, visiting hill farms on cold, foggy mornings in winter. 'Meet me in the garage in ten minutes,' she said.

I arrived to find Virginia talking to Lord Cottesmore's driver who tipped his cap and introduced himself.

'Afternoon, Miss. Ronald Harper at your service. I understand you would like to take the Riley out for a spin.'

He walked to the back of the garage and pulled a large, dusty tarpaulin off a compact two-seater drophead coupe which looked brand new.

'My brother bought this for Henriette, and had it shipped out from Liverpool two months ago,' announced Virginia coming to stand by my side. 'The fact that she cannot drive is irrelevant to her father, who assumed we would teach her once she arrived at Benningtons, but my niece prefers to be chauffeur driven around the area, so the vehicle has sat under wraps ever since.' Her grunt added to her slightly sarcastic tone. 'While our young lady is indisposed you might as well put it to good use.'

I looked across the bonnet at Ronald who winked. 'Right Miss, I will fill it with fuel and bring it round to the front straight away. Would you like the hood up or down?'

I was having trouble finding my voice. I could not believe my good fortune. 'Up . . . I think. No . . . down. It will be nice to get some fresh air.'

'Very well, Miss, shall we say in about fifteen minutes?'

I returned to my bedroom and freshened up in the en-suite, tiled bathroom. The room was lovely, facing south across the driveway and lawns, with a spacious, airy balcony which I could access through glazed double-doors bordered with voile drapes. A finely woven mosquito net was loosely tied and suspended above a four-poster bed which, when undone, cascaded like gossamer around the bedframe for my protection. Maud had already unpacked my case, so I grabbed a cardigan from the dresser and went in search of the Riley.

The feeling of freedom as I drove through the countryside around Benningtons was something akin to riding my first bicycle around Riveldene. On that occasion I had fallen off, rather spectacularly, and punctured both my knees and my pride. That memory triggered a quick reduction in the Riley's speed, and I returned to the house at a sedate fifteen miles per hour. Ronald was waiting by the garage, leaning against the bonnet of the Rolls Royce with a chamois leather in his hand. 'How was it, Miss?'

'Grand, Ronald, just grand.' I jumped out and slammed the door, my feet floating on air. 'I will need it tomorrow afternoon if that's alright.'

'Your wish is my command, Miss.' He walked around the car, brushing his hand against the bodywork. 'Nice little number, isn't she?'

'Oh, yes,' I sighed. 'Henriette is a very lucky girl.' She is also very spoilt, I thought but kept that opinion strictly to myself. 'Ronald, can you give me directions from here to the Bengal Club in Calcutta. I would hate to get lost tomorrow as my meeting is very important to my future career.'

'No problem, Miss, I will leave a detailed map on the passenger seat if I have to go out, but it is quite easy. The Club overlooks the Maidan, and anyone can tell you where that is.'

I walked into my small laboratory and looked at my watch still trying to work out what a Maidan was. I had a couple of hours before dinner and decided to spend the time reading up on anti-syphilitic compounds and setting up my vacuum flask ready for the morning.

Once dinner was over, I made my excuses and took the opportunity to catch up on my mail. Sitting at my bedroom bureau, lit with an oil-lamp spluttering in the breeze, I wrote a long letter home. Ma and Pa were going to be relieved to learn that I had fallen on my feet after so many negative letters, so I embellished my prose with as much luxury as possible and glossed over the actual reasons for my stay at Benningtons.

The only blot on my landscape was the silence from Edinburgh University on my sponsorship request. I tried not to worry about it, but time was running out and without backing, my PhD studies were far from certain.

I scribbled a note of thanks to Elsie and Arthur then doused the lamp. In the morning, Henriette would get her first injections and internal irrigation. Once that was over and my patient was resting, I planned to write a long letter to Frances in Poona inviting her to Calcutta for the Christmas holidays which were rapidly approaching. I hoped she would accept as I missed her calming influence and we had so much to catch up on. After that, I would attempt to locate the Bengal Club and enjoy the ambience of Calcutta's oldest and most prestigious gentlemen's club which, I had learned at dinner, was frequented mainly by military and Government dignitaries, providing, of course, they were male and white. I had no idea where my life would lead me from there, but luck had been on my side so far and all I could hope was that it would continue long into the future.

By six a.m. I was washed, dressed and in my laboratory melting arsphenamine in the vacuum flask with quantities of methyl alcohol, distilled water, and caustic soda over a heated water-bath. I had checked the exact measurements from detailed notes in my medical compendium and double checked that I had everything I needed. My syringe, needles and irrigation tube were bubbling away in a sterilizer and the bottle of potassium permanganate wash stood sealed and ready on the counter.

I stood back and examined my work. The preparations were very familiar to me, having been done many times in my past, but I still felt apprehensive. The upper-class status of the Cottesmore family added undue pressure and my stomach churned from the tension. My inferiority complex had always got the better of me when dealing with people above my station, as it had when Tom had asked me to visit the Jhalanpur Suite. Henriette's family were no exception.

'Get a grip, Mac,' I said to the countertop. 'You need a steady hand and a calm head this morning.' I checked my notes for the umpteenth time, then packed my medical bag, removed my laboratory apron, and went in search of breakfast. Maud met me on the stairs.

'Good Morning, Miss. Breakfast will be ready in about half-an-hour. Lady Cottesmore is out riding but she should be back soon.'

'Thank you, Maud. I need to change anyway.' I was about to walk on, then stopped. 'Maud, where are you from?'

'Chichester, Miss. I came out with my employers three years ago.'

'Do you like it in India?'

'Oh yes, Miss, especially at this time of year, and my brother is coming out after Christmas to work for Lord Cottesmore as a stable boy. I am so excited.'

'I bet you are.' I continued up the stairs.

'If you have time, Miss, a walk to the lake at this time of day is lovely and the migrating birds are amazing.'

'Thank you, Maud. I'll do just that.'

We went our separate ways and ten minutes later I was crossing the meadow in the cool morning air. I was not sure what made me turn but, as I scanned the rear of the house, I glimpsed Henriette standing at her bedroom window watching my progress. I waved but she failed to respond. She just stood there, a pale shadow of her former self and my heart sank.

I walked on, wondering if there was some way to make her defiler suffer for what he had done. A letter to Ruby was on my 'to-do' list, so I made a mental note to ask if she remembered the tea-planters' names and where in Assam they lived. Henriette may have been a pompous little brat before leaving

England, I reflected, but contracting syphilis had put paid to her cocky demeanour overnight, and her fall from grace had been truly spectacular.

'No man has the right to do what he did,' I declared to myself, my words fragmenting on the breeze as I halted by the lake and scanned the horizon. 'This moron needs to be castrated and I know just the person to do it.'

Chapter Twenty-Five

The syringe hovered above Henriette's buttock, the plunger extended between my thumb and forefinger. Virginia stood at the end of the bed with her hands lightly resting on her niece's shoulder-blades and her feet firmly rooted to the floor. I could feel her gaze willing me to be kind as my patient whimpered and gripped the bedding with clenched fists and white knuckles.

I looked up and slowly nodded. Virginia closed her eyes, clamped her teeth together and applied the full force of her arm muscles onto Henriette's shoulders while I took a deep breath and lowered the hollow needle towards the pink, nubile skin. It pierced the surface and penetrated deep into the gluteus maximus muscle, the needle shaft disappearing completely. Ignoring an ear-splitting scream, I raised my thumb and with steady, gentle pressure, depressed the plunger all the way home, emptying the syringe barrel and knocking Henriette out quicker than chloroform.

'I need to be quick before she comes around,' I said, slowly withdrawing the needle and placing an alcohol-soaked pad onto the puncture site. 'Press here, Virginia, while I refill the syringe.' I left her stemming the flow of blood and began sterilizing the syringe needle before placing it back into the vial of arsphenamine solution and refilling the barrel to the required cubic centimetres. Seconds later, the needle pierced the other buttock and I pressed the plunger again, this time in total silence.

Two down, four to go, I thought, sitting back on my heels as sweat dripped into my eyes. I wiped my forehead with the sleeve of my gown, plugged the weeping wound with another antiseptic pad and heard the metallic clatter of the used syringe as it dropped into the surgical bowl by my side.

Virginia lowered herself onto the edge of the bed and rubbed her arms trying to relax her muscles. 'When are the next injections due?'

'In three days, depending on the bruising,' I whispered. Our eyes met. I had no idea what I looked like but Virginia looked as if she had just given birth. We sat in silence as the minutes ticked by, neither wishing to move and both feeling emotionally exhausted and thankful that it was all over.

I dressed the small wounds then filled my ice pack with crushed crystals brought up from the icehouse after breakfast and laid it, in its thick cotton cover, across Henriette's coccyx. Her pulse rate was high and her breathing laboured, but this did not concern me. Her colour was good, and her quiet groans into the pillow indicated that she was coming around.

'I intend to give her five drops of laudanum dissolved in wine, three times a day to mask the pain.' I said, climbing off the bed.

'Will she become addicted to it?' Virginia reached for her silver cross again.

'No. It is a very mild dose of opiate and she will have no idea what she is taking. Now, can you remain with her while I clear up? I do not want Henriette to see this syringe.' I held up the surgical dish. 'Her discomfort will be bad enough without seeing the instrument that caused it.'

I returned to find my patient fully awake, but I could see her bottom lip clamped tightly between her teeth and deep lines across her forehead. 'Right, Henriette, I want you to drink this.' I handed over a small glass of red wine knowing it would taste foul, but it went down in one gulp. 'We are going to leave you now so you can sleep. If you need us, ring this.' I picked up a small brass bell lying on the bedside table then checked her pulse. I smiled and raised my thumb. 'You will be more comfortable if you remain on your stomach, and whatever you do, do not try to get up.' The icepack had been against her skin for long enough, so I removed it from her buttocks and emptied the contents into the wash-hand basin.

Virginia was already standing by the bedroom door as I returned. She blew her niece a kiss. 'You were very brave, Hettie, and I am very proud of you. Now rest, darling, and I will send Maud up with some soup at midday.'

I followed Virginia from the room and headed for my writing case.

Dear Frances,

Life goes on apace here in Calcutta and I am gradually finding my feet. This afternoon I will be meeting the Surgeon-General of Immunisation at the Indian Medical Service. (You may remember that Vijay contacted him on my behalf.) We are to meet at the Bengal Club for tea - all very grand - so I hope to have even better news when I write next time.

Elsie Thornton continues to drive me crazy, but I did meet a junior Sanitary Inspector at one of her dinners last Friday. A charming chap who works for Arthur Thornton and has invited me to accompany him on his next field trip to the outlying villages, north of the city, to see for myself how the local people live. You would like Jonathan Davies - he reminds me a bit of Jim Hamilton. Which reminds me, you never mentioned Jim in your last letter. Is there any news on that front?

How long do you get off for Christmas and would you like to join me here in Calcutta for the holidays? I have already mentioned the idea to Elsie, and she is more than happy for you to stay at the bungalow throughout the Festive Season. In fact, having a headmistress under her roof would put another feather in her cap with the other cantonment wives!

Do say you will come; it would make my day and you could then pass judgement on some of the Paris creations that Elsie's tailor has been instructed to make for me. Personally, I could do without the expense but I'm afraid my tartan and blue velvet evening gowns have had one outing too many since I arrived, and I doubt my emerald dress from Simon Arzt would enhance my reputation with the old fogies at the Indian Medical Service.

I am about to write to Ruby in Delhi. Have you heard anything from her?

Now, about your Deputy Head trying to stir up trouble for you. It might be better if she found a post elsewhere and resigned. I doubt she will ever come to terms with being passed over for an outsider and she will be a constant thorn in your side if she stays. Either way, make sure she never gets to see your flimsy purchases from Aden, or she will have a field day ruining your reputation with the school Governors!!!

Well, what else can I tell you about my life here in Calcutta? . . .

The Maidan, I discovered, was a large green space of over four-hundred hectares situated between the Hooghly River and the Victoria Memorial. Within its boundary there was a military parade ground, the Calcutta racecourse, the city's main cricketing venue and a well-used hockey pitch, all surrounded by extensive parkland.

I had intended to post my letters at the central post office before reaching the Bengal Club but failed miserably to find it in all the traffic. I had by then lost my bearings and had to ask a local ayah, pushing a pram along the side of the Maidan, where the Club was located, only to discover that it was behind me.

The imposing three-storey white building overlooked the park, as Ronald had said, and with fifteen minutes to spare, I drove the Riley through the grand gates and parked next to a Phantom Rolls Royce.

The sky was blue, so I left the car's hood down and strolled across to the porticoed entrance which provided welcome shade from the late autumn sun. I could hear a Sitar softly playing somewhere in the interior as I approached the uniformed concierge standing behind a polished ebony desk. He bowed, pen in hand, his elbow resting on a thick, leather-bound visitor's book.

'Good Afternoon, Memsahib.'

'Good Afternoon. Could you tell me if Sir Peter Bonham-Cavendish is here? I am to meet him for tea.'

'Please wait, Memsahib. I go and check.'

While I waited, I cast my eye around the well-appointed entrance hall and noticed a square wooden mailbox sitting on a circular table by the door. I wandered over to read the brass plaque. The gothic script was short and to the point. *Members Only*, it said. I shrugged and turned, coming face-to-face with a tall young man striding through the door.

'Doctor Stuart-Mackenzie, I presume.'

His voice was refined, his dress informal but smart and his nails neatly manicured as he stretched out his hand.

'Sir Peter?' I enquired, completely thrown, having expected a much older man.

'Do you have some mail to post?' he queried, his hazel-coloured eyes peering at my shoulder bag. I gingerly extracted five letters and held them up. 'Go on, it won't bite.' The tip of his tongue touched the corner of his mouth as he looked sideways at the mailbox.

I felt like a schoolgirl caught pinching sweets from the tuck shop and quickly fed the envelopes through the slit in the box.

'If anyone asks,' he called over his shoulder, walking towards the desk, 'the letters are mine.' He scribbled his name in the visitor's book and passed me the pen. 'Sign here, then follow me.'

We passed the concierge coming the other way. 'Namaste, Omar. My guest has signed in. If anyone wants me, I will be on the terrace.' His pace had not slowed during this interlude and I concluded that my host approached life at break-neck speed.

'Is that your Riley Ascot outside?'

'I . . .um . . .yes, . . . sort of.' I mentally kicked myself for sounding so pathetic. 'Actually, I have it on loan.'

'Really.' He pulled out a wicker chair for me then held up his hand. 'Nippy set of wheels, Doctor. I wish I had friends like yours.' He beckoned the turbaned waiter over and ordered a pot of Earl Grey tea, some toasted teacakes, and some strawberry jam. 'I assume that meets with your approval.'

Having tried and failed to follow up with his previous statement, I closed my mouth and simply nodded. He was like a whirlwind, and strongly reminded me of a certain Rajputan Prince.

'Fine,' he said, settling into his seat, 'Now, why I am here?'

I was becoming heartily sick and tired of having to pamper to the egos of all these bigoted men and this one's superior expression and sexist demeanour did nothing to ease my frustration. With little thought to the consequences, my Scottish intransigence rose to the surface and took over.

'Because,' I said, 'as a fellow Scot and physician, you are ideally placed to recommend me to the Governors of the Calcutta School of Tropical Medicine where I intend to do my PhD.'

He crossed his legs and placed his hands in his lap.

'And why should I do that?'

'No reason. Except that I would make a damn good addition to their scientific research programme, and Prince Vijay Kumar Singh II seemed to think you would be worth having on side. Perhaps he was wrong.'

My sparring partner was trying to keep a straight face but failing miserably. I threw care to the wind and went for the jugular. 'Aren't you a bit young to be a Surgeon-General?'

'Not so young that I cannot recognise a gallus wee besom when I see one.' His laughter bellowed across the terrace and out onto the lawn. 'Vijay said that you didn't take prisoners and he was right.'

A large tea-tray appeared, the tea cakes still steaming from the oven. Sir Peter moved forward in his chair.

'Tea?'

'Would you like this wee besom to pour?'

'And be accused of being a male chauvinist into the bargain? I think not, hen.' He eyeballed me over the teapot, laughter lines wrinkling his temples.

'Tis good to see that you ken your place,' I remarked, my Highland accent coming to the fore. 'So, am I right?' I picked up a knife from the tray.

'About being too young for my post?' My eyelids blinked as I buttered a teacake. 'Definitely, but I found myself in the right place at the right time when my predecessor suddenly dropped dead with a heart attack and there was no one more qualified to take over. We were in the middle of a cholera epidemic at the time and the IMS needed a replacement, so I volunteered. Like you, I am not known for hiding my light under a bushel.'

'Well, at least we have that in common. Call me, Mac, by the way. Just in case you were wondering.' The taste of strawberry jam reminded me of Riveldene Vicarage, and I had a sudden twinge of homesickness.

'Thank you, Ma'am.' He touched his hairline in a form of salute. 'and Sir Peter will be fine for me.'

The cheek of the man, I thought but swallowed my pride. 'Very well, Sir Peter, perhaps we could now have a serious conversation on how you can help me.'

We talked through tea, then through drinks and then through dinner. By the time we parted in the Bengal Club carpark we had become firm friends and I knew Sir Peter would do whatever he could to smooth my path with the college Governors. The night air was chilly, so we combined tactics to raise the Riley's hood and I then climbed behind the wheel.

'Are you going to tell me who owns this little beauty, Mac,' he asked, closing the driver's door.

'Sorry, Sir Peter, need to know basis only.' The engine sparked into a throaty roar and I released the handbrake and backed out. 'Thanks for tea and dinner,' I shouted above the din. 'Let me know how you get on.'

It was well past eleven when I climbed the stairs at Benningtons, the only sound being the Grandfather clock ticking in the hall. I tiptoed along the landing and peeped in on Henriette. She was still awake and in need of more laudanum.

I returned to my laboratory and mixed a new dose, then sat, holding her shoulders, as she emptied the contents of the glass.

'Have you slept?' I asked, straightening her bedclothes.

'I think so.'

'What about food?'

'I had a coddled egg just after you left this afternoon. My aunt wanted me to eat some of cook's fish pie but I had no appetite, not after that second dose of this stuff. It tastes awful.'

'I know, Henriette, but it helps reduce the pain. Would you like some water to wash it down?'

'No thank you, but could you help me to the lavatory?'

I left her dozing and wondered if a large shot of whisky would have been a better option. Back in my room I analysed my day. Peter Bonham-Cavendish had been a real find and I mentally thanked Vijay for bringing us together. I had enjoyed his company immensely, particularly as we were from the same generation, but I did wonder how much sway he would have with the ageing members of the college board.

It was late, I was tired, and I needed my bed, so I shrugged my shoulders and curled up between the freshly laundered sheets. I could only hope my new friend's charisma would win the day.

Chapter Twenty-Six

W e were sitting on Henriette's bedroom balcony, watching Virginia in the paddock, going through a dressage routine with her favourite gelding Sapphire.

I had spent some of my free time making a pillow ring from some old sheeting I found at the back of a cupboard in the laundry-room, an inflated rubber inner-tube which Ronald had lying around in the garage and some wadding from a discarded cushion.

My patient was now sitting on it, the upholstered ring supporting her lower body while her bruised buttocks hovered above her seat.

I had been at Benningtons for ten days and Henriette was to have her final two injections the following day. I then planned to stay on for a further three days to monitor her progress before returning to the cantonment and the problems of my own life. At least I was now solvent. Virginia had been true to her word and a money draft for fifty pounds had been credited to my account.

The skin around the top of Henriette's thighs and genitalia was now stained a dull pinkish brown from the daily potassium permanganate douches I had administered, and she was still taking diluted laudanum for the pain, but the dosage had gradually reduced and would cease by the time I left. She had lost half-a-stone in weight and had dark rings around her eyes, but her swollen glands had receded, and her lesions were drying and shrinking.

So far, there were no signs of pregnancy either. No morning sickness or enlarged breasts, but it had only been a month since the ship's Gala Ball so, if my assumptions were correct, that was not a surprise. I was beginning to gain her trust and hoped that she would eventually open up about what happened aboard the ss Narkunda particularly as Ruby had reminded me of the names of the tea-planters and I was keen to have my suspicions confirmed.

Ruby's letter had been amongst my mail sitting on the hall stand at the Thornton's bungalow when I dropped by the previous day. I had deliberately timed my arrival to miss Elsie and Arthur and had left a brief note apologising for missing them and confirming that the fictitious birth was now imminent.

Ruby's note was short and, as usual, lacking substance, but she confirmed that Maurice Blackthorn's tea plantation was in Cachar in Assam and Cyril Montgomery's in Palampur in the Himachal Pradesh Province. I filed this information inside my head and waited patiently for Henriette to let slip a name.

While she dozed, I scanned through my other post. There was good news and bad. The bad news was that Edinburgh University were unable to help me with funding as the budget in the current financial year had already been allocated. They suggested I approach them again in the Spring. According to Ma, my brother's eyesight had deteriorated further since the smallpox epidemic and he was now incapable of holding down a job. Pa, meanwhile, had damaged his back trying to mow the lawn. The good news was from Aunt Karr, who had been in correspondence with the British Headquarters of the Countess of Dufferin's Fund and had told them all about me. This information was being passed on to their counterparts in Delhi and I was to contact a Dr Agnes Scott. I had no idea what the Countess of Dufferin's fund was, but I thought Gloria Hodgson might, so I planned to write to her at the Cama Hospital in Bombay without delay.

Henriette woke and tried to get up. 'Here, let me help,' I said, quickly rising.

'I feel so helpless,' she replied, once on her feet, 'but I think I can manage now.'

I watched her slow progress into the bedroom and wandered if I should introduce the night of the Gala Ball into our conversation when she returned. She must have been reading my mind, as she questioned me on the very subject once back on her rubber ring.

'Doctor Mac, were you at the 'East Meets West' Ball on the ss Narkunda?'

I slowly filled my lungs and chose my words carefully. 'Yes, I was. In fact, I remember seeing you looking gorgeous in a floaty outfit with some cymbals attached to your fingertips.'

Her half-smile did not reach her eyes. 'Yes, I was supposed to be an Egyptian dancer.' She paused to take a deep breath. 'You know, the dance of the seven veils.' She paused again. 'I am not sure I remember seeing you there. What were you wearing?'

'Oh, just a rather plain missionary outfit,' I lied. 'I doubt anyone would have remembered it.' I bit my lower lip and pretended to go back to my post. 'Did you have fun?'

'No, not really.' She hesitated, her hands trembling on her lap. 'To be honest, I don't remember much about it.' She looked beyond the paddock, obviously reliving the events of that evening.

'Henriette, do you want to talk about it?'

She gripped the arms of the chair, the artery at her throat pulsating rapidly. 'I'm not sure I have anything to tell you.'

I stretched over and touched her arm. 'Henriette, you are my patient and you are obviously worried about something. As your doctor, I am concerned for both your physical and your mental health and anything you say to me is in the strictest confidence, that I promise.' Our eyes met and a tear slide down her cheek. 'Oh, Hettie, whatever is it?' I knelt by her side and took her into my arms as the tear turned into a torrent and all her pent-up emotions poured out onto my blouse. Her words, when they came, were fractured and punctuated with sobs.

'I can remember being on the promenade deck. There was an officer in a Bedouin costume calling out peoples' names and a sitar group sat playing under a canopy. A tall lady dressed like Cleopatra made a very grand entrance.'

'Yes, I remember that too.' My stomach flipped as I realised Henriette's reminiscences were about to lead me straight back into the arms of Tom Wallace and I could do nothing about it.

'There was this man. A passenger dressed as a Turk who kept giving me drinks and asking me to dance for him. He was older than me and good looking.' Her words were muffled and lacking conviction. 'I guess I was flattered by his attention and I must have been a bit tipsy from too much champagne on an empty stomach, because I felt dizzy.'

'What happened then?'

'I don't know. The rest of the evening is a complete blur. All I know is that I woke up on the floor of the hurricane deck with the ship's fire alarm ringing in my ears.'

I eased her from my chest and held her by her shoulders, staring directly into her eyes, any thought that she had gone willingly into this man's arms shattering as a new, evil scenario formulated in my mind. 'Hettie, what do you think happened?'

'I don't think I want to tell you, Doctor Mac. It all sounds so crazy.'

'Leave me to decide if it is crazy or not. What is it that you believe happened?'

'I think I was drugged.'

God alive, I thought. That bastard. 'Do you know who this passenger was? Did he have a name?' Her frown deepened. 'Take your time, Henriette. Go back in your mind to the last memory you have.' She lowered her eyes and stared at her hands, concentrating as hard as she could. Suddenly her head shot up, fear flashing across her eyes.

'There were two of them. The other one was dressed as a Roman Centurion and kept calling the Turk, Cyril, and egging him on.' She paused and shook her head, trying to bring the memory into focus. 'This man, Cyril, kept asking me if I had a boyfriend, if I were a virgin. They were both laughing, and he kept pulling at my costume.' Her hand shot to her mouth as she remembered something else. 'He had his hands all over me. I tried to stop him, but he was too strong. I couldn't get away.'

My arms enveloped her body and I rocked her backwards and forwards, thinking back to a gut-wrenching comment made at dinner in the Bengal Club by Sir Peter Bonham-Cavendish about syphilis and some non-scientific beliefs on recovery.

It was now obvious to me that Henriette had not been a good time girl, she had been drugged and raped, possibly twice, while I lay in the arms of Tom Wallace. I imagined her waking, bloodied and alone somewhere in the upper recesses of the ship while Major Stokes burned to death in his cabin. No one there to help her. No one had cared, certainly not me. We were all too busy battling the fire to bother about a young, abused girl staggering back to her cabin, dishevelled, hurting and in a state of shock. It was insane, and the injustice of it all made my innards turn to ice. Cyril Montgomery had stolen this young girl's innocence and infected her with a life-threatening disease, and I thought I knew why. The myth was that sex with a virgin could cure syphilis.

Inwardly, I was adamant that he would pay for his sins, but I also knew it could take years. The syphilis, embedded in his loins, would kill him, slowly and painfully. His joints would swell and become gnarled, painful rashes would appear all over his hands and feet, his nasal tissue would erode and his nose decay, leaving him horrifically disfigured, and the pestilence would eat away at his skull until he went out of his mind and died. In my opinion, Cyril Montgomery deserved nothing less, but until then, he was free to infect other girls wherever he went. I could not allow that. He had to be stopped.

Henriette lay limp in my arms, a ragdoll with all her stuffing hanging out. She would need counselling, I thought, if she were ever to come to terms with the consequences of her rape. She would eventually find peace, but I would not. Not until her rapist was dead or behind bars.

I gently stroked her hair and murmured words of comfort and care, letting her know that she was not alone and that she was not to blame. She had been a defenceless victim not a willing participant, and her family needed to know the truth. The boil needed lancing and I had the scalpel.

'Hettie, this man needs to pay for what he has done to you.' Her body went rigid, but I continued, undeterred. 'He cannot be allowed to get away with this heinous crime or he will continue to harm other young women and pass on the disease. You do not want that on your conscience, do you?' Her head rocked in agreement. 'I know you feel battered and bruised right now, but you are getting better, believe me, and you are safe. He can never harm you again, but you must face the truth head-on and find the strength to put him in prison.'

Her swollen eyes looked into my face, begging for absolution.

'No-one is going to judge you, Hettie, so stop judging yourself. One day, this will be a distant memory, but today, you must trust in the people who love you and let them help you find closure.'

Lord Montgomery was in his study when I found him, sitting in his wing-backed chair smoking a cigar.

'May I come in?'

'Of course, Doctor Mac. Please, take a seat.'

Virginia joined us, searching my face as she closed the door, her expression that of a mother whose child had disappeared. I waited till she settled then cleared my throat.

'What I am about to tell you will be hard to hear, but Henriette has given me permission to explain what actually happened to her on the ss Narkunda and why it is important that you know the truth.' I had their undivided attention. 'Lord and Lady Cottesmore, your niece was drugged and raped by a man twice her age on the night of the ship's Gala Ball.' They both looked horrified. 'I know who this man is, and I also know from Sir Peter Bonham-Cavendish that men like him believe they can be cured of syphilis by having intercourse with a virgin.'

Virginia's sharp intake of breath shattered the silence.

'Henriette specifically remembers him asking her that very question.' I paused as I allowed the implication to sink in. 'It is also possible that she was then raped a second time by his travelling companion. However, proving any of this will be difficult without witnesses. It will be Henriette's word against theirs.'

Shell shock would be the best way to describe both their reactions.

'Lord Cottesmore, I know you will want these men brought to justice, as do I, but I have no idea how to go about it. Do you have any contacts in the Indian Police Service who can help us without dragging Henriette's good name through the gutter?'

Chapter Twenty-Seven

I stepped out of the rickshaw and looked up at the crumbling façade of the Calcutta Police Headquarters. I was here to see one Charles Tegart, a close associate of Lord Cottesmore and Calcutta's infamous Police Commissioner, who was now in charge of Henriette's case. He was Irish and renowned for getting the job done, often paying lip-service to orthodox interrogation techniques when questioning suspects.

Cyril Montgomery was the current suspect at the top of his 'to do' list.

We had first met at Benningtons two days earlier when he arrived to take a statement from Henriette. She was terrified, insisting on having me present, so I sat quietly at her side, stroking the Commissioner's Staffordshire bull terrier whose podgy backside had taken up residence on my left foot, as my patient slowly described what had happened to her. The Commissioner then interviewed me, taking down my details, Ruby's details and the details of the officers and crew of the ss Narkunda who I could remember. He then informed me that I would be called to act as a witness and expected to write an in-depth report on my involvement in Henriette's medical care. That report was now in my bag and I was about to meet him again.

Walking into the dark lobby I nearly tripped over a punkah-wallah sitting crossed legged by the wall, his foot operating a large, material fan suspended above my head which was supposed to be creating a draught. The duty officer took my name and escorted me down a dimly lit corridor and pointed to a metal chair beside a shabby, sickly-green closed door. I could hear Charles Tegart reprimanding a member of the staff, his loud, gravelled voice bouncing off the walls as a rather timid second voice kept trying to butt in with the words, 'Yes, Sir.' The door nearly flew off its hinges as a pimply-faced squaddie backed out of the room, swerved around my chair and rushed towards the entrance.

Commissioner Tegart, his all-white uniform spotlessly laundered, and his epaulet pips recently polished, poked his head around the door frame and invited me into his inner sanctum. His dog's ears pricked up as I entered and before I could sit down the animal was sniffing around my ankles and slobbering all over my shoes.

'Well, Doctor MacKenzie, I have some interesting news.'

His lilting Irish brogue sounded just like Duncan Fitzpatrick, which was not what I needed at that juncture. I laid my medical report on his desk and sat, keen to hear what developments had come to light.

Ruby had been interviewed by the Police Investigation Branch in Delhi and had been able to fill in a number of blanks left from my statement. This had triggered a request for information from the Police Excise Division who had been keeping both Cyril Montgomery and Maurice Blackthorn under surveillance following their recent trip to Britain.

'Unfortunately, Doctor MacKenzie, Excise have an undercover operation going on right now and they do not want us barging in and blowing their man's cover.' He opened a buff-coloured folder on his desk and flicked through a couple of pages while still explaining. 'Currently, their officer is in contact with two European crew members off a ship that docked here in Calcutta recently and is sure that they are agents for a Glasgow firm supplying cocaine to a drug-cartel somewhere here in India.' He stabbed his index finger onto a line of type and, using his spectacles, read what was written below. 'Messrs Gowan and McLean, located in St Vincent Street, Glasgow are to supply one-thousand ounces of cocaine at a cost of twenty-five rupees an ounce.' He peered at me over his reading glasses. 'It says in this report that Fraser Gowan has already been arrested and interrogated by the Scottish police and has confessed to this illegal trade. The Excise Division are now using information gleaned from Gowan to track the drugs to India.'

I had an image of Fraser Gowan stretched out on a rack like a heretic of the Spanish Inquisition in the dungeons of Edinburgh Castle. 'This is all very interesting, Commissioner, but what has it got to do with Cyril Montgomery and Maurice Blackthorn?'

'Ah, now that is where we have been lucky.' He turned another two pages. 'Maurice Blackthorn has a sister who works at Messrs Gowan and Maclean and both tea planters were seen in Glasgow shortly before they boarded your ship at Tilbury. The Scottish Police have copies of their rail tickets.'

'So, you think these two rapists are part of the drug cartel?'

'That is what we're trying to find out, Doctor MacKenzie. A tea plantation is the ideal place to store drugs away from prying eyes and there is some suggestion that this is a two-way trade. Opium out, hidden in legitimate tea-chests and cocaine in, smuggled aboard passenger-liners by ship's crews.'

I was flabbergasted at the thought of illegal drugs sitting in the hold of the ss Narkunda while I slept overhead.

'Now, Doctor, can you prove that the drug given to Lord Cottesmore's niece was also cocaine?'

My attention snapped back to the present. 'No. No, I can't. Even if it were in her bloodstream that night, it would have dispersed within days.'

'Well, without solid evidence, this rape charge has no guarantee of success.'

'Not even with the fact that she was infected with syphilis?' I was getting angry.

'Doctor MacKenzie, right now, your patient cannot prove that she was actually raped by Cyril Montgomery, or for that matter, by Maurice Blackthorn. Without incriminating evidence, it is her word against theirs, and from what you and Miss Tavener have both stated, her costume that night is not going to help her case.'

I had to agree and could see no way of ever proving Henriette's account of events. 'If only someone had been on the hurricane deck that night,' I said, almost to myself. 'It beggar's belief that on such a crowded ship no-one saw what was going on.'

Charles Tegart sat back in his chair fingers entwined. 'In my opinion, Doctor, this young lady may have to put the whole episode down to experience and move on.'

'But what about the charges for drug-trafficking?'

'They are on-going and I must remind you that what you have heard in this office cannot go any further.'

My clenched fists were the only outward sign of my
frustration as I left the station trying to work out how I was
going to tell Henriette the bad news. As I climbed into a
rickshaw, I spotted Salvador D'Souza, the ship's Goan steward,
on the other side of the road. I called out and beckoned him
over, watching him risk life and limb trying to dodge between
the traffic.

'Salvador, whatever are you doing in Calcutta?'

He raised his thumbs to his forehead and bowed. 'Namaste,
Memsahib Doctor.' I returned the greeting. 'I come see Police
Chief, Memsahib Doctor. I sent by Bombay Police.'

'Why?'

'I not sure. Police Chief, he want information about
Narkunda ship.'

My mind was racing. 'Is the ship still being repaired?'

'No, Memsahib Doctor, it go away yesterday. I am to work
sister-ship, Ranchi, when it arrive in Calcutta next week.'

My voice quivered with my next question. 'And Doctor
Wallace, Salvador. Was he on board the Narkunda?'

'Yes, Memsahib Doctor. It was doctor who brought police
to ship. He now on his way to Aden.'

A steel band crushed my ribcage and tears pricked my eyes.
I swallowed hard and directed Salvador towards the
Commissioner's office, then told the rickshaw driver to pedal
me back to the cantonment.

Elsie was waiting on the verandah with a message from
Jonathan Davies. He was about to leave for the Hugli-
Chuchura District and wanted to know if I had the time to join

him. I asked Elsie to respond positively on my behalf and rushed into my bedroom to change and pack my medical bag.

I arrived at Howrah train station with only minutes to spare and joined Jonathan on the East India Railway's Howrah to Bardhaman train which would carry us twenty-two miles north of Calcutta to Hooghly Station. On the way, I brought him up to date on Henriette's case and then asked if he knew anything about the Countess of Dufferin's Fund mentioned in Aunt Karr's letter. He was a mine of useful information.

The fund had been founded by Queen Victoria in 1885 when she instructed the Marchioness of Dufferin and Ava to improve the plight of Indian women during pregnancy and childbirth. It aimed to provide scholarships for doctors, nurses and midwives and for the construction of female hospitals and dispensaries throughout the country.

The Countess of Dufferin, as she was known, was the wife of the Viceroy of India at the time and had worked tirelessly to bring western medical practices to Indian women, whatever their religious beliefs, and her legacy had been nurtured and expanded through subsequent Vicereines ever since.

We arrived in Hooghly station at midday and a Sanitary Officer transported us to the local field hospital where I met the resident doctor and nursing staff on duty. While Jonathan chaired a meeting of local dignitaries and water engineers on a proposed sewerage scheme, I was taken on a ward round by the nursing sister, my constant queries highlighting the sad lack of equipment, medicines and surgical procedures within the hospital's walls.

The building was cramped and dingy and lit only by oil-lamps. The nurses and auxiliary staff were doing their best to keep the wards clean and sanitary but, as the lavatories had no running water and there was an infestation of rats from the local open sewer close by, their efforts were an uphill battle. I noticed that none of the patients were women.

'Why no women?' I asked.

'Our population is predominantly Hindu and Muslim, Doctor MacKenzie. Most women are in purdah and cannot be seen by men outside their own families,' explained an IMS junior doctor, bandaging a young man's gangrenous foot. 'Some of our missionary nurses go into the zenanas to treat the women, but in the poorer areas they are left to their own devices or have to rely on Dais.

The word Dais triggered Gloria Hodgson's graphic description of the hideous practices of these indigenous midwives and I asked if one of the hospital's missionary nurses was available to talk with me about them. I was led into the dispensary where a woman dressed in a habit and wimple stood by a set of rusty metal scales checking the weight of a teenage boy with rickets. I sat on a matching stool, subconsciously noting the peeling plaster and glassless window as she fielded my questions.

I learned that pregnant Hindu and Muslim mothers, some as young as thirteen, were left in filthy rooms with only high-level slits for ventilation until the baby was born. The women and girls often suffered from anaemia, osteomalacia or eclampsia, venereal or tropical diseases, all of which could kill.

Assuming the babies did survive childbirth, the Dais used opium pills, known locally as *bal golis*, to stop them fretting.

The more I heard the more horrified I became and, by the time Jonathan and I stepped back onto the train to return to Calcutta my mind was made up. I would broaden my research to include all causes and effects of death in childbirth and infant mortality.

Jonathan smiled. 'On that basis, Doctor Mac, I suggest you talk to this Agnes Scott at the Countess of Dufferin's Fund as soon as possible. They may well sponsor your research as it encompasses everything that they are in existence to achieve.'

I wrote a long introductory letter to Doctor Scott that evening and sat outside the main post-office waiting for it to open the following morning. When I returned for breakfast, an embossed envelope was sitting on my plate. I was to attend an interview at ten o'clock on Wednesday the 11th December at the CSTM. After waiting for weeks, I had just thirty-six hours to gather my thoughts and write my proposal. I adjourned to my room and made copious notes on everything I had learned since arriving in Bombay, including my own experiences with the effect of smallpox in England. I then condensed this into a concise presentation for the benefit of the Governors.

Chapter Twenty-Eight

Henriette looked as if the bottom had fallen out of her world when I recounted Commissioner Tegart's comments regarding her rape prosecution. We were strolling across the meadow getting some exercise at the time, Hettie using one of her uncle's crooked walking sticks and gingerly putting one foot in front of the other. I watched the colour drain from her cheeks and felt like Judas, knowing that I had been the one who had pushed her into bringing the case to his attention.

'Do you think your ship's steward could have seen something which would help my case?' she asked, pausing by the lake. She was clutching at straws, but I did not blame her.

'I have no idea, Hettie. All I know is that something about the Narkunda is of interest to the police service here in Calcutta.' I wished I could have told her about Cyril Montgomery's possible involvement with the drug-cartel. It would have given her something positive to hang on to, but my lips were sealed.

I picked up a blade of grass and twisted it around my finger searching vainly for another angle as a sudden thought flashed into my mind.

'Hettie, what happened to your costume from the Gala Ball?'

Her eyes opened wide and she shuddered even though the temperature was a pleasant sixty-five degrees. 'Goodness knows. I threw it under my bed when I returned to the cabin. What happened to it after that is anyone's guess.'

'No matter, Hettie, Commissioner Tegart has his own way of doing things.' I was having difficulty keeping my eyes open after another sleepless night and rested on a log letting the tranquillity of the lake wash over me. 'I'm sure he will come up with a solution.'

My words may have convinced Henriette, but they were wasted on me. As we made our way to the house, I decided to try one last theory.

Maud was in the laundry-room ironing one of Virginia's day dresses when I found her.

'Maud, when you unpacked Henriette's cabin trunk, did you find a fancy-dress costume? Something flimsy with veils attached to it.' I sounded like Ma vainly asking if I would ever give her grandchildren.

'Yes, Miss.' I was suddenly wide awake. 'I put it in the fancy-dress box with all the other party regalia. It looked rather grubby, but I was nervous to wash it with all those baubles on it.'

Devout protestations to God bounced around my head as Maud led me up to the attic. She dragged a large wicker hamper from its stowage and opened the lid. And there it was, laid out like a shroud, on the top of a pile of theatrical costumes and props.

I carefully dropped it into a clean pillowcase and left Benningtons without saying another word to Henriette. There was little point in raising her hopes, I thought, only to dash them again if my plan failed.

Sir Peter was in a meeting when I arrived at the offices of the Indian Medical Service, but I was asked to wait and supplied with a cool, freshly made lemonade. I had just finished it when he appeared.

'Dr Mac, whatever brings you to the hallowed halls of the IMS?'

'I need to pick your brains.'

'Then you had better come in.' He held the door for me and waited while I unravelled Henriette's costume.

'Sir Peter, I am looking for a gifted chemist who can lift stains from this material and check for evidence of cocaine.' I doubted if the Surgeon-General of Immunology was often stumped for words, but, on this occasion, he was speechless. 'I am not at liberty to explain the reasons for this request. All I can say is it is highly important to a police investigation and very urgent.'

'Right,' he said, leaping into action. 'You should contact Professor Karlsson at the Institute of Serology and Microscopy. You will find him at the Calcutta Medical College on Chittaranjan Avenue. He is a highly respected Swedish scientist and a thoroughly nice fellow. I'll let him know you are coming.'

'Great, Sir Peter. Remind me to buy you dinner when this is all over.' I was out of my seat and folding the costume back into its cover before he had time to blink.

'I assume you know where the college is?' he said, half-standing.

'Correct,' I replied, opening the door. 'Oh, I almost forgot. I have one other request before I go.'

'Really, will it cost me money?'

I chuckled. 'Hardly. I wondered if you would be my supervisor if the CSTM agree to take me on as a PhD student.'

The five story, Romanesque building on Chittaranjan Avenue was a hospital and college combined. I wandered about the central atrium with its diamond designed tiled floor and exposed upper levels towering above my head, trying to find someone who could direct me to Professor Karlsson's laboratory. It was midday and the general staff and students all seemed to have gone for lunch. A floor plan attached to the entrance wall was of no help as it was all in Hindi, which only emphasised the fact that I had done nothing since arriving in Calcutta to organise some private language lessons.

A stick tapped my shoulder as I stood trying to make sense of the plan. When I turned, an elderly Indian with rheumy eyes, dressed in a pristine white dhoti and turban and carrying a walking cane enquired if I needed help. I explained my dilemma and he immediately pulled on my sleeve and dragged me across to the staircase and pointed up the stairs.

'Third Floor, Memsahib. Left side.'

I thanked him and took the stairs two at a time, my lungs pumping and sweat beginning to wet my collar. Walking along the open-sided corridor with the fret-iron balustrade protecting me from falling onto the concourse below, I searched for the right room, passing a continuous line of glass-fronted display cabinets full of medical bottles and anatomical specimens on the way.

I finally found it and knocked, but there was no answer. Tentatively opening the door, I peeped inside and saw a tall man in a white laboratory coat bent over a microscope.

'Please come in, Doctor MacKenzie. I understand you are looking for Professor Karlsson?'

'I am,' I said, manoeuvring around the long expanse of workbenches until I was by his side. He straightened his spine and shook my hand.

'Then you have found him. What can I do for you?'

His ice-blue eyes, fair complexion and slight Nordic accent confirmed his Scandinavian roots and his well-toned frame towered over me like a lighthouse. 'May I speak to you in confidence?'

'Of course. Most of our work here is strictly confidential.'

'Then let me explain.'

Hans Karlsson listened intently to Henriette's story and then examined the various stains under a bright light. We adjourned to the canteen for some lunch and continued our discussion as students and medical staff came and went in a never-ending stream of humanity, much like that on the street outside. Intrigued, I learnt how Hans Karlsson had ended up in India after he had studied biochemistry as a student in Gothenburg before specialising in forensic serology at Uppsala University. The Swedish police had been sad to lose his talent when he married, but his new wife hailed from Madras, so they moved to India, and he had continued his research in Calcutta ever since.

The test results would take a couple of days, so we agreed to meet at the end of the week and with that we parted, both

keen to get on with our day. I was devoid of all energy and the
verandah bath-chair looked very inviting as I walked up the
steps of the bungalow. I flopped onto it and mulled over
events. Elsie found me there, fast asleep, two hours later.

When I woke on the day of my interview, my nerves were in
shreds. I felt nauseous. Various outfits were strewn around in
disarray as I tried to decide which one to wear and my hair
seemed to have a mind of its own.

Elsie told me to stop pacing up and down the verandah for
fear that I would wear a hole in the wooden floor as I waited
impatiently for my rickshaw to arrive. When it did, my legs
refused to work and I was frozen to the spot, convinced I
would be packing my bags and departing for Riveldene on my
return. I had to be virtually carried into my seat.

At the college entrance I managed to drop the coins for the
driver into the gutter, then I caught my shoe on the jagged edge
of a step and head-butted the entrance door. It was like some
slapstick scene from a Laurel and Hardy film.

An egg-shaped lump was growing on my forehead, I was
seeing stars and my right big toe felt as if it had been
amputated. This was not a good start, I thought, and if it did
not improve, I would be writing my own rejection letter before
I even reached the interview room. I stood stock-still, took a
deep breath and willed my pulse rate to drop below one
hundred and twenty beats a minute, then asked directions to
the ladies' lavatory. Once there, I soaked a hankie in cold water
and hoped that the cold compress would reduce the swelling
on my forehead. My reflection looked tired, green around the
gills and stressed. The past weeks had taken their toll and the

young woman who had been so full of optimism and self-determination on leaving Riveldene was now reduced to a damaged pessimistic realist, riddled with self-doubt.

What I needed was one of Aunt Karr's confidence-boosting lectures, but she was thousands of miles away along with her sherry and Dundee cake, so I had no choice but to believe in myself. I rinsed my face, pinched my cheeks and mentally repeated my personal mantra.

'You are Doctor Elizabeth Stuart-MacKenzie and you are at the Calcutta School of Tropical Medicine to help advance the cause of medical science.'

After several repeats of the mantra, the tension which had been crippling my stomach muscles since dawn began to dissipate and my heart rate returned to normal. I retraced my steps to the entrance lobby trying not to hobble and asked where I would find the Physiology Department. Breathing deeply, I followed the directions and arrived at the waiting room, on time, and ready to prove my worth.

Chapter Twenty-Nine

'Doctor Stuart-MacKenzie,' said a smart young man looking around the empty waiting room. I rose from the cracked leather armchair where I had been sitting for over an hour and stepped forward.

'That is me,' I said, smiling nervously.

'No, I am sorry,' he replied courteously, checking the notes on his clipboard and scanning the empty chairs. 'I am looking for Doctor E. Stuart-MacKenzie who is here to meet Doctor Chakramachari.'

'Yes, that's me. Doctor Elizabeth Stuart-MacKenzie.' I walked forward my hand outstretched.

'But you're a woman.' His mouth fell open.

'I sincerely hope so,' I declared, sensing resistance. 'Is that a problem?'

'Uh, I'm not sure.' He rubbed his nose. 'We were expecting a man.'

'Well, you have got a woman instead. So, perhaps you would introduce me to the Deputy Director of Physiology without delay. My interview was scheduled for ten o'clock this morning and I have been waiting here patiently ever since.'

'One moment, please.' He expression reminded me of my brother's when Pa caught him scrumping in the Manor orchard.

I waited, tapping my foot and screwing my damp hankie into a ball in my pocket, silently repeating my mantra over and over again. When he returned, he was accompanied by a refined Indian in a starched collar and tie, a three-piece brown suit and matching lace-up shoes. He introduced himself as Dr Chakramachari, bowed, apologised for the delay, asked for my medical certificates and testimonials and led me through to a large, wood-panelled room where three other ageing gentlemen sat at a long green-baize table.

'Doctor Stuart-MacKenzie, please take a seat,' he said, pointing to a lone chair in the middle of the room before taking up a position alongside the other examiners. I expanded my lungs, walked sedately to my allocated position, lowered my posterior onto the upholstery and crossed my ankles in a very ladylike manner.

The four men examined my documents with intense scrutiny, eyeing me at intervals as some point of interest came to light, then they each sat back and deferred to the Chairman.

'Doctor Stuart-MacKenzie, your Curriculum Vitae is very impressive, particularly as you are a woman.' The others nodded. 'Perhaps you could tell us what motivated you to take up a career in medicine and why you wish to join this research establishment?'

Having practised my speech through the long night hours I was word perfect. My response was well executed, and I completed it without hesitation, reiteration or confusion. I kept my eyes on the Chairman and began to relax as the expressions facing me varied from initial male amazement to grudging respect.

'Very interesting,' stated the gentlemen on the right, 'but what about your role as a wife and mother?' His bushy eyebrows met at the bridge of his nose. 'How could you possibly complete a PhD and practise as a medic and bring up a family?'

My teeth were welded together as I inwardly told myself to stay calm. 'That is a very relevant point,' I replied, driving my cheek muscles into a smile. My adversary's chest puffed out and he raised his chin, awaiting my answer. 'I can understand why you believe a woman's place is in the home. However, Sir, we are now living in the twentieth century and enlightened men such as yourselves,' my eyes scanned the table, 'are realising that women should also be given the opportunity to expand their horizons.' He tried to butt in and failed. 'Of course, men are not anatomically able to have children but not all women in my generation wish to procreate either. They prefer to use their unique professional abilities to further enhance the plight of those women who do. For instance, Edinburgh University already accepts woman to study medical research.'

His chest deflated as his contemporaries shuffled in their chairs, guttural coughs cutting across the silence.

'Well put, Doctor MacKenzie,' said the gentleman to the left. 'However, this modern thinking,' he wafted his hand in the air, 'in female emancipation may be all very well in England, but here in India we must respect the status quo.'

'Why?'

'I beg your pardon?'

I heard the sharp intake of breath and mentally crawled back into my box. 'Forgive me, I did not mean to be rude. What I meant was, although this may still be the case today, this world-renowned college has an opportunity to show by example that India can move into a more progressive period by providing the same opportunities to women as those in our homeland.' My smile was now pure treacle.

It went on like this for over ninety minutes, the conversation batting backward and forwards between the table and myself, all the board's negative questions being countered by my positive answers. I had had a long time to hone my skills while waiting for this interview and the Board of Governors were struggling to maintain their chauvinist arguments against a constant stream of evidence-based reality.

The wrecking ball finally came from the Chairman. 'Doctor Stuart-MacKenzie, we realise that you have travelled a great distance to come here today, and you have supported your position with great precision and detailed analysis. However, the decision to accept your application has to be ours and there are many other factors, both in relation to our facilities and finances,' his emphasis on the latter drove a knife through my ribs, 'which we must take into consideration.' I could feel a Damocles sword hovering above my shoulders. 'It is now lunchtime, so I propose that we adjourn until two o'clock. I can assure you, Doctor, we will think long and hard about your application during the recess and will have an answer for you on your return.' The other automatons, nodding like mechanical donkeys, could not wait to see me gone.

We parted on well-mannered terms and I left the building feeling as if I had received a knock-out blow at a World Champion boxing match. I headed for the Maidan and sank onto the grass under the shade of a tree, not knowing whether to laugh or cry. The interview spun, like a vortex in my mind, every point scored and point lost being recorded for posterity.

'It really didn't matter what argument was put forward,' I muttered, staring at the tree trunk, 'that lot would never countenance a woman joining their ranks. I threaten their profession and their manhood, and there is nothing I can do about it other than chain myself to the college railings.'

Unlike Emily Pankhurst, I had no energy left to fight, so began to consider my options instead. I could stay in India and work as a junior doctor within the Women's Medical Service under the authority of a male Civil-Surgeon or I could privately administer medical advice to upper-class British colonials who would pay for my expertise. Or I could go home to Northumbria.

I had no intention of kowtowing to some spotty-faced surgeon from the IMS who could not recognise a bedpan from a surgical bowl nor pamper to the hypochondriacs of the Colonial upper-classes, no matter how sympathetic I was to Henriette's situation. That left my only choice as being to head home and try to pick-up my life as a GP in Riveldene. It had been quite an experience coming to India, but it seemed the adventure was over. At least, I thought, walking back through the park, I now knew what an advantage it was to own a bullock to cut the lawn.

With a heavy heart, I re-entered the interview room convinced that I had been born fifty years too soon. It was empty and quiet, only the sound of the electric fans, whirring above me, providing any sign of activity. I steeled myself for the bad news and decided, whatever happened, I was going to stick it out until after the holidays so that I could enjoy the Christmas festivities with Frances.

The far door opened, and the Board of Governors walked in, looking like a set of Supreme Court judges about to rule on a sentence for treason. I held my breath and tried to appear relaxed. The Chairman took the floor.

'Your application, Doctor Stuart-MacKenzie, has been an extremely difficult one for us to adjudicate . . .'

He rabbited on about my excellent references and impressive qualifications, trying to persuade me that the Board had seriously considered my application, when we all knew that they had made up their minds to reject me the moment they realised I was a woman. I lost interest and watched a fly buzz around the circulating fan-blades above his head.

'In the end,' he concluded, 'it all boils down to finance.'

Surprise, surprise, I thought and recalled Lady Geraldine Stewart-Symes, sitting in her garden in Aden, pointing out that money, and only money, was the key to unlocking the door to future success. I knew exactly where the Chairman was going with his summing-up and just wanted it to be over. At that point, the door to my rear opened and a figure wearing official court dress, his ceremonial sword hanging by his side strode into the room and passed my chair.

'Good afternoon, Gentlemen, I do apologise for interrupting this interview.'

The four Governors sprang to their feet and stood to attention their heads erect. The visitor nodded in my direction and I found myself staring into the well-known countenance of Lord Cottesmore.

'Lady Irwin,' he announced, 'has been bending my ear for the past hour, from Delhi, and I wanted to be fully conversant with her views before relaying them to yourselves so that there would be no misunderstanding. Please, do sit.'

The Board members looked at each other then sat in unison and watched Lord Cottesmore as he progressed around the table to the rear.

'Now, where are we on this interview with Doctor . . .' he leant over the Chairman's shoulder and peered at my certificates spread across the baize cloth. '. . . Doctor Elizabeth Stuart-MacKenzie?' His eyes met mine over the back of the Chairman's head and he winked, then flicked his tailcoat to one side and sat down at the end of the line.

The Chairman, desperately trying to regain control leant into the table, his eyes straining sideways to meet Lord Cottesmore's and stuttered a response. 'Your Lordship, I was explaining to the young doctor,' he pointed in my direction, 'why our finances play such an important role in any decision we make here at the school.' His smile was sycophantic.

'Really? Well then, allow me to add some input on this subject from the wife of our Viceroy, Lord Irwin, in her capacity as President of the Countess of Dufferin's Fund.'

I had no idea why Lord Cottesmore was in the room dressed as if he had an audience with the King, why everyone was bowing and scraping in his presence and what Lady Irwin had to do with me wanting to carry out scientific research in Calcutta. All I could do was stay silent and watch events as they unfolded.

'At the quarterly committee meeting of the Dufferin's Fund yesterday,' began Lord Cottesmore, 'the Secretary, Doctor Agnes Scott, advised her Ladyship that a young Scottish doctor,' he nodded once more to me, 'had given up her successful medical career in Northumbria to travel to India in order to carry out much needed research into female deaths during childbirth and infant mortality.' He raised his right forefinger. 'A state of affairs, gentlemen, that Lady Irwin assures me, is a disgrace to the good name of the British Empire.'

The gold braid covering Lord Cottesmore's chest kept catching the sun's rays from high level windows running along the length of the room, adding emphasis to his obvious rank and status. The others looked quite drab in comparison.

'As with Vicereines before her, Lady Irwin has a responsibility to uphold the mandate given to the Marchioness of Dufferin from our dear late Empress, God rest her soul, and considers such overdue research to be germane to her cause.'

Lord Cottesmore's words were met with a wall of silent resistance but he appeared to be undeterred. I, meanwhile, felt as if I was on a funfair roller-coaster.

'Therefore, Gentlemen, I am instructed to inform you that the Countess of Dufferin's Fund will sponsor fifty per cent of the annual cost of a scientific programme specialising in such research and it is proposed that Doctor Stuart-MacKenzie be the lead researcher in this project.'

The Board appeared to be lost for words, the obvious next question hovering like an elephant in the room. I waited for one of them to comment and when no-one did, I spoke up. 'My Lord, although this is a very generous offer by Lady Irwin and her committee, where does she expect the other fifty percent to come from?'

'A very astute question, Doctor, if I may say so, which Lady Irwin has provided an answer.'

We all waited expectantly.

'The balance can be provided by the India Research Fund, can it not, gentlemen?'

I had no idea what the India Research Fund was but looking at the downcast faces of the Governors I had a pretty good idea. Game Set and Match, I thought, watching them all mumble their reluctant agreement.

'Excellent, then that is settled,' Lord Cottesmore announced. 'I am sure the Vicereine will be delighted to know that she has your unconditional support.' He removed a pocket watch from his dress-coat with an exaggerated flourish, stood up and bowed. 'Doctor Stuart-MacKenzie, gentlemen, it has been a pleasure meeting you all today. However, I must now take my leave. I am expected on the Maidan in twenty minutes to take the salute at the army passing-out parade.'

With a swish of his tailcoat he marched from the room, leaving a hole the size of Vesuvius in his wake. The Chairman shuffled my papers into a pile and placed his hands, palms down on the top. 'Well, Doctor, it would seem that you have influence in high places, and I congratulate you on obtaining such prestigious support.' His words dripped acid. 'The Board will now review your proposal in the light of this unexpected financial patronage and decide on a practical timetable for the programme to begin. We will be in touch.'

The limp handshakes and strained expressions did nothing to dampen my joy. I stood in the empty room and savoured every minute of the past half-hour, blessing Doctor Agnes

Scott for her timely intervention. Life is stranger than fiction, I thought, and had to pinch myself.

My stomach rumbled, reminding me that I had missed both breakfast and lunch, so I went in search of a street vendor and some freshly fried samosas. Jonathan Davies was standing at the curb, leaning against Henriette's Riley as I appeared.

'I believe congratulations are in order,' he said, holding the passenger door open for me.

'News travels fast,' I quipped, getting in, my smile lighting up the pavement. 'But you are right, Mr Davies. You are now looking at the CSTM's newly appointed lead obstetrics researcher and she happens to be starving.'

'That is easily rectified.' He pulled out into the traffic and did a U-turn in the middle of the street causing mayhem all round. 'Next stop, the Calcutta Club for lunch and a Pimms.'

'Sounds good to me,' I yelled above the roar of the engine. He honked the horn at a bullock blocking our path and slowly eased the coupe past its bony frame. 'Jonathan, what the blazes is Lord Cottesmore?'

'You mean you don't know?' Jonathan was astounded.

'No, I don't. I didn't think it was my place to ask.'

'Well, Doctor Mac, my godfather is His Royal Majesty's Governor of Bengal.'

'Oh, crikey. Is that all?' I quipped and burst out laughing.

Chapter Thirty

Professor Hans Karlsson met me at the entrance of the Calcutta Medical College looking rather pleased with himself. He had Henriette's costume packed in a laboratory bag and a file of papers under his arm and announced that we were both to meet Police Commissioner Charles Tegart at the Central Police Station immediately.

I was itching to know if he had been successful with his tests, but he remained steadfastly dumb until we walked into the Commissioner's office and took a seat, the Staffordshire bull terrier giving the chemist a wide berth and plonking its backside on my shoes again. Hans Karlsson found this very amusing and watched with interest as I tried to shift the animal off its perch. I gave up and waited for my toes to turn blue. Charles Tegart was too interested in the professor's report to even notice what his mutt was up to.

'You say here that the blood stains were of little use in determining evidence of narcotics.'

My buoyant mood lost some of its bounce as Hans Karlsson looked at me and shrugged his shoulders. 'Turn to the next page,' he said.

Tegart read on, his expression blank, but slowly, his eyebrows lifted, he pushed his spectacles down his nose, and he glanced over the frame at the chemist with a lop-sided smile. 'Will this stand up in court, Professor?'

'It depends who is being cross-examined,' replied Hans Karlsson. 'A clever defence lawyer might try to discredit the findings, but he will need to be pretty sure of his ground if he hopes to get the evidence thrown out.'

I had no intention of being ignored any longer. 'Would someone mind telling me what you are talking about, seeing as I am the one who brought the garment to your attention in the first place?'

'Are you going to put her out of her misery, Commissioner, or shall I?' quipped Hans Karlsson.

'Oh, for goodness sake,' I exploded. 'Just tell me. Do we have proof or not that my patient was drugged?'

'We do, Doctor Mac,' replied Charles Tegart. 'At least, the professor can say without a shadow of doubt that the stain on the bodice was a type of white wine which had minute traces of coca paste and gasoline in it.'

'Gasoline?'

'Yes,' confirmed Hans Karlsson. 'It is used to extract the alkaloids in the coca leaves. Other chemicals such as ammonia, sodium permanganate, sulphuric acid, ether and caustic soda are also used, as well as cement of course.'

'Cement?' I was feeling quite sick wondering how anybody's stomach lining could survive such an onslaught. 'If you are so sure of your facts, why do you have reservations?'

'Because the traces are so small, they could be questioned as being part of the stain.'

'Are you suggesting that my patient splashed her champagne onto her bodice, but the cocaine could have got there by other means?'

'Yes, from someone's fingers, for example, or the bodice could have brushed against the powder on a previous occasion.'

'In other words, a good defence lawyer could accuse her of being a user?'

'Exactly.'

Charles Tegart's smirk had ominous undertones. He placed the report back in the file and locked it into his desk drawer along with the garment. 'Then I will have to disprove this theory, won't I?' He looked at both of us and tapped his nose. 'Thank you Professor Karlsson. I take it you are prepared to act as an expert witness?'

'I am.'

'Then let us leave it there for the time being. One other matter, Doctor MacKenzie.'

I held back as the chemist withdrew.

'You make no mention in your report as to any signs of forced entry.'

For a moment I had no idea what he was referring to, then the light dawned. 'No, I didn't, but it was extensive. The skin of her vagina was badly scarred and the loss of blood on the costume is substantially more than I would expect from a broken hymen alone.'

'Good, then you need to add that to your statement.'

I was cross with myself for not including this vital information earlier and thanked Charles Tegart for raising the matter. The bull terrier finally decided to move back to his cushion in the corner and I rubbed my toes as I posed another question. 'Did Salvador D'Souza see anything suspicious that night?'

'How do you know about him?'

'We met outside here on my last visit. He was my steward on the ss Narkunda.'

'Well, Doctor, not only did he see Cyril Montgomery in possession of cocaine that night, he was instructed to fetch it from Montgomery's cabin while Cyril befriended Henriette. Ships' stewards are supposed to hear nothing, see nothing, and say nothing.'

'Then who persuaded Salvador to spill the beans?'

The Commissioner referred to his notebook. 'A Doctor Tom Wallace, the ship's surgeon. I assume you know him.'

I had to hang onto the table edge.

'When Doctor Wallace was informed of the suspected rape by the Bombay Police, he took it upon himself to interview all the stewards and lascars on the ss Narkunda and he then accompanied De Silva to the police station to make a statement.'

'Do you now have all the evidence you need, Commissioner Tegart?'

'I believe I have.' He looked so smug I could have kicked him and his dog. 'I will be informing Lord and Lady Cottesmore of this fact later today.'

'Then perhaps you would also inform them that I played a significant role in bringing these criminals to justice? And a thank you would not go amiss from you either.' My MacKenzie spirit was back in place.

'You'll be asking me next for a job in the Calcutta Investigation Branch.' Charles Tegart was only half-joking.

'Sorry, Commissioner, but I shall be tied up doing medical research. I trust you can manage without me?' All I heard as I left the room was a mumbled 'cheeky hussy.'

Frances had accepted my invitation, her letter resting on my lap as I soaked my toes in a bowl of hot water.

Dear Mac,

I would love to come to Calcutta for the holidays. Please extend my sincere gratitude to the Thorntons for their generous invitation.

We break up for Christmas next Wednesday and I am now looking at train times for the following weekend as I need a couple of days to tie up any loose ends and plan next term's schedules. Can you meet me at Howrah Station as I have no idea where to find you and even intelligent Headmistresses are known to get lost in the big city!

Do you have any suggestions for Xmas gifts for your hosts or will we have time to shop in Calcutta?

Must dash as I have morning assembly. See you very soon.

Much love

Frances.

Ps: It will be so nice to get out of my prim, boring school wear and into something a tad more frivolous. F x

I had never even thought about Christmas gifts and chewed my fingernails trying to come up with ideas. Elsie was easy. All I had to do was talk to her tailor and get him to make her a winter fur muff or purchase a pair of kid gloves to match her latest creation, but Arthur was quite another matter. Jonathan might know his preference in cigars, I thought, and scribbled a note in my diary then concentrated on a gift for Frances. I settled on a piece of jewellery and decided to invite Elsie to join me on a shopping expedition the following day.

'Mac, that would be splendid,' she enthused on her return from playing bridge. 'We can spend the morning in the Whiteway Laidlaw Departmental Store and then have lunch at the Grand Hotel. I will get Arthur to provide a car and driver. We might as well shop in style.'

I had obviously made Elsie's day and could only hope it would not be another Ruby Tavener experience. A chill ran down my spine and I went to check on my bank balance.

The day was turning into one of general housekeeping and my next job was to try on one of my new dresses. I was about to do so when the ayah announced that someone was asking for me at the front door. I walked through to the hall and found a slight, grey-haired Indian lady in a beautiful midnight-blue silk sari standing at the entrance. We both made a Namaste and I enquired who she was. She pulled a local newspaper out of her bag and pointed to an advertisement I had placed in it for a language teacher, with a reference number for replies. Arthur had been contacted by the classified section informing him of a response and he had passed on his address, which had brought this charming woman to our door.

I immediately invited her in, asked the cook to prepare a refreshment tray and lead her into the drawing room. She glided across the Kashmir carpet, her silver-edged skirt brushing the pile as she went to sit down. Everything about her reminded me of Princess Darshwanabai's aunt and I instantly knew I could work with her. Over tea and biscuits, we discussed my needs and she informed me of her long illustrious career as a language teacher at the Calcutta University. As she had now retired, she had time to tend her garden and take on private clients. If I was in agreement, she recommended a daily lesson of two hours in order to make inroads into the language.

We agreed terms and that my lessons would take place each weekday morning commencing the following Monday and she handed me a list of books which I needed to purchase. I watched her float down the front path like an aging ballerina and realised that my second-hand bicycle was about to get some serious use. Hopefully, the tyres aren't flat, I thought, and made a quick detour to the garden shed.

It was a relief to know that everything was falling into place and once Henriette was fully recovered, I would be free to concentrate on whatever the Board of Governors had to throw at me. I still had to write to Agnes Scott thanking her for intervening on my behalf and there was the thorny problem of Henriette possibly being pregnant, both of which needed my immediate attention.

At Benningtons, Virginia handed me a Gin & Tonic and plonked herself on the sofa. 'How is Hettie doing?' she asked.

'Really well, Virginia, and thank goodness, her period has just started.' We both raised our eyes to heaven. 'I rather think the injections messed up her monthly cycle.'

'So, all that is left is the court case. Have you any idea when it will be heard?'

'No,' I replied. 'Cyril Montgomery hasn't been arrested yet. I don't even know if the case will be heard in Calcutta or if we will have to travel to Himachal Pradesh.'

'Well, at least Hettie will be able to enjoy Christmas, and after hearing about the evidence you discovered, this evil man should be behind bars sooner rather than later and then we can all get on with our lives.'

Lord Cottesmore arrived looking less official than before, poured himself a whisky and came to join us. 'I see our new research scientist had paid us a visit,' he said to Virginia, raising his glass in my direction.

'Actually, James, she was here to check on your niece, who, I am pleased to say is on the mend.'

'Excellent, you have been an absolute blessing, Elizabeth.'

'As were you on Wednesday, Sir.' I reciprocated and we both toasted the occasion. 'I have no idea how to thank you for what you did. I was already mentally packing my cabin trunk and booking my passage home.'

'Don't mention it, dear. The Board needed a kick up the backside and Sir Peter Bonham-Cavendish and I decided it was time they got one.'

My drink hovered halfway between my mouth and the drink mat. 'What has Sir Peter got to do with it?'

Virginia leant over and tapped my knee. 'I think you are about to see the devious side of my husband's character, Elizabeth. I know that look of old.'

Lord Cottesmore's cherubic expression was devoid of any covert thought, but he could not fool his wife. 'Right, James, spill the beans.'

'There's really nothing to confess,' he said, shrugging. 'I simply made the Board of Governors believe that the Countess of Dufferin's Fund was stumping up half the money to sponsor

Elizabeth's project. They fell for it as I expected they would and stumped up the balance.'

I nearly fell off the sofa. 'You mean the Countess of Dufferin's Fund is not backing me?' I was gutted.

'Well . . . no . . . not yet.'

'Oh, goodness, and I have just posted a letter to Doctor Agnes Scott thanking her for their offer of support.'

Lord Cottesmore burst out laughing. 'Then I had better have a word with Lady Irwin, so she is not left in the dark.'

Virginia was not amused. 'James, you are impossible and take far too many risks with other people's lives. Poor Elizabeth now has no idea if she to be offered the post or not. It really is not good enough.' Her husband had the temerity to look chastened. 'Please tell me where she is supposed to find the rest of the money at such short notice or are you going to sponsor her?'

He looked across at his wife and drummed his fingers on the chair arm. 'Virginia, at least have the decency to credit me with some intelligence. I did not get to be the Governor of Bengal without a modicum of good sense.' He turned to me and smiled. 'Never fear, Elizabeth, I would not leave you in the lurch. Sir Peter is speaking to Agnes Scott right now in Delhi. When she hears that the India Research Fund are part-funding your project; one, I might add, that the Dufferin Fund has been trying to get off the ground for years, she and Lady Irwin will jump at the chance to get onboard.'

I sat back, holding my chest as it thumped alarmingly. 'Do I look like a country bumpkin because I certainly feel like one? All this political intrigue is going right over my head.'

'Nonsense,' replied Lord Cottesmore. 'You are the sharpest female I have come across since meeting Gertrude Bell in Mesopotamia all those years ago.' He paused and wagged his finger at me. 'Listen to me, young lady, after what you have done for Henriette, we now regard you as an honorary member of this family and I have no intention of allowing misogynistic men to put obstacles in your way.'

'I don't know what to say.'

'There is nothing to say.' He raised his glass once more as a warm glow brought colour to my cheeks. 'I have every confidence in Sir Peter's persuasive powers with the ladies in Delhi, so you have nothing to fear.'

He may have been confident but until I received a letter of formal acceptance from the CSTM I knew I would never rest. Meanwhile, I had promised to invite Sir Peter to dinner and wondered if the Grand Hotel had an upmarket restaurant that was within my price range. I planned to enquire when Elsie and I had lunch there after our shopping trip.

Chapter Thirty-One

It was all hustle and bustle in Whiteway Laidlaw Departmental Store as Elsie and I joined other Calcutta shoppers preparing for Christmas. With just over a week to go to the big day, tinselled garlands and coloured baubles were hanging from every ceiling and pillar, giving the interior a very festive and colonial air.

Elsie's pile of purchases was growing by the minute and I had found the ideal necklace for Frances made from beaten silver and lapis lazuli gemstones. Arthur's cigars were gift wrapped and I had managed to sneak a pair of camel hide gloves into my basket for Elsie while she was otherwise engaged ploughing through a selection of table decorations across the store.

We were both ready for a long, cool drink by the time we arrived at the Grand Hotel, so we ordered a chilled "Highball" and perused the lunch menu. The prices were not excessive, so I tentatively reserved a table for two on the Wednesday evening and scribbled an invitation to Sir Peter on hotel headed paper. The concierge assured me it would be delivered to the IMS offices that afternoon and I felt rather proud of myself as I joined Elsie in the dining room.

Once home, we set to decorating the bungalow, commandeering Arthur's help with a rickety stepladder and drawing pins while the ayah stuck numerous strips of coloured paper into rings, looping them together to make long decorative chains. Once the gardener had dragged a small mango tree in its wicker pot onto the verandah we decorated that as well.

My medical skills were called upon later in the day when the cook twisted his ankle falling off a stool whilst hanging paper lanterns from wires either side of the footpath and Elsie dripped blood all over the sitting room carpet from trapping her finger in the stepladder's metal hinges. However, by evening we were relaxing on the verandah with a glass of hot, spiced wine while candle-lit stars floated above the path and soft Christmas music emanating from the wind-up gramophone player in the drawing room.

'What have you got there, lass?' asked Arthur, the smoke from his pipe spiralling into the rafters.

'Just some Hindi language books I bought this morning,' I replied, fingering the pages which, in the dim light of the verandah, I could hardly see. 'I want to get a head-start before Monday.'

'Very commendable, dear,' said Elsie scratching her bun with a knitting needle. 'Does Frances eat pork?'

'I've no idea. She eats curry because we seemed to have eaten nothing else on the ship and she is definitely not a vegetarian.'

The evening drifted on in like vein, the homely chat bringing back thoughts of Riveldene. I imagined Ma and Pa decorating the Vicarage and church in my absence and longed to see them. It must have showed because Arthur, getting up to replenish his pipe, squeezed my shoulder in a rather paternal way.

'You be missin' your folks, lass?'

'It's the music, Arthur, and all these decorations. This will be my first Christmas away from home, but I am so grateful to you and Elsie for provided me with a home-from-home in my first months in India.'

Come the New Year, I thought, I really had to find more permanent accommodation but without knowing what my annual salary would be that would be difficult. I hoped Sir Peter would throw some light on my future income over dinner.

We met in the lobby of the Grand Hotel and went straight into the restaurant, Sir Peter in his tuxedo and bow tie, and me in one of my new Paris creations. We caused something of a stir amongst the other diners as we crossed the room to our table, which made me smile recalling my brief moment in the limelight dressed as Scheherazade.

'So, what happened in Delhi?' I asked as soon as we had ordered.

Sir Peter waved to some acquaintances at another table before answering. 'Doctor Agnes Scott was very impressed with your letter of introduction and had already made an agenda note to talk about your plans at the next committee meeting. She was, therefore, surprised and delighted to learn of the college's proposed obstetrics research programme.'

'I assume you left out the bit about pulling the wool over the Board's eyes.'

'Naturally. The whole objective was to make both sides believe they had to contribute or lose face.'

'Fine, but what will Lady Irwin say when she hears that you have taken her name in vain?'

'Unless you tell her, she will never know, Mac. Anyway, she would probably applaud Lord Cottesmore's action seeing as she is not averse to using the same tactics with the ICS.'

'But how confident are you that Lady Irwin and the committee will actually sanction half of the budget?' I was still convinced the whole idea would fall at the last hurdle.

'Mac, will you stop worrying and eat your dinner. Agnes Scott could hardly sit still when she heard the news and was already calling an Extraordinary General Meeting as I left Delhi. Lord Cottesmore is probably getting a call from Lady Irwin as we eat.'

I changed tack. 'Was your visit to Doctor Scott the only reason you shot off to Delhi in such a hurry or did you have other official business to deal with?'

Sir Peter looked both ways, leant across the tablecloth and beckoned me to join him over the condiment set. 'Actually,' he whispered, 'the real reason I went was because I rather fancy Agnes Scott.'

I came upright like a meerkat on alert. 'Good God, she's well into her sixties, isn't she?'

'Certainly old enough to be my mother,' he joked and held my gaze, daring me to argue.

I stared back, refusing to look away first. 'And does she fancy you?'

'I doubt it, I don't think I'm her type. However, she has agreed to be a joint-supervisor with me for a certain Scottish doctor who is about to do her PhD in obstetrics.' I was speechless.

'Close your mouth, Mac, you're catching flies.'

'Peter Bonham-Cavendish, you are impossible.'

'I know, it used to drive my mother wild, but at least it has made you smile. Now, is there anything else you want to know, or can we talk about something more interesting?'

'Yes, there is. I want to know what the WMS annual salary is for a female doctor in this city.'

Chapter Thirty-Two

I recognised Tom Wallace's handwriting immediately I saw the letter, lying so innocently on the bungalow's hall dresser. Gingerly picking it up I locked myself into my room and slit the envelope with my medical scalpel. It had been posted in Aden five days earlier according to the stamp on the front, which seemed odd, but reading the letter made that all too clear.

Dear, dear, Mac,

I have no idea if you will want to return this to sender so I have posted it in Aden and will be back at sea tomorrow. I could not leave India without explaining my situation even though you refused to listen to me in Bombay.

I have relived that day in Karnala Fort many times and now realise that you were not as impervious to the feelings we had for each other as you made out. You were a very good actress, Mac, and, at the time, your casual attitude cut me to the core. Over the intervening weeks I have had time to analyse what happened that day and now suspect your Scottish pride stopped you from showing the hurt and pain you were suffering, believing that I had used and abused you for my own self-gratification.

This could not be further from the truth and I need to make you understand that. You were not some plaything I had a dalliance with to pass my empty hours. On the contrary, I never expected to meet anyone like you, and when I did, it was as a colleague and a friend. I should have told you then that I was married but you had captured my heart and I could not watch you walk away.

It was selfish and I have no excuse for wanting you physically and emotionally, irrespective of the consequences. In the cold light of day, I have lost your trust and damaged your personal reputation in the eyes of others and for that I am deeply sorry, it was not my intention.

Whatever you think of me, Mac, I am not an abuser. Until we met, I had been a faithful husband and a loving stepfather and will continue on this course because my family need me to be there for them. Years ago, I put their happiness before my own. It seemed the right thing to do at the time and I do not regret making that sacrifice, but I never imagined then that I would meet someone with so much spirit, so much strength of character and so much depth of love as you have.

I doubt that you will ever forgive me, and that is only right, but know that I will always treasure the gift that was you and keep your memory close throughout my days.

Do not treat all men with contempt because of one man's momentary weakness. I know you so well, Mac, and cannot allow my mistakes in life to affect your happiness and future relationships. You deserve so much more.

Be successful in whatever you do, and God bless you for being the woman you are.

Tom

x

I was in pieces, like a scattered jigsaw puzzle. Tom's words had penetrated my defences and exposed the cracks in my self-esteem. Whether I liked it or not, he had not been to blame for my behaviour out at sea. I could have said no, I could have remained aloof, I could have asked the question, 'Are you married?' but I chose not to. It had been too easy to blame him for my loss of self-respect and dented pride when, in truth, I had been complicit in our relationship and my own lack of self-control.

Henriette had been the victim, I thought, not me. She was the one who had been drugged, raped and scarred for life. I, on the other hand, had gone willingly into the arms of a man who just wanted to love me, care for me and give me his protection even though he knew it had no future.

I brushed my fingers lightly over the surface of Tom's ivory and malachite bracelet. 'Learn to live with yourself, Mac, and take responsibility for your actions instead of blaming others.'

The purging process took all night and by morning I had come to terms with myself and learnt a few lessons along the way. Had I loved Tom? Yes, I had, and in other circumstances we could probably have been very happy together, but life was never going to be that easy for me. Either I wanted a career, or I wanted to be looked after. I could not have both, so it was high time I realised that and set some personal ground rules.

Chapter Thirty-Three

Frances looked radiant as she stepped from the train, her hair flowing down her back and her silk stockings evident below her calf-length gabardine raincoat. Life in Poona obviously suited her, and I was thrilled to see her friendly face as she walked down the platform waving madly. After hugs and greetings, we made our way to the street where Arthur was sitting patiently in his car.

'Welcome to Calcutta, lass, how was the journey?' He picked up her case and dropped it into the boot.

'Fine,' replied Frances, 'but crowded with everyone heading home for Christmas.'

'Well, you are here now, and Elsie is expecting us home for tea, so make yourselves comfy in the back and let's get out of this mayhem.'

Frances's eyes were everywhere as we crossed the Hooghly River pontoon bridge and drove along the embankment before turning into the city and out towards the cantonment.

Elsie was hovering on the verandah as we pulled up outside the bungalow and rushed down the path and through the picket gate as the brake was engaged, giving instructions to Arthur at the same time as wrapping her new guest in a bear hug. My eyebrows arched as Frances grimaced, our expressions out of Elsie's line of sight, then we were ushered into the house where an array of sandwiches, cakes and nibbles were laid out on the dining room table.

'Goodness, Mrs Thornton, there was no need to go to so much trouble,' exclaimed Frances, whose cheeks matched the colour of the Christmas poinsettia in the centre of the spread.

'Nonsense, dear, you'll be raight hungry after your long journey and out on ya' feet no doubt. Off you trot now and freshen up. Mac will show you to the bathroom, then come and tuck in. No need to stand on ceremony in this house.' With that she breezed out leaving us feeling as if we had just been attacked by a whirlwind.

'Come on,' I whispered, grabbing her hand and heading for my bedroom. Frances fell onto the spare bed laughing as I closed the door and leant against the frame. 'Phew, sorry about that, but I did warn you.'

'Oh, Mac, she is a delight, and she even has your accent.' Frances was rubbing the tears from her eyes as I threw a pillow at her head.

'The bathroom is down the hall on the left. Take you time while I go and fetch your luggage.' She grabbed her bag and was about to leave when my hand stopped her. 'Frances, the Thornton's have no idea about Tom.'

She nodded and placed her fingers to her temple. 'My lips are sealed, D'Artagnan, never fear.'

Her parting comment brought back the image of Major Stokes calling us a coven of witches in the ship's dining room as he went to join Cyril Montgomery and Maurice Blackthorn for lunch. I wondered again if they had caused his death on that fateful night, then shook my head and went to get the bags. My conspiracy theory that Major Stokes had threatened to report them for drug-smuggling sounded ridiculous.

Elsie fussed around Frances like a mother hen, wanting to know all about the girl's school and if any daughters from the top-drawer of colonial society were being educated there, information she could then casually drop into conversation to impress her social circle. Frances, having been forewarned, was discretion itself and gave very little away.

We couldn't escape Elsie's clutches until after dinner when I suggested an evening stroll around the neighbourhood to see the varied festive lights. Frances opened the conversation as I closed the garden gate.

'It seems ages since we last saw each other, Mac, and my life in Poona has been a series of continuous ups and downs ever since.'

'Mine too. You go first because I wouldn't know where to start.'

'OK. Well, the school is solidly Victorian in both architecture and curriculum, the girls are spoiled, juvenile delinquents as you would expect, and the Governors are a bunch of senile old men with Edwardian views on female suffrage.' She eyed me sideways. 'Apart from that, it's a great place to work.'

We linked arms. 'Sounds fascinating. What about your Deputy Head, Miss Beckinsale?'

Frances grunted. 'Miss Beckinsale, Mac, is a squint-eyed, grey-haired spinster who would not know the difference between a seamed stocking and a pair of long-johns, and they are her more redeeming qualities. The girls have taken to calling her Beaky behind her back.'

'Does she know?' Frances shook her head. 'What do they call you?'

'I dread to think. With a name like Trotter, there is ample room for teenage minds to get very creative.'

I waved to a couple sitting on their verandah having a night-cap, recognising the wife as one of Elsie's circle who usually opened her mouth before engaging her brain, like the time she told me nothing good had ever come out of the north of England. 'So, has Beaky found alternative employment or is she still fighting a rear-guard action?'

'The latter. Her determination to see me gone knows no bounds. Last week, she wrote to all the parents telling them that my lax attitude to discipline was jeopardising the school's reputation. The letters were placed in the girls' luggage as they left for the holidays.'

'What did you do?'

'I instructed the girls to show some initiative in disposing of them.'

'And did they?'

'It would appear so. I saw one skewered to the horn of a bullock in the street outside the train station when I left.' Her chuckle was infectious.

'You really are a breath of fresh air, Frances. I haven't laughed like this for goodness knows how long. Do you think you will stick it out?' Despite the levity I imagined this form of vengeful behaviour would be very draining after a while.

'Oh, I think so, although you may have to visit me in prison when she is found head-down in the school pond.'

We continued around the block as a full moon lit our way. 'Do you get homesick at all?'

Frances twisted a ring on her middle finger and looked pensive. 'Yes, I do, but then I knew I would before I left Peckham. When I feel a wave of nostalgia creeping over me, I find something energetic to do, like refereeing a hockey match. You have no idea how distracting it is watching twelve-year old girls knocking seven bells out of each other. There are times, Mac, when your skills would come in very handy in the school infirmary.'

'Perhaps I should pay a visit to the school when I'm in the vicinity,' I suggested.

Frances stopped in her tracks. 'Is that possible, Mac? It would be great to have you stay for a few days. Maybe you could drill some sense into their devious heads,' she paused, 'and I mean that literally.'

'I'm not sure about trepanning young girls' skulls, Frances, but if I do get offered this research post, I will be travelling all over India and the Sassoon Women's Hospital in Poona will be on the list.'

'But you told me your application had already been approved. Has something gone wrong?'

'Frances, you will never believe the shenanigans that have been happening here in Calcutta.' We made our way back to the bungalow as I filled her in on Lord Cottesmore's covert operation.

'Good Lord,' she muttered as we crossed the verandah. 'And I thought my girls were devious.'

The days flew by with long rides in the early morning, visits from Elsie's social circle during the day, sightseeing tours around Calcutta when Jonathan could act as our guide and lengthy dinners in various establishments most evenings.

Christmas Eve was the main event and Elsie excelled herself as the hostess, producing dish after dish of steaming food while Arthur tried to get Frances and me tipsy. All I could remember about the night, as we sat unpacking our gifts from under the mango tree on Christmas morning, was informing the Thornton's vicar that Santa Claus was actually a Turkish priest who dropped gold coins down the chimneys of his poor parishioners' mud huts somewhere in the Eastern Mediterranean. I don't think he believed me.

We were approaching New Year's Eve and I was back trying on various outfits for Frances's approval, in preparation for the Gala Ball at the Calcutta Club.

'What do you think to this one?' I held up a satin and lace creation.

'An improvement on your tartan number, Mac, but not a patch on your emerald silk dress and feather boa.'

I bit my lower lip and opened the wardrobe door, recalling bubbling flutes of Veuve Cliquot on the aft deck of the ss Narkunda.

'Tom's malachite bracelet would go perfectly with it, Mac.' Frances was watching me intently from the bed.

I lifted my Simon Arzt dress out of the wardrobe as a tear slid down my cheek.

'Are you going to tell me what happened after I left Bombay?'

I looked up and saw her pained expression. Frances had become a true friend and one I knew I could trust.

'Tom told me he was married.' I tensed, my fingers gripping the coat hanger, waiting for her shocked reaction. Instead, she took the dress from my hand and hung it on the wardrobe door then curled her arms around my shoulders.

'I know, Mac. I just didn't know if you did.'

We stood our hands entwined. 'Who told you, Frances? How long have you known?'

'Jim told me on the night of the Gala Ball. They have been close friends for years and they were in the same naval actions during the war.'

'Tom didn't tell me until the day before I left Bombay. I think he had tried to tell me before, but I was too interested in myself to listen.' Frances squeezed my fingers. 'At first I blamed him for treating me like a whore but in retrospect, I brought it all on myself.' I had to swallow hard to stop my emotions taking over. 'Did you know he has step-children?'

'Yes. Jim was at Tom's wedding and told me the whole story.'

I blew my nose, lowered myself onto the bed and rested my elbows on my knees, my head in my hands. 'Will you tell me, please?'

Frances brushed her hand over my hair and held it against the middle of my back. 'I don't want to rub salt into the wound, Mac. Are you sure?'

I nodded, my eyes screwed tightly shut and my fingernails digging into the palms of my hands.

'OK, if you insist. Tom married Enid Wallace after the war. She was his sister-in-law with two small sons and had been widowed when Tom's brother, Jack, committed suicide after returning from the Somme. His right leg had been amputated and he had lost the sight in his right eye from a bomb blast and suffered with chest pains from breathing mustard gas in the trenches. He was only twenty-six, Mac.'

I thought of all the young limbless soldiers I had seen returning from the Somme and the young women widowed before their time. 'How did Jack die?' I asked, desperate to learn every detail of Tom's story.

'He hung himself in the family garage. His youngest son found him when he went to fetch his tricycle.'

A cold chill rippled down my spine. 'The child will live with that memory for the rest of his life.'

'I know, and he won't be the only one. The Great War has caused so much pain to so many. Anyway, after Jack died, Enid Wallace had no way of earning a living, the older child had learning difficulties and the youngest suffered from nightmares and screaming fits. She ended up having a nervous breakdown.'

'Dear Lord. What an awful story.'

Frances sighed and continued. 'Tom couldn't stand by and watch. He decided to take his brother's place and marry his sister-in-law to give her financial security and his nephews' a surrogate father.'

'How long have they been married?'

'Ten years. He married Enid in 1919.'

'Are they happy?'

'Jim doesn't think so. Enid never fully recovered from her illness and, no matter how he tried, Tom was always second best. His decision to go back to sea was deliberate to give her space because being there only made matters worse, even though he would never abandon her or the boys.'

'But that's so unfair. Tom has a right to a family life as well.'

'I agree, and so does Jim, but for Enid, living with Tom was purgatory.'

'Why?'

'He and Jack were identical twins.'

'Oh, my God! And I thought Tom was a selfish, heartless bastard who cared nothing for me or my reputation.' My hand shot to my stomach and I rushed to the bathroom.

Frances quietly closed the bathroom door and handed me a glass of water and a damp face flannel. 'I hate to see you in this state, Mac, it would have been better if I had said nothing.'

I gargled into the lavatory pan then washed my face, shaking my head in disagreement. 'Why didn't he tell me, Frances? There were so many opportunities and I would have understood.'

'No, you wouldn't, Mac, and he knew that. He was in love with you and wanted to grab some happiness while he could.'

'It hurts like hell, Frances.' We were back in the bedroom amongst the detritus of my wardrobe. 'Tom and I were in the right place at the wrong time, weren't we?'

'Yes, you were, but think about it logically, Mac, what would you have done about your career if things had been different?' Frances was busy hanging clothes back on the rail.

'Heaven knows, Frances. I had spent most of that last week at the Taj Mahal Hotel wondering how I could let Tom down gently. Classic, isn't it?'

She ran her hand over the emerald silk and shrugged.

'Enough about me,' I said, trying to lighten the mood. 'What about you and Jim. Has that got a happy ending?'

Frances stood looking out of the window with an empty coat-hanger in her hand. 'I guess we are a work in progress. Unlike Tom, Jim is a widower. His wife died in 1916 crossing the road in Manchester. She was run over by a tram in the fog.'

'For goodness sake, Frances, haven't you got any good news?'

'Sorry, but you did ask. They never had children so Jim thought a spell away at sea would help him come to terms with his loss. He has been a Navigation Officer with P&O ever since.'

'Where does that leave you?'

'Taking one day at a time.' She turned and smiled. 'Apparently Florence Nightingale swept him off his feet and he is now considering a post ashore, working for the ICS Maritime Division.'

'Oh, Frances, that's wonderful. Do I need a new hat?'

'Whoa!' Her hands flew into the air, her palms outstretched. 'Before I go rushing off into the sunset with a Mancunian who has designs on my body, I need to get my feet firmly under the Board of Governors table in Poona'

'So Ruby was right all along.' I grabbed my emerald dress, intent on getting it pressed before the Gala Ball.

'About what?'

'About watching the sunrise over the Horn of Africa?' I smiled.

The Calcutta Club was lit up like a Christmas tree as we arrived in our evening finery. Oil lamps hung from hooks all around the entrance and illuminated paper lanterns glowed like stars in the night air. A chamber orchestra was playing in the lobby and red, green and tinsel garlands wound themselves around pillars, mantlepieces and chandeliers in every room.

I introduced Frances to Virginia, Lord Cottesmore and Henriette while Jonathan marked her card for a Gay Gordons later in the evening. My card was filling up too with such partners as Arthur, Jonathan and Henriette's father who had arrived from Tanganyika for the festivities.

Sir Peter breezed past at some point and whispered in my ear, much to the annoyance of his charming lady partner. 'It's in the bag, Mac, and you look ravishing.' As he was dragged away to the buffet table, he gave me a thumbs-up sign and pointed towards the door. At first, I had no idea what he was talking about, then squealed, coughed demurely to hide my outburst and went in search of Lord Cottesmore.

He was in the drawing room in conversation with a group of other dignitaries. I hovered by the door not wishing to interrupt but eager to get his attention.

'Ah, and here she is,' he announced beckoning me over. 'I was just telling some members of the IMS about your recent success in obtaining full funding for an obstetrics research project. Allow me to introduce these distinguished surgeons who are, frankly, amazed.'

The admiring glances and genuine compliments went straight over my head. All I could think about was the fact that Lord Cottesmore had pulled it off. I had all the sponsorship I needed, and my future was secure.

Frances was reclining on a sofa, her chest heaving from her excursions on the dance floor when I found her. I repeated what I had just heard, beaming like a Cheshire cat. She sprang to her feet, grabbed two glasses of champagne off a steward's tray and pulled me onto the terrace where she raised her arm and made a toast. 'To your success, Mac. What a great way to end the old year.'

Suddenly loud squeals and shocked cries interrupted us and we peered into the ballroom to see male guests leaping about the dance floor like Spanish matadors, their jackets held out in front of them, as twelve tiny pink piglets scurried between everyone's legs, much to the amusement of all watching.

'It's a club tradition,' announced a lady furiously waving a fan under her nose. 'If you catch one you can keep it.'

The laughter was infectious, and my sides ached from all the hilarity when one little piglet, making its escape through the ballroom doors ran straight under Frances's skirt and remained hidden there trapped between her shoes. She lowered one hand to the floor and lifted the cute animal into the air like a sports trophy.

'What are you going to do with it now?' I was hanging onto my diaphragm.

'Take it back to Poona for the girls to use as a mascot.'

'For goodness sake, Frances. Miss Beckinsale will have you committed for being completely off your rocker.' I hiccoughed.

'Let her try,' she replied as a snout buried itself into her neck. 'With a surname like Trotter, what else would I suggest for a school mascot?'

We collapsed, giggling, onto a nearby swing chair with the piglet imprisoned between our hips. At that point, the sound of two hundred guests counting down the seconds to midnight rent the air.

'THREE, TWO, ONE – HAPPY NEW YEAR'

'Make a wish,' demanded Frances.

I closed my eyes, crossed my fingers and wished that my life from then on would be less complicated. I turned to look at Frances and found her doing likewise. 'Penny for them?' I asked when she opened her eyes.

'What do you think?'

'That you've just made a pact with the devil to bring about Miss Beckinsale's demise.'

'You must be psychic, Mac.'

A conga-line of revellers loped across the lawn and disappeared behind the cricket pavilion as our crystal glasses were refilled.

'Happy New Year, Frances.'

'Happy New Year, Mac. Let's make it a good one.'

The piglet was placed in a wicker cat-box and left in Arthur's car while we went back to enjoy the rest of the Gala Ball. I was 'Stripping the Willow' with Jonathan when my eyes locked onto Cyril Montgomery edging around the dance floor. I stopped dead in my tracks, leaving Jonathan charging down an archway of raised arms all on his own. He circled round and grabbed me by the waist, assuming I had forgotten what to do, then followed my eyes to the other side of the room.

'What is it, Doctor Mac?'

'Henriette's rapist. He's just gone through that door.' I pointed towards the terrace. 'Find Hettie while I tell Lord Cottesmore.' We split up, both now fully sober.

'Your Lordship?' I had hardly got the words out when there was a high-pitched scream from the terrace. I rushed out, Lord Cottesmore on my heels and did an emergency stop by the steps. Cyril Montgomery was out cold on the lawn and Jonathan was walking around in circles rubbing his knuckles. Henriette saw me and rushed into my arms.

'Who is that, Elizabeth?' asked Lord Cottesmore.

'Cyril Mont . . .'

He was down the steps, digging his toes into the tea-planter's ribs and shouting for backup before I could finish.

Charles Tegart appeared by my elbow, took one look at the scene and demanded an explanation. When he heard the name, he pulled Henriette off my chest by her shoulders and asked if she had been harmed. She shook her head, fear gripping her throat and he gently led her back into the ballroom. Frances was there by the door and immediately took charge in a very matronly way.

Montgomery was just coming around as Police Commissioner Tegart read him his rights, pulled him to his feet and manhandled his wrists into a set of handcuffs. I moved forward and watched as he frisked the man from head to toe. A small snuff box appeared from an inside pocket, the interior full of white powder. I shook with fury and vented my anger by slapping the tea-planter hard across his face, twice. He sneered at me, wheal marks appearing across both cheeks as I went for his throat. 'Rot in hell, you bastard,' I whispered, my thumb and forefinger squeezing his Adam's Apple, 'and take your syphilis with you.'

'That's enough, Doctor MacKenzie. Let the authorities deal with him.' Tegart peeled my fingers off Montgomery's throat and led him away. Jonathan's knuckles, meanwhile, were bleeding profusely.

'Jonathan, follow me. We need to clean and disinfect that wound. NOW!' I headed for the Calcutta Club kitchen screaming for alcohol and hot water.

As I dabbed his knuckles with a clean napkin, I asked him what had happened.

'I followed the screams and saw her being dragged across the lawn by that villain. He was drunk and heading towards the trees, so I grabbed him by his collar, spun him round, kicked him in the goolies then gave him a right upper cut as he went down.'

'Public School training?' I enquired.

Jonathan's lips cracked then he grimaced as raw alcohol sanitised his knuckles.

Back in my bedroom at the Thornton's I told Frances the whole story filling in the gaps left out by Henriette.

'Jesus, Mac, why was he at the Calcutta Club?'

'Apparently, he had been under constant police surveillance since leaving Himachal Pradesh and had been at the Calcutta Docks taking delivery of a shipment of cocaine off the ss

Ranchi. I guess he thought he would celebrate New Year at the Club before returning home.'

'What happens now?'

'Knowing Charles Tegart, he will be convicted of rape and drug trafficking and go to jail for years.'

'What about the other chap. Maurice, was it?'

'Yes, Maurice Blackthorn. The Cachar Province Police will arrest him tomorrow.'

Frances pulled back her eiderdown and climbed into bed. 'Mac?' She puffed up the pillow and lay down. 'Did you expect any of this to happen when you left Riveldene last October?'

I doused the bedside light and opened the curtains. Dawn was just breaking on the first day of the new decade. 'Not in a million years, Frances. Not in a million years.'

I woke at nine o'clock feeling out of sorts. My head ached, my mouth was dry and I felt nauseous. Putting it down to a surfeit of alcohol from the Gala Ball I crept to the bathroom trying not to disturb the others and pressed my face into a wet flannel, hoping I was not about to suffer a dose of influenza from wandering around the Calcutta Club grounds in the middle of the night in only a silk shift. It was winter after all and not the wisest thing to do if I were to be fit and well to take up my new role at the CSTM.

I had been hung-over before, but this was different. My skin felt clammy, my muscles ached, and my stomach contents bubbled away like a simmering cauldron. I groaned as I lay against the cool lavatory pan wishing the world would end, trying to remember what I had eaten the night before. Perhaps I have food poisoning, I thought, picturing the platter of cooked prawns in curried sauce and chided myself for not dousing them in fresh lime juice. I could hear Tom's instructions as if he were standing alongside me and relived our days in the Taj Mahal Hotel suite as I waited for the nausea to subside. It didn't and I was violently sick for the second time in two days.

I froze, staring into the bowl as another possibility flashed across my medical brain.

'NO,' I murmured, holding onto my stomach and rocking backwards and forwards. 'No, no, no, no, no. Not now. Not after all I have been through. Not after everything I have achieved.'

I rested my forehead on the cold floor tiles and closed my eyes.

'Dear God, what the hell do I do now?'

****

Acknowledgements

Rachel Lawston gets my sincere gratitude for her talented, patient and creative input as my graphics designer and Jenny Crickmore-Thompson, who professionally edited the first draft of the novel and whose critique helped move the story along.

To my close family and friends, especially Elizabeth Lodola and Lorraine Ure, whose reader critiques leading up to publication were invaluable, thank-you all for your input and support, it means a great deal. As for my husband, David, who argued his point of view with vigour and sound common sense and put up with my many moods whilst undertaking the extensive research, I can only reiterate, 'Like my previous novels, without you, this novel would never have seen the light of day!'

Finally, I pay tribute to the many long-suffering and doggedly determined female doctors, nurses and midwives throughout India whose dedication to their profession improved the plight of women and infants throughout this sub-continent and brought western obstetric knowledge and education to a country rife with female and infant mortality. They were the medical pioneers of their time and are owed a huge debt of gratitude. Your gender salutes you.

About the Author

Susie Baggaley was born in Nottingham in 1948 and by the age of nineteen had become an executive air-stewardess before starting her own successful company managing residential property for private owners working overseas.

Her passion for sailing became a lifestyle when, after twenty-three years, she sold her company, and went ocean-cruising with her husband, David, crossing the Atlantic Ocean four times and covering over 50,000 nautical miles on their private yacht. During the long hours at sea, Susie wrote articles for the sailing press and regular blogs for family and friends. Writing fiction was a natural progression beginning with her first novel, DEAD RECKONING, in 2015.

Susie continues writing from both the current family yacht based in the Mediterranean, and from her home in Devon. After a lifetime of travel, her wealth of experiences forms the basis for her intricate plots and characters. PORT OUT, Part I of the CALL ME MAC trilogy, is the Author's latest novel to be published.

Novel Reviews

If you have enjoyed this novel, I would be most grateful if you could spread the word by reviewing it on whichever site you purchased
Call Me Mac – Port Out.
Thank you
Susie Baggaley

Author's Books

Fiction

Call Me Mac - Book 1
*Dead Reckoning
*Rum Punch

Non-Fiction

Islas Baleares Pilot Book
by David & Susie Baggaley

(*published by IMRAY/RCCPF*)

Dead Reckoning & Rum Punch by Su Garcia

Baggatelle Publishers Ltd
www.baggatellepublishers.com

Printed in Great Britain
by Amazon

15925343R00180